Second Chances
at
Brambleberry
Creek

BOOKS BY ELIZABETH BROMKE

Elizabeth
BROMKE

Second Chances
at
Brambleberry
Creek

bookouture

Published by Bookouture in 2022

An imprint of Storyfire Ltd.
Carmelite House
50 Victoria Embankment
London EC4Y 0DZ

www.bookouture.com

ISBN: 978-1-80314-647-8
eBook ISBN: 978-1-80314-646-1

For Grandbob

PROLOGUE

PRESENT DAY

Amber

Amber Lee Taylor stood in the farmhouse kitchen at Moonshine Creek. Conversation swirled around her like dandelion seeds on a breath of wind. She clutched the yellow-paged notebook in her hands tighter.

The others' wild chatter churned up anxiety in Amber. Her cousin, Morgan Jo, was at the helm, rippling with excitement about the discovery of the notebook that once belonged to their grandfather. Morgan Jo's boyfriend, Emmett, beamed like a proud husband. Morgan Jo's best friend, Julia, gushed about what a treasure it was to find your ancestor's written account of life. "Who *knows* what's in there!" Julia said, adding to Morgan Jo's palpable elation.

Amber nodded along, but carefully, since she was just as scared to open the precious book as she was to drop it. Amber *knew* that she wasn't only holding her late grandfather's recipe book. She was holding a key to the past. And if she wasn't careful, Amber might just fall into the pages and get swept away in her grandfather's words.

Evening was falling across the farm, a great sweeping property that had been built by Amber's ancestors and had withstood time and change with relative grace. Once upon a time, these acres had been a refuge to bootleggers trying to get through Prohibition without succumbing to the law. It wasn't always the scene of a crime, though. Bookending the property's years as a secret establishment, the rambling bluegrass hills eventually played home to a thriving tobacco farm and all who lived there.

Most recently, however, Moonshine Creek was a family home, accommodating the newest generation of Coyles. Now, since the passing of matriarch Memaw and grumpy ol' Grandad, Amber lived there with her cousins. The property continued to support its descendants, feeding them sweet fruit from its legacy orchard and tart berries from the brambles, which climbed like spiders over a tumbledown fence that framed the farmhouse itself, as well as over a nearby barn and a back building once used as a tobacco hangar.

Everything about Moonshine Creek was inherited. Everything there, an heirloom. Especially the big house that sat at the front and center of the property, white and sprawling and so chock-full of family lore that you couldn't step a foot inside without *smelling* history.

Sometimes Amber thought it was a little odd to *live* in an heirloom. Almost like living in a haunted house, except the ghosts were your memories of your grandparents and fuzzy images of other ancestors who you'd heard wacky stories about.

Amber's older cousin, Morgan Jo, prattled with animation. It was Morgan Jo's best friend, Julia, who'd discovered the notebook that Amber now held. Julia was a sweet, blond little thing. Like a Barbie doll, or maybe Barbie's little sister. *What was her name?* Amber hadn't been one to play with Barbies as a kid. She'd rather bake cookies with Memaw and eat the dough until her belly ached.

Morgan Jo's boyfriend was there in the kitchen, too. Emmett Dawson. Emmett was exactly what you pictured when you thought about a small-town country boy, except grown up. With thick sandy hair and lake-blue eyes, tan skin, and a great body. Amber wasn't ashamed to admit that she had a crush on Emmett, even if he *did* belong to Morgan Jo.

Morgan Jo. The imperfectly perfect one. Yep, Morgan Jo had been *that* cousin. Straight As in school. Went to college on scholarship. Great hair that didn't need dying or perming because it was the perfect shade of auburn and swung in thick, wild waves. Morgan Jo's pretty green eyes set off a spray of freckles that Pippi Longstocking would kill for.

The three of them chattered on about all the "what-ifs," praising Julia for her discovery and Morgan Jo for her perfection, and Emmett for his mere existence.

Meanwhile, Amber dared to study the ink-stained, ragged-edged notebook. If it was possible to be a *fourth* wheel, then Amber was it. Standing at a measly five-foot flat, she was often mistaken for being half her age. But then she'd turn around and whoever had called her *kiddo* took in her ample bosom, got a little confused and realized Amber wasn't fifteen, she was probably thirty, which was accurate.

Amber tried hard, though. She regularly added highlights to her stick-straight dishwater hair, which was usually set in big round curls that were meant to balance out Amber's apple-shaped form. She tried so hard, in fact, that she ended up becoming a hairdresser. Not that it helped much.

There was more to fashion than hair, luckily, and Amber opted for the most stylish shape of eyeglass frames she could afford—tortoise-shell-framed rectangles that transitioned to sunglasses in the sun. What's more, she spackled on her makeup and played up her cleavage with Victoria's Secret bras, purchased en masse during their semi-annual sales.

Amber did everything she could to be more than she was.

"Well?" Morgan Jo was talking directly to Amber now. "Let's see it. What does it say?" She hooked one hand on Amber's shoulder and used her other hand to open the cover of the notebook.

Doing as she was told, Amber thumbed through its dry, yellowed pages. Several pages presented stilted, crooked lettering, but the words stopped only about a dozen sheets in.

Amber carefully moved back to the first page, her fingers tracing her grandfather's writing like it was a treasure map.

This was big.

This could mean they'd recover the recipes they thought were lost. Grandad's wine recipes. The recipes they could parlay into something more than a hobby. The recipes that could become the foundation for a family business—a vineyard and winery.

"Oh *my*," Morgan Jo exhaled the words on minty breath over Amber's shoulder. "I can't even believe it." Without reading past the first page, Morgan Jo released Amber's shoulder and left to go dig around until she found an open bottle of her mom's wine in the back of the fridge. She pulled the cork and held it up. "Amber, get some wine glasses. We're celebrating."

Amber slid the notebook onto the kitchen table and squeezed past Morgan Jo and Emmett, who were giggling like teenagers as they each took a sniff of the wine, which was something cheap from the market.

Amber sometimes felt a pang of envy over Morgan Jo and Emmett Dawson. They were perfect together. Amber allowed herself to smile, though. You couldn't *not* be happy for the sweet pair, even if they were annoying, their bliss was contagious. Inspiring, even. Amber wished she had that for herself. Instead, she enjoyed a stable, consistent, six-year-long relationship with Grant Maycomb, a security guard for Western Federal Bank.

Julia joined Amber at the cabinet, and together they withdrew four glasses. Amber set them in a row across the kitchen counter and leaned into the butcher's-block island. Julia remained near her, perhaps seeking respite from the radiating romance.

Emmett set about pouring the wine, and Morgan Jo slipped in between Julia and Amber, looping each of her arms around them. Morgan Jo squeezed them in. "Girls, this is just the beginning."

Beneath the warmth of her cousin's touch, envy and fear and anxiety eased away, and excitement bubbled up inside of Amber.

Emmett passed out the glasses. "Should we toast?"

Morgan Jo raised her glass. "To family."

Amber smiled at that and then looked at Emmett who stared at her cousin with so much affection and love that Amber felt a familiar question rise up in her chest. She pushed it away. Emmett and Morgan Jo might have passion, but Amber and Grant had contentment. They'd been engaged for six years, after all.

She shook the thought and tried instead to focus on the future. Not the present moment, but the *future*.

Emmett raised his glass. "To love," he said, unabashedly and heroically, and in a way that made even Amber's stomach flip in her stomach. Morgan Jo flushed pink.

Julia, who could be counted on to even things out, raised her glass, too. It was becoming something of a game, this toast. "To business." She grinned and winked at Amber, who had an idea for her own contribution.

Trying for something thoughtful, Amber raised her glass. "To Memaw and Grandad."

The four of them pushed their glasses to the center, and Morgan Jo caught Amber's eye. Together, the cousins shared a look that could fill a whole wine barrel. It was the beginning of something, Amber knew. Maybe the beginning of her *future*.

CHAPTER ONE

SIX MONTHS LATER

Morgan Jo

Morgan Jo Coyle stood in the barn at Moonshine Creek. Her best friend, Julia, sat on a leather-seated camping stool. One of its three legs was shorter than the others, and every time Julia shifted her weight, the stool rocked backward, and Julia threw her arms out, thinking she was falling.

"Find a different chair, maybe," Morgan suggested as the giggles overtook her. She wasn't giggling from joy, though, more from being so dog-tired that she was slaphappy. They'd been working on organizing the winery staging area since five that morning. This was an important part of opening the business, taking the barn from what it was—a dusty storage space once used for housing livestock—and turning it into a winemaking operation.

Now it was going on two thirty.

The two of them were supposed to have stopped when Morgan's boyfriend, Emmett, came in from the field. That would be their lunch break, which they'd take in the big house.

The big house, the main home on the farm which now belonged to Morgan, her mom, and her cousins, was the centerpiece of Moonshine Creek. White and tall and rambling, outsiders figured it'd once been a plantation. But no. Never had a real, live, haunting southern plantation-tainted Nelson-Coyle family history. Not that Morgan knew about, anyway.

Presently, Morgan pictured her mom in the kitchen, whiling away at a lunch so refreshing Morgan's mouth watered just thinking about it. Probably sweet iced tea. Or maybe lemonade. A light-but-wholesome lunch fair. Maybe tuna salad. Maybe not. Morgan's stomach growled.

Emmett had only dipped his head into the barn once, at about one, to say he was almost finished pruning the grapevines —could they hang tight a little longer?

Julia, who still worked full-time at her *real* job as a physical therapist was losing steam, like Morgan. As if she could read Morgan's mind Julia said, "Should we drag that boyfriend of yours into the house and force-feed him? We need a break. I'm sure he does most of all."

Morgan nodded and picked her way across the packed dirt to the wide-open barn doors. She rubbed her hip and down the top of her thigh. Therapy on the years-old wound and a subsequent operation had ramped up, thanks to Julia, who Morgan visited at the outpatient facility three days a week.

Morgan's physical therapy focused on strength, and that meant that half their sessions involved weightlifting. The other half were stretching, basically. All that plus the work at the farm meant Morgan could rely upon ongoing bursts of pain along her ligaments and down deep in her bones. It was a good pain, though. The kind that meant that she was moving in the right direction. Hopefully.

Standing in the open doorway and letting the afternoon breeze cool her face, Morgan searched the landscape for signs of a tall, dirty-blond-haired man. She didn't need to shield her eyes from the sun, which had by now begun to droop on the west side of the barn behind her. It cast a stout shadow just past where Morgan faced, looking towards the orchards and vineyard.

Six months earlier, Morgan, Julia, Emmett, and Morgan's cousin, Amber, had discovered a notebook that once belonged to their grandfather. In it, he'd scrawled bits of wine recipes. The unearthing was so profound and moving, that Morgan and her little crew of three had agreed they were going to do something with the find. With inspiration from her late grandmother's hopes for Morgan and the resource they had in the farm, the logical thing to do with Grandad's recipes was to bring to life the wine he'd made so long ago.

Morgan was determined to open a full-scale boutique operation based exclusively on the toils of her ancestors. Everything from buildings to crops to recipes: the business would be so closely connected with Morgan's family history that when a customer toured the grounds or sipped the drink, they'd be transported to a different time.

It was critical to Morgan that she preserve her grandparents' legacy. Any deviation would feel like failure or, worse, disloyalty.

Over the course of the winter, Morgan's main goal had been to assess what they had growing, what kind of shape it was in, and where exactly everything started and ended. Turned out her memories from growing up on the farm were less useful at predicting what they'd have to work with. Emmett was great, though, in that he helped along the way— reading up on vineyards and consulting the internet every step of the way.

It was his idea to start in the fields with the vines that they meant to turn into vineyards.

By January, they'd pruned back well over two-hundred vines. Come February, they'd managed another two hundred.

From there, it was easy enough to tell that whatever Morgan's ancestors had done, it was planned.

And besides the berry vines and grapevines, fruit trees and bushes of many varieties thrived within and without the network of brambles.

The would-be vineyards wrapped around four sets of micro-orchards precisely, like a grid. Woven in between the grape vines, too, were what seemed to be wildflowers with bright, vibrant buds and heady fragrance emanating out. It was only beyond the grapevines that Morgan and Emmett discovered the other types of berries she'd always known of. Strawberries, blackberries, and blueberries grew on the inside rows then again out deeper into the woods, away from the orchard, out past the tobacco fields all the way to where the old railroad curved and ran south toward Tennessee.

From what could be told, there was no rhyme or reason to the wild berries beyond the vineyard, but it seemed clear that the Nelsons had planted grapevines, strawberry vines, blackberry and blueberry vines with intention.

The hard part was sussing out what was what.

At least, at *first*.

But just as soon as April hit, little blue buds began to appear on two separate rows. Cross referencing with Emmett's help revealed that these must be blueberries and blackberries. There had yet to be sight of any strawberries or grapes, however. So, all they could count on at this point was that Grandad's threadbare notes were right. Of course, there were the memories Morgan shared with Amber and those of her mother and aunts. They'd all sworn that growing up they'd run through the fields, plucking sweet berries as they went.

According to all the information Morgan had rustled up, the farm should produce vines and vines of sweet red grapes.

However, the information and the memories were fast becoming desperate pleas in Morgan's heart. If this whole vineyard and winery business was going to go up that fall, she'd better have *something* to show for it.

Or else, Morgan would have failed yet again. And Morgan wasn't sure how much more professional failure she could take. Especially since *this* professional attempt was wrapped up tight in her *personal* life.

CHAPTER TWO

1992

Bill

Dank warmth hung down from the rafters above Bill Coyle, who stood at the workbench in his barn. Above him, up on platforms once meant for farm animals, old tools rusted in beds of crusty, aged hay. The smell of must and mold couldn't be ignored, but the fifty-three-year-old found such an odor to be a comfort.

On the rough-hewn wood top of Bill's workbench sat a notebook his daughter, Barb, had given him for his birthday. To the front cover, she'd taped a note:

Dad,

One day, your grandkids will want to know your secrets. Maybe you could start with the recipes for that delicious wine of yours. Happy birthday, Old Man!

Love,
Your favorite daughter

He grinned to himself. Bill wasn't a fool. He knew a father didn't have favorites. Still.

Inside of the notebook he found the typical white pages lined in pale-blue ink. It reminded Bill of his schoolboy days. Sometimes, notebooks didn't have lines but rather just blank white pages as if whoever sold the notebooks really expected someone to pay for that. Anyway, Bill liked the lines for a practical reason, too. They'd keep his thoughts orderly for the colossal task ahead of him.

A crude, square carpenter's pencil was locked in his prematurely gnarled hand as Bill considered where to start.

There was only one place, and that was at the beginning.

Bill eyed the cylinder he'd just filled. It was half empty with liquid the color of eggplant. Bill loved eggplant, but this juice wasn't from an eggplant, it was from a bushel of purple grapes.

He then turned his gaze to the low shelf that sliced through his line of vision. Across it sat six cloudy glass bottles of crystal-clear moonshine.

Contraband, some might call it.

Inspiration, Bill called it.

A reminder of where he lived and who'd come before him here.

He'd hand-labeled all six bottles with a black marker: *Nelson Farm Creek Moonshine 1939*. The last batch that existed. Of all the things Bill Coyle owned, these six bottles were probably the most valuable. They were the last of an original store of moonshines that his father-in-law had bootlegged and managed to keep hold of. Feds hadn't gotten their hands on the stuff. The old man had kept enough to get him through the war and then some, and all that was left over was Bill and Essie's to keep. To enjoy, too, bit by bit.

Funny how illegal things tasted better than their counterparts.

His gaze traveled back to the big jar with grape juice fermenting inside.

"The moonshine might be worth something, but wine's sweeter all the way," he mumbled to himself with a dry laugh. Then Bill pushed the round lead pencil tip to the paper and started scrawling his very first secret.

CHAPTER THREE

PRESENT DAY

Amber

Amber carefully painted a rope of gray-brown hair onto a foil, then folded it up and clipped it into place. A slow examination all around that one foil assured her she could move to the next. It was over an hour into her mother's appointment, and Amber was only about halfway through the foils.

Amber's phone chimed in the back pocket of her jeans, but she hardly noticed. Her focus remained on the new foil, the new rope of gray-brown hair, her color, and her brush.

"Sorry this is taking a while, Mom."

"Amber, you take your time. I got nowhere to be. Until tonight, I mean." Barb surreptitiously glanced at the clock sitting on Amber's station. It read just past two.

"So, are you excited for tonight?"

Her mother pursed her lips. Beneath Amber's hands, the fifty-something woman turned stiff as a board. She glanced up at the mirror, and the pair shared a brief moment of eye contact. Barb's eyes fell back to her magazine. "Mhm."

Amber pushed the heel of her hand into her aching lower back.

Amber wondered what in the world she would do if she weren't a stylist but still had to work out of the home. Sure, she was technically helping Morgan Jo and Julia start the winery, but that felt like a long shot, and Amber's role in it was little more than honorary.

If only Grant hurried up and agreed on a date, then Amber could get on with being a housewife and, one day, a stay-at-home mother.

The *ultimate* dream gig. Amber could just picture herself in her little kitchenette in the basement, fixin' lunches for a string of towheads and shooing them out the door to catch the bus that stopped at the corner of Smoking Pipe and Eleventh Street.

Fumes from hair bleach snapped Amber from her reverie.

"You haven't been to My Old Kentucky Dinner Train in forever," she pointed out to her mother as she started the new foil. "Are you excited for *that*, at least?"

My Old Kentucky Dinner Train was as romantic an experience as any Amber could imagine, which was why she'd bought it as a gift for her parents' wedding anniversary. Although could you celebrate your wedding anniversary if you were *divorced*? Amber couldn't be sure, but that was one of the challenges in matchmaking your own parents: awkward questions were sure to arise.

She'd wrangled her siblings, Tiffany and Trav, into pitching in, and all together they'd put up one hundred dollars, cash, delivered directly to the maître d' up in Bardstown. Amber had been careful to enclose all five twenties in a white envelope labeled: *Hank and Barb Taylor Wedding Anniversary Dinner.* She just hoped her plan worked.

Her mother replied with a snort. "Well, *obviously* I'm excited to *eat*." She patted her thick waist, reminding Amber exactly where her own figure had come from. Amber knew, however, that she and her mom weren't alone in enjoying a wholesome down-home meal. It was only human to be driven to eat, and Amber struggled to trust any man or woman who could resist such a biological urge. That's why she had precious few skinny friends and why she kept her skinny family members, even her own sister, at a safe distance.

Amber thought about her parents' marriage and what little she knew of their wedding. She'd like to ask her mother everything. What color was Barb's dress *exactly*? Amber already knew it wasn't snow-white. Was it ivory? Cream? Beige? The pictures might as well have been snapped in black and white, their quality was so questionable. What about flowers? What type? Did they serve chicken or beef? Both? Lobster? Probably not lobster.

"Mom?" Amber asked. "Exactly how long were you and Daddy engaged for before you got married?"

"What're you getting at, Amber?" Her mother eyed her from beneath a bang of foils.

Amber had better keep doing foils. If she stopped, the first ones might overprocess. She kept her gaze on her work and let her mouth do the answering. "I just wonder what it'll take to get Grant to hurry up."

"If you're trying to remind me that I was pregnant before we were married, don't bother. I knew it all too well. And anyway, *my Lanta*, child. Just let it be." Barb clicked her tongue to kingdom come and shook her head, too.

"I don't care about that. I just wonder why some people get married fast and why some people wait."

Hopefully Dad didn't only marry Mom because he got her pregnant, but maybe he did?

In fact, there'd been a scandal close to Amber's birth. None other than the story of Aunt CarlaMay and Morgan Jo. Morgan Jo, the love child.

"This is inappropriate," Barb snapped. "We got married because it was the right thing to do."

Amber's smile and hopes and dreams fell away. *Obligation? That's why? Fear of social repercussions?* Amber didn't want to believe that. She wanted to believe she was the result of passion and love and some undeniable need. What if, instead, she was just a mistake?

"But you loved each other, right?"

Barb sighed, and Amber could feel the woman's breath on her hand. That breath—that life—it was Amber's only connection to the story of her coming into this world. That face, hidden behind the foils. That woman. After all, once Travis and Tiffany were born, things had gotten bad. Their dad had left for sunnier pastures.

Once he'd made it out to California, Amber'd never heard from him again. He'd sent checks, but Barb was always griping that they weren't enough to cover all three kids. Maybe two, the twins, but not all three. Not Amber and her braces and special eyeglass prescription. Not her backup plan—beauty school—once she was rejected from pastry school. It was probably a good thing that she hadn't gotten in. Pastry school was a million times more expensive than beauty school.

Anyway, her father, Hank, had moved back to Nelson County the autumn before. Amber learned this only because she'd overheard her mother talking to Travis on the phone one day. The conversation stuck like a dagger in Amber's heart. Amber could remember it word for word now. *"Travis, your dad called me. He's hoping to see you today or tomorrow, you know."*

Amber'd been confused. Why wouldn't Hank want to see all of them?

Launching her way into the kitchen, Amber asked her mom for an explanation. Barb had said Hank was thinking about reuniting with them, yes. He was interested in visiting with Travis.

It was then that Amber's curiosity about her father grew into a beast. Knowing him and learning why he'd left had become a compulsion.

Her brother and sister didn't share Amber's interest though. That's when she figured there might be another way to draw Hank back into the fold. Barb.

Amber had set about greasing the wheels to establish a date, and their wedding anniversary was the next opportunity. Now, here they were. The day of.

Her mother pointed to the open foil that was only half finished. "Don't fry my hair, Amber Lee."

Amber blinked. "Oh. Sorry." She finished the foil and folded it. "So, what did Daddy think when he found out?"

"Found out what?"

"*Mom*. What did Daddy think when he found out you were pregnant with me?"

"Well, he proposed, didn't he?"

"That's it? He wasn't, like, *mad* or really excited—or?"

Barb let out a long breath and again lifted the flap of foils on her forehead. "I'll put it this way. Things went smoother for me than for Carla, because of Hank. *Everybody* loved Hank."

She hadn't answered the question, but for whatever reason, Barb's response satisfied Amber.

"Lemme check your foils." Amber set about peeking at the first few as she thought back on the full-blown family scandal. Though Amber had only ever heard whispers of the drama, she wasn't so dumb as to not put together the pieces. She wasn't so dumb as to not see the hurt on Morgan Jo's face every birthday party or Christmas when a new friend showed up and asked, "Morgan Jo, where's your dad? Ain't he s'pose to be here today?" The question, ever unwitting and ever heartbreaking, sometimes turned into: "*Who* is your dad?"

Amber's folks might be split up, but at least she had two of them.

And at least she *knew* who her dad was.

And hope remained for their reunion. Amber had little to complain of, really.

Realization then hit her like a truck full of bricks. "Oh. So, you'd come out ahead of Aunt Carla, by comparison. Whereas she was a harlot, you were just..."

Her mother finished the sentence for Amber, the fleeting look of happiness pinkening the woman's half-hidden cheeks. "In love." The words whispered like smoke swirling up into the chemical air of the salon.

Then, as Amber stood there, painting her mother's gray-flecked hair and willing away the throbbing in her back, another thought tickled her brain. As little as Amber knew of her parents' marriage, she knew far less of their divorce.

Hank and Barb had split just as quickly as they had gotten together. Amber wasn't quite four years old. Too young to understand. But anyway, at least with the Taylors' marriage, everyone could appreciate the *why* surrounding it. The pair's love had burned as red as a garland of derby roses.

That was the exact reason Amber had set this whole thing up.

To get her parents *back* together, to remind her dad that he had three children, and at least one missed him something awful.

CHAPTER FOUR

PRESENT DAY

Morgan Jo

Up to now, Morgan and Julia had made good progress in the barn.

Currently, the greater plan for the family vineyard and winery was to prep the crops and to convert half the barn into a working winery space. This meant a lot of cleaning, a lot of organizing, and a lot of figuring out how in the world a vineyard really operated.

So far, they'd cleared out some boxes, stacked others, and used a shop vac on everything from rusty nails that had fallen into crevices to spiderwebs that traced across every last nook and cranny. It felt like a baby step toward the top of Mount Everest. But it was a step in the right direction, at least.

As Morgan stood in the mouth of the barn, she saw her mother appear at the back door of the big house. Morgan waved to her. "Please tell me that's lemonade!" She could spy the beverage glasses CarlaMay carried out, and the wide smile on her mother's face gave away that it was.

Morgan felt euphoric as she lifted her face to heaven and whispered to herself, *Praise be.*

She then left the barn and met her mom halfway to take the tray while her mother darted back in the house for napkins.

Tall sweaty glasses of lemonade anchored each corner of the tray, and in the center was a small platter with sandwiches piled high. Apparently, they'd be eating in the barn rather than the house.

CarlaMay was back in a flash, joining Morgan as she entered the barn.

"I don't want you all to starve, so I figured I'd just bring lunch out here," CarlaMay explained.

Julia moved to stand up, her arms flailing again as the rickety antique seat rocked beneath her slight weight. "Thank you, Miss Carla," she said, finding purchase on the ground and joining the other two at a workbench that spread across one wall. It was the workbench they'd already vacuumed, scrubbed, stained, and let set. Their biggest accomplishment yet.

"I don't know why you all are even bothering with this ol' barn," CarlaMay said. "Shouldn't you focus on the fruit, first?"

The barn, though, would have to become the storeroom and the actual winery. After harvesting the grapes, berries, and some fruit from the farm, Morgan would process it in the barn, where they'd also bottle and prepare to sell the bottles. Maybe it'd become a distribution center, maybe it'd become something else. The goal for now, though, was to get the fruit into wine by that fall.

So, they'd need a place to bring the fruit and to start the fermenting process, obviously. The barn was logical. Anyway, Emmett had taken over the field operations, becoming nearly obsessed with pruning, checking, watering, studying, plucking. Morgan figured it was his escape from the law offices. Emmett, like Julia, had maintained his day job, too. He was a partner at his uncle's law firm in Bardstown. Money was good there, but Emmett's heart belonged to the land.

And to Morgan, of course.

The last several months had seen the two become closer than ever. As teenagers, the pair had been devoted high school sweethearts, but then came college and a breakup. Over ten years later, once Morgan returned to Brambleberry on the heels of her grandmother's passing, she and Emmett picked right up where they'd left off. And they never looked back. So, between time spent working on the farm and date nights around town, Morgan and Emmett were inseparable. Between them, there were no secrets. Except for one, that was.

Emmett wanted a family, and sooner than later. Morgan didn't know about the family part—medically, at least. Several years back, Morgan's grandmother, in a fit of dementia or anger —no one really knew—accidentally discharged a gun. The bullet lodged in Morgan's hip bone, but the consequences were wide-ranging. She ended up with further surgeries to restore the parts of her leg and torso that were damaged. Now, a limp was the only visible proof that Morgan had been through something awful.

Who knew what lurked beneath her skin, though?

Paranoid the injury could affect Emmett's feelings about their future, Morgan had decided against reminding him that maybe she was broken on the inside somewhere.

It was easier to focus on the *now*. Turning the farm into a vineyard and squeezing every romantic moment she could get out of Emmett.

But as much as she threw herself into the present, the project exhausted Morgan, who hadn't done much physical labor in over five years now. Plus, the project hadn't allowed for the personal reprieves she'd become used to. In Tucson, and even across other cities where Morgan had lived before she returned to Brambleberry Creek, her evenings and weekends were composed of modern self-care, such as pedicures and reality TV.

Back home in Brambleberry, however, things were different. Morgan fell back into her old routines of getting up early and working from dawn to dusk and then some. Weekends just meant extra help for extra work, like gutting the barn and mowing the grass and tending to the regular maintenance of the farm as a whole.

So, when CarlaMay asked why they even needed to use the barn at all, Morgan's exhaustion came to a head.

Presently, Morgan snapped at her well-meaning mother, "Mom. It's the next thing we need to do. Clear the barn. Prep it for the operation." Even as she said it, though, Morgan followed CarlaMay's gaze over the back half of the barn they hadn't even started on.

More boxes piled high in both corners. Old farming equipment bled orange rust onto the dirt floor, probably poisoning the water table. Who knew? Metal drums of oil lined the walls. In the rafters above sat tools that long ago should have been hauled off to a scrapyard.

Grandad Bill hadn't been a hoarder, but he was most definitely a pack rat. The things he'd left behind were orderly enough, but this was the reality of leaving *anything* behind after you kicked the bucket.

Well, anything other than fruit trees.

Grapes might ferment into tasty wine, but corrosion ate away the bowl of a once-good wheelbarrow, rendering it so useless it became more work than it was worth.

Morgan sighed. "I know. It's a lot."

"We've got time, though," Julia chimed in through a mouthful of BLT. "We aren't opening until fall. It's barely April." Opening was feeling like a stretch even to Morgan, who was utterly committed to getting a vineyard and winery operation going in time for harvest season. If Morgan could pull this off, she could start monetizing the farm. But more than that, she could finally feel like she was *doing* something. Something she was meant to do. Upholding family tradition, proving her worth, and making some sort of impact.

As such, Morgan felt like the world rested on her shoulders. While she worked every day of the week—and had since November—on making progress, her team was otherwise occupied. Emmett had a law firm to run in Bardstown. Julia had her therapy clients. Even Amber, their fourth partner, worked at least four days a week at the salon. Sometimes even five. It was up to Morgan to drive things forward, get the business up and running, and—with any luck—bring on a little more help.

CarlyMay pointed to the sandwich and glass of lemonade that sat on the workbench nearest where Morgan stood. "Sit down and take a break, Morgan Jo. You're liable to burn right out."

The three of them ate in silence for some time. Emmett came in a few minutes after Morgan had finished her sandwich. Saturdays were fast becoming precious to Morgan, when she could have both Julia and Emmett on hand.

He gave her a peck on the cheek but not after greeting Julia and thanking CarlaMay for the refreshments first.

"How's it going out there, Emmett?" CarlaMay replied.

"Pruning is rough. This'll be our third round of it, and I'm not sure we'll have much to work with come summer."

Morgan froze mid-bite. "You said you thought we'd have a full harvest."

"That was before I saw the bugs."

"Bugs?" Morgan let her eyes close. She could use a nap and a face mask right about now. When she peeked back at Emmett, she dared to ask, "What do you mean *bugs*?"

"The good thing is that they're drawn to the flowers and the fruit trees—and away from the vines. But it's early season, and I'm not even accounting for birds or deer. We're liable to get swarms of them come summer, and it makes me wonder what's been going on the last several years since Mr. Bill died." He looked purposefully at CarlaMay.

It was widely known that Grandad Bill, for all that he wasn't, took impeccable care of the farm, insomuch as he was able. That said, everyone assumed he'd never taken much interest in keeping the vines alive and well. It was way, way too much work for an old man to do all his own.

CarlaMay looked thoughtful. "I've got an idea." She went for her phone in her pocket. "I'm going to call up Travis. Maybe he'll know, since he helped out with things when Dad was alive." When CarlaMay tapped her phone to life, her expression twisted. "Oh my," she whispered.

"What is it?" Morgan asked. She hated those types of phone interactions, the ones where you got a call or a text and it was bad news up and down and left and right. Bad news was painted over her mother's features. "Mom, what?" Morgan crossed to her mom, peering over the woman's shoulder to read a text message that glowed like gold in a mine.

Under her breath Morgan muttered a swear. "This is the *last* thing we need."

CHAPTER FIVE

PRESENT DAY

Amber

Barb's words drifted into Amber's ears and curled down around her heart. *In love.* Her parents got married because they were *in love.* Not only because it was *the right thing to do.*

Amber wasn't a mistake.

Sure, mistakes had happened along the way. Maybe a fissure opened between her parents, but the plates beneath the surface remained snug. Barb and Hank hadn't shifted away. It was just that dang ol' fissure making them think it was more than a crack, making them think it had opened into a canyon. It hadn't though. The fissure remained a crack, and Amber knew this for many reasons. Firstly, her mother had never remarried. She hadn't even dated. Amber had watched her mother age and keep her heart locked safe inside of her chest.

As for Hank, well, Amber couldn't be positive, but Barb had said he wasn't married. So at least there was that.

This simple truth proved to Amber all she needed to know.

Hope for her parents' marriage not only existed, it persisted.

All they needed, Amber figured, was a little soil to fill in the cranny.

Plus, if Amber could pin down why her parents couldn't make it work, maybe she could repair her own relationship. If her own parents could fix themselves a wedding and three babies all within three years, then Amber could surely get herself down that aisle *after* six years of engagement.

From there, it'd be gravy. If she and Grant could make it six years of being engaged, well that had to bode well for a good long union, right? There were whole marriages that hadn't lasted seven years. Just ask Marilyn Monroe.

Or Barb and Hank.

Sometimes, late at night when Amber was falling asleep in the bed between a snoring Grant and her purring pair of felines, she wished she'd gotten pregnant out of wedlock just in order to light a fire beneath Grant's butt. But it wasn't her style to trap a man. Amber wasn't like that.

In the salon, as her mother's hair processed, Amber leaned against the countertop and stared out to space.

"Oh, hon, look at this." Her mom flashed the phone screen at Amber. A big poufy, princess-style wedding dress filled it.

Amber made a face. "It's big."

"It's flattering." Her mom tapped her pinky nail at the bustier which had to have more boning than a Christmas roast.

"How long did it take you to pick out your dress, Mom?"

"Oh, I don't know. Probably half an hour."

"Half an hour? Not like, a month? Or a week at least?"

"It wasn't about the dress for me." Barb lifted her foil and ran the back of her hand over her forehead. "It wasn't even about the wedding."

Amber felt a stab of *something* down deep inside. Envy? Or was it guilt? Guilt that she was more concerned with having a wedding than a marriage...? Could that even be true? Did she really just want a wedding?

Or was it anger that bounced around her insides like a table full of billiard balls clicking and clacking? Anger that her mom and dad gave up on something *so* damn important. That had nothing to do with Amber's engagement or wedding or marriage.

Did it?

"Why, Mom?"

The foils flapped back down over Barb's eyes and her phone slid back to her lap, the screen aglow with a silly game. "Why, what, hon?"

"Why did Dad leave?"

Barb made a strangling sound and cleared her throat. Her finger paused over the phone screen for a split second then went right back to tapping and sliding. She sighed. "Things *happen.* That's why."

It was meant to shut Amber up, but it didn't. "Okay, but you're willing to go back out with him?"

"I'm willing to go eat dinner with the father of... Amber, it's *dinner,* honey. I've eaten dinner with enemies before. I can do it once. For you."

"Okay, but who initiated the divorce? Like, whose idea was it?"

"I don't want to talk about that right now, Amber Lee."

"How come we've never talked about it, though, Mom? Here I am, engaged to be married, and you don't think we ought to talk about what ended *your* marriage? Maybe it'll help me."

Barb was smarter than that. "Speaking of *you,* have you and Grant talked any more about a date?" Her voice rang sharp.

Amber had a mind to grab a razor and shave off a chunk of that woman's hair. "I don't know what you want me to tell you, Mom. *No.* We haven't."

Beneath Amber's slowly moving hands, Barb twisted and looked up. "Amber Lee, why the hell *not?*"

This was the first time her mother had made a full-on

affront about it. Up to now, no one had fussed. They'd accepted that things would progress just about as fast as an old hog trudging through muck when it came to the Taylor-Maycomb wedding planning. That's just the sort of couple they were. They were working on things. Grant was trying to lose weight and save up some money. Amber was trying to hunt for a good apartment in town for the pair of them. Those sorts of big life changes took time. Years, even.

Amber's phone chimed again in her pocket.

"You gon' get that?" Barb asked.

Irritation swam through Amber's veins. "No, I'm not," she said stubbornly, but she pulled the device out with the idea to silence it anyhow.

"Well, who is it? Is it Grant?" Barb asked.

Without much more than a glance at the screen, Amber said, "No. It's Tiffany."

Then Barb's phone went off. It had been sitting her lap. Tiffany's name flashed there, too. "Oh, my." Barb plucked it up and thumbed the call to life.

Amber's breath caught in her chest. In this family, if someone texted twice then started in on the phone calls, you could be assured it was bad news. As if the Coyle family hadn't had enough bad news lately. Amber finished the foil she'd started and went back to her phone to see what Tiffany had said, but she was cut off by her mother's expression.

Barb's mouth had dropped open into a wide O, and she lifted the foil that hung down over her right eye. Then, she stared directly at Amber in the mirror as she hollered loudly, "*You're jokin'*, Tiffany Jeanette."

"What?" Amber hissed.

The other two hairdressers in the shop had stopped what they were doing. Their clients had lowered their own phones to their laps. Everyone was waiting expectantly to hear what morsel of gossip had just befallen Barb Taylor. And *who* it was about.

CHAPTER SIX

1992

Bill

REGALAR WINE MADE WITH GRAPE

The first thing you do is get a crock. These days they don't but sell 'em except as antiques. You'll find 'em all over the county but they'll want a hundred dollars. People don't use 'em for anything but to set in the house.

Anyway, you'll need a crock but you could get a plastic drum.

Next you'll need is grapes. It don't matter the kind, red or green or a mix unless yer particular. Now if you ain't got vines on yer property then you can go to the A and P. They hold the grapes they don't sell. Used to be they'd feed 'em to the hogs if they didn't sell but they don't do that no more. Or they'd feed 'em to a cow. Anyhow that's what you need to get yourself is the crock and the grapes and also a flour sack. And that'll be the first thing anyway.

Bill lifted the pencil and stared down at his writing from the bifocal bottom part of his glasses. It was a little scratchy to read, but all the right information was there so far. His hand wasn't cramped but he wasn't exactly used to writing for a while, and now he was itching to do something else.

Before he could figure what that was, the barn door juddered open behind him.

A tall, familiar figure emerged. With shaggy dark hair like a hippie's and Coke-bottle glasses, the man looked half teenager to Bill. But he was twenty years old and probably just suffered from a rotten upbringing. The product of comic books and those damnable arcades Bill had seen once in the shopping mall over in Shelbyville.

Bill let forth a grunt. "What're *you* doing here?"

Bill Coyle wasn't the sort of man who looked down his nose at his daughter's husband. He'd never threatened any boy or man who came around for his other girls.

When it came to Hank Taylor, though, the respect just wasn't there for Bill who couldn't help but see the young guy as less than a man. Bill had felt this way since the first time he met Hank Taylor nearly a year back, just months before the wedding.

Seeing the guy now, standing there in Bill's barn, well—Bill didn't feel any different. Even as Hank had put out a hand to shake. There it was, Hank's hand, soft as a baby's bottom. Bill could remember asking the kid point-blank, back when they first met, "What is it you do for a living to have such fine soft hands?"

He worked as the manager at the video store on Main Street. The *video* store. Bill knew that you couldn't do much worse than invest in technology. Every last piece of it was a fad, sure to burn out faster than a halogen bulb. A real man worked with his hands and God's green earth. He didn't fiddle around with plastic.

Of course Bill wasn't so stupid to be an outright jerk to the kid. "Hello," he said now, in the middle of his secret-recipe writing, and pushed his hands down the pockets of his trousers.

"Hi, Mr. Coyle," Hank replied, too chipper. He gave a little jump toward Bill.

"What, you got ants in yer pants or somethin'?" Bill laughed at his own joke.

Hank laughed, too, which told Bill he was being funny and not mean, which Bill never aimed to be. "What, Barb send you out here for a lashin'?" Bill pointed his fingers like a gun at Hank. Another great joke.

Hank laughed again. "Well, you know how it is in there." Hank threw his head toward the main house.

"What?" Then Bill clicked his tongue. "Oh, you mean them women. Sure. Well, I'm used to it." He lifted an eyebrow. *Maybe Hank wasn't so used to being 'round women?*

"Oh, right, right," Hank said in a way that told Bill he hadn't a single clue what to do with a woman. It was just as well. Barb was wild like Essie. She could use a steady Eddie, or a *geek*, even.

"You know with a newborn, it's nice to have some adult interaction." Hank stopped there.

Bill just grunted.

"What you got goin' in here?" Hank took a confident step toward the workbench. Bill wondered if the notebook was *Hank's* idea instead of Barb's. Maybe she only signed the note.

Was Hank interested in the workbench? The notebook? Or...

Bill followed him tight and pointed to the crock of grape juice. "You know what that there is?"

Hank leaned forward, and some of his brown mop swished into his face until he brushed it back. Bill really wanted to groan. Instead, he did the right thing and said, "You need a haircut, I think."

Hank laughed like Bill had cracked another joke then studied the liquid closer. "Is that homemade wine?"

Bill stood up a little straighter. "Well, I wouldn't call it *home*made. Maybe *barn*-made." He guffawed and clapped Hank on the shoulder, squeezing hard. "But you got it half right. That there is gon' be red wine. Just as soon as I finish it."

"Wow. I have *always* wanted to learn how to make this stuff." Hank reached across the workbench and grabbed one of the bottles of moonshine next.

Bill swiped it right out of the kid's hand. "Don't play with that. It's not a *toy*."

Hank went white like a sheet. "Sorry, Mr. Coyle."

"And call me Bill, for the last time."

"Sorry, Bill."

Bill gave his head a shake and returned the bottle just so to the shelf. "That was Essie's dad's moonshine. He bootlegged it right here, himself. We don't have a hell of a lot left. This is all."

"That's so awesome."

Bill snorted at the word. *Awesome*. "Well, it's *history* is what it is."

Hank moved his face back to the wine. "History that's happening right now."

The boy didn't make a lick of sense. "I don't know a thing about moonshine and if anyone's making it now," Bill started.

Hank cut him off. "Actually, I was talking about your wine."

"My wine?" Bill looked at Hank, surprised.

"Well, yessir. I'd love to know more about it."

When was the last time somebody told Bill to talk more? Maybe never.

CHAPTER SEVEN

PRESENT DAY

Amber

Amber didn't believe it, even in the face of video proof, she didn't believe it.

She *so* did not believe it that she opened the internet on her phone and searched for wedding venues in Nelson County.

The other girls in the shop were whispering, and whispers were never a good sign. Not in a small town, anyway. One might think them respectful, but Amber knew better. She'd just become the talk of the town.

Her mother, meanwhile, was gabbing on the phone, loud as a tractor in the springtime. "Tiffany, where did you get that video?"

And because her mother not only lacked the couth to keep her voice down but *also* preferred to have her phone calls on speaker, Amber could hear her sister's replies plain as day. So could the rest of the shop.

"Mom, I *took* it."

Behind them, the door to the shop swept open. Like a magic trick, Tiffany floated in through the doors, her red-dyed hair whipping across her face with the spring breeze. She lowered her phone and Barb did the same. Amber tucked her phone away. A line of sweat prickled up her spine.

Barb shook her arm out from beneath the cape and waved Tiffany back to Amber's station. "Get over here," she hollered. "You went to the bank? *And?*"

Tiffany frowned at Amber. "You're calm."

"I'm working," Amber replied, her face as serious as a heart attack.

"I just told you I caught your fiancé kissing on Crystal Finnegan behind the ATM at Western Federal Bank, and you're *working?*"

Amber took a deep breath. Tiffany was prone to outbursts, and she was also prone to gossip. "I don't believe you."

Tiffany snorted and fell into the next empty seat over. "Mom? Really?" She flapped a hand uselessly at Amber. "She doesn't believe me?"

Amber checked a foil on her mom's head, then folded it back up. "Under the dryer for ten minutes."

"Under the dryer!" her mom cried. "I won't be able to hear you all."

"There's nothing to hear, Mom! Tiffany is making up lies."

Tiffany pushed her phone screen up to Amber's face. "This. Is. Not. A. *Lie*. Amber, *look*."

Amber had already seen the footage, but it was blurry. "You don't know that's Grant."

"Well, I know two things. I know Grant was supposed to be standing at the back of the teller line, and I know that he wasn't there. And I know a guy who looked an awful lot like Grant was swapping spit with a girl who looked an awful lot like Crystal Finnegan."

"That's three things." Amber rolled her eyes. "And anyway, Grant might be on lunch, which explains at least two of your concerns."

"Do you even care if he cheats on you?" Tiffany boomed.

Now that Amber was done on her mama, she had a chance to sit and think. "Just give me that again." She indicated her sister's phone. Amber rewatched the video once, twice. Three times.

In it, she could see clear as day the face of a girl she'd graduated with. Crystal Finnegan was a nice girl, and she'd never had a problem with Amber and vice versa. In the video, Crystal—it was positively Crystal—played with a strand of her silky blond hair, laughed, and looked into the eyes of the burly, short-statured man she'd been facing.

Amber squinted as the man glanced behind him. She caught a brief image of a familiar face.

It was definitely Grant. The video wasn't blurry on Tiffany's phone. The evidence was indisputable.

A flood of emotions coursed through Amber's body. This gossip wasn't gossip; it was fact. It was real. And it *was* about her. But even in the face of such damning evidence, Amber didn't want to believe it. She did not want to believe that the person she'd loved for the past six years could be capable of betrayal. *Not Grant. He was so... unassuming. Soft.* And ultimately, Grant was not, well, *attractive.* Even Amber could admit this.

As she watched the video for a fourth time, she began to roll things over in her mind. If Grant was kissing another girl, when did it start? How did they connect? Why did he want to kiss Crystal Finnegan? Was it because Amber wasn't a beauty queen? Well, Grant was no specimen of the male order. Amber *knew* this. It was partly why she'd wanted to be with him.

Low expectations.

Low standards.

Low, low, *low*.

She never considered the possibility that even if he had a low threat level, that he could still be low-down rotten. Her stomach flipped and her throat closed up. She felt like crying all of a sudden. "It's him," she murmured. She blinked away tears that had forced themselves up into her eyes. She rubbed the heel of one hand across each cheek. "Grant's *cheating* on me?"

The salon had gone coldly quiet. When Amber looked up, she saw her co-workers and their clients were staring at her.

Barb pushed her hair dryer up and tossed her phone onto the seat, standing and crossing to her daughter. She wrapped her arms around Amber in a great big hug, and it felt good, even though it made Amber cry harder.

After a few moments of crying and hugging her mom, Amber pointed back to the dryer. "Go on. We don't want to mess you up."

Tiffany gave Amber a hug next, and again came another onslaught of tears. "You want Travis to go slash his tires?" Tiffany asked, sweet as a cupcake.

"Does Travis know?"

Tiffany nodded dolefully. "I sent the video to everyone."

Amber choked on a sob. Her tears dried on instant. "What!? You sent the video to everyone? *Who's* everyone?"

"Travis, Geddy, Morgan Jo, Aunt Dana, Rachel, and Aunt Carla."

Amber squeezed her eyes shut. *Just great.* Her brother, her cousins, and her aunts.

This was just like Tiffany, to take somebody's tragedy and turn it into front-page family news. "I think I'm gon' be sick..." Amber rushed to the shampooing sinks at the back corner of the shop and heaved air until Tiffany joined her, rubbing her back.

Her mom hollered from the dryer, "Amber—honey! It's okay!"

"Mom, put that dryer back on your head and just sit!" Amber called back. She couldn't do this—juggle two things at once, like this. Another heave came up from her stomach and she pulled her hair back into a single rope.

"Breathe," Tiffany told her. "Just breathe."

Amber did breathe, and it helped. She took one long last breath then stood up and squeezed her eyes shut. She pulled her glasses off and rubbed the back of her hand over her eyes before resituating them. "So, everybody in the family knows he was kissing her?"

"Yep." Tiffany wasn't one lick sorry, either. That much was clear.

"What about Grant?" Amber asked.

"What about him?" Tiffany grunted.

"Did he see you?" she asked Tiffany. "Does *he* know you filmed him?"

Tiffany acted like it was entirely irrelevant whether Grant saw that *she* saw. Amber, however, knew better.

When Amber arrived back at Moonshine Creek that afternoon, once her mama's hair was trimmed, blown out, and curled, and after she'd cleaned her station, things went from bad to worse.

The big house rushed with an energy Amber was unused to. She liked people being around, but she didn't much care for surprises, and walking in through the front door to find Morgan Jo, Julia Miles, Aunt Carla, Aunt Dana, Rachel, and Travis sitting there in wait... well, it unsettled Amber. Normally, she went straight down to her basement apartment, but she was so dang thirsty she'd come in through the front door only to be met with the winces of a thousand Coyles. Starting toward the kitchen, Amber figured if she could just make it past the set of sofas in the front room, she could get her drink and get on downstairs.

But Barb stood at the picture window, holding court in the living room like she'd beaten Amber there by half an hour or more. Barb cleared her throat and clasped her hands in front of her stomach. "Thank you all for being here," she said.

Tiffany peeked out from the far side of her mother from an upright chair, adding, "Yes. Thank you all."

Amber frowned and stopped in her tracks, gripping the back of another sitting chair that faced the rest of the room and in which slight Rachel, her cousin, drowned. It felt as safe a place as any to be standing behind one of Memaw's old sitting chairs. Back when her grandparents were alive, sitting chairs weren't actually for sitting, they were just for looks. Amber came to learn this the hard way—not because Grandad had griped at her but because she'd sat in a small wooden "sitting" chair only to have it crash beneath her weight, humiliating her in one, painful drop.

Still unclear about what everyone was doing but trained up enough to follow her mother and sister's lead, Amber joined in. "Thank you all for comin' over. Are we—are we eatin' early?"

Barb made a face.

Aunt Carla left the room for a moment and returned with iced tea and a stack of plastic tumblers on a platter.

There was just one person distinctly missing from the group. Someone who was usually home by now on a Saturday.

Amber fidgeted her hands at the back of Rachel's chair then edged around it and leaned against the sliver of wall between the front door and the picture window. Oddly, no one made eye contact with her.

Except her mother.

Barb cleared her throat again and gave Amber a short nod, as if it was Amber's turn to say something again.

It was all the indication Amber needed to put two and two together. Shame filled up her belly and pushed into her chest like heartburn. "Oh. Right. I guess you all know about Grant by now." She looked at the floor and kicked an imaginary speck of dust. "Is he here somewhere?"

"No," Aunt Dana said. "We locked the basement entrance from the chain on the inside, too."

Travis piped up from his seat at the window. "I'm watching for him here, but I've got a straight line of sight to the back door, too." He pointed dramatically with his finger straight down the hall toward the mudroom that opened to the backyard.

Amber knew she ought to thank her brother, but she was upset. "Listen, we don't even know the full story."

"Sure, we do." Morgan Jo crossed her arms. "We know what we've known all along, Amber."

Amber frowned at her cousin. Morgan Jo was everything that Amber wasn't. She was pretty and tall. Her hair had those natural waves to it that Amber could hardly get even with a great salon-quality curling iron. And another thing, Morgan Jo was a country girl. She could wield a hammer and ride a horse and do all the things that any true Kentucky girl should be able to do. Plus, she had Emmett Dawson. Emmett, hands down, was the sexiest man Amber had ever seen in her life. He wasn't just brawny and tough, he was smart as a whip, too.

"Oh, is that so, Miss Morgan Jo? And what exactly have you known all along about Grant? You've known that he doesn't have a fancy degree. That he's short. You've known that he's been here for me since day *one*, Morgan Jo. Meanwhile..." Amber looked around the room, taking in everyone's stares as she pressed on, "... I don't know a single one of you who had a man like that."

"Amber Lee Taylor," Barb hissed. "You hush up and sit down. Each one of us has a thing or two to say to you, and you'll hear it all."

Amber froze. This was like that show she loved. *Intervention*. It was an intervention. But why should she have to face the condescension and disapproval of her relatives? Amber was a good family member. She worked a job and helped around the house. She didn't do disgraceful things or get in anybody's way. She never interfered with anyone else in the family. So, why were they interfering with her? Just because they caught Grant on video kissing Crystal Finnegan?

"I can handle Grant," she said earnestly.

"Oh really?" Barb asked.

"Of course. I'll talk to him."

"No, you won't." Travis stood up and pushed the knuckled of his right hand into his palm. A loud crunching sound ensued. "I will."

Amber fumed. "No, you won't do any such thing, Travis Roy Taylor."

Travis, who was mainly used to taking orders from his sisters, mother, and aunt, sank back into his perch by the window. "Well, I *will* talk to him whenever you need me to."

Amber fell back into the love seat, next to Tiffany, who reached for her hand. "Amber, just listen."

"It was time something changed around here for you two," Aunt Carla declared. "Not a one of us liked Grant. Not even Geddy, and Geddy likes everybody." Geddy, another of Amber's cousins, *did* like everybody. He loved easily and forgave fast. But now that Amber thought about it, she'd never once seen Geddy joking with Grant at a family function or giving him a high five during a game of cornhole.

"Emmett can't stand him," Morgan Jo admitted.

Amber glared at her.

"Why? Because Grant doesn't want to help with the vineyard?"

"Are you taking up for Grant?" Barb asked.

"No," Amber balked. "I'm just saying that if this is what you think about Grant, then I guess it's what you think about me, too."

"You *do* help with the vineyard, Amber," Morgan Jo pointed out. "This isn't about *you*. It's about your good-for-nothing boyfriend."

"Fiancé," Amber corrected.

"*Ex*," Morgan Jo said.

Amber swallowed. She looked around the room. No one made eye contact with her except for Morgan Jo.

"So that's why you all are here, then? To tell me to break up with Grant, because you thought I couldn't break up with him on my own. That I wasn't strong enough or something?"

It was Rachel, pipsqueak Rachel with the fine mousy hair, straight as a pin, round glasses and sallow skin, who raised a thin hand. "Actually, we're here because it's Saturday."

"Saturday?" Amber's stomach growled.

"Yes, Saturday." Rachel rose up from her seat and she pointed in toward the kitchen, where Amber spotted a stack of plates and cups and a baking tray lined over in shucked corn cobs. "Family barbecue."

A little smile broke over Amber's mouth. "So, we *are* eating early."

CHAPTER EIGHT

PRESENT DAY

Morgan Jo

The Coyle family milked the Amber-and-Grant drama.

Aunt Barb parlayed it into a reasonable excuse to stand her ex-husband up. She had declared there wasn't any chance she could go out on a date what with her daughter wounded like a November buck.

Morgan didn't blame the woman. There was something to be said for sticking by your family, and Uncle Hank wasn't family any longer. For whatever reason, Morgan sympathized with her aunt over her cousin on the matter. Not that Morgan didn't like Hank Taylor—she didn't even know him. But instead because Morgan knew what it was to be in a relationship with someone who wasn't right for you. Bad romances made it a lot harder to move into new relationships, because you were so caught up in wondering if you were making the same mistake all over again.

The feeling must be even more powerful when it was an *ex-husband* in question. The father of your children, too.

Everyone had tried to encourage Barb to go ahead with the

date, but all it had taken was a quick text to Hank. Barb said the matter was settled. They'd raincheck.

This all, of course, had peeved Amber right off. Curiously, Morgan noted, it did not peeve off Tiff and Trav. "You owe me my twenty bucks back, Amber," Travis had the gall to say.

Morgan had shushed him. They needed to redirect their focus to enjoying the afternoon and evening with family, especially after such heady drama. Travis agreed easily enough, and Amber's attention was occupied on her personal matter so much that she didn't make too big a deal of the canceled date.

The family moved on from the impromptu intervention and set about taking up with their usual Saturday routine. The best thing they could do now was pretend like everything was fine. Once Grant showed up, Travis was assigned to confront him and handle things.

With the plan in place, an uneasy rhythm settled in.

It was April on the farm, and it was a balmy seventy degrees out. Perfect. Well, perfect for Morgan, who'd done a stint in the oven that was Tucson. It was nice to enjoy the seasons again.

Aunt Dana, Aunt Barb, and Morgan's mom set about getting the grill wiped down and prepped. They'd do a cookout. "We got to capitalize on warm days. Who knows when a cold snap'll hit with hail or even a good snow," CarlaMay remarked. Although rarely would they get snow this late in the year, and in fact, down in Brambleberry, winter snow wasn't even all too common.

Morgan fretted openly. "I hope we don't get a bad rain. We've got the vines just ready."

"Rain'll do 'em good, though." Emmett had rejoined them from the fields. He'd said it wasn't his place to involve himself in the Amber drama, so he stayed out there, finishing his pruning work and studying the plants with such care that Morgan wished she were a grapevine. Then again, when night fell and it was just the two of them walking the farm or cuddling on the sofa, that's exactly how Emmett treated her, too. His attention was unwavering.

"We don't want root rot. They need to stay dry," Morgan pointed out, her face drawn and hands on hips.

"It's been dry. Time we get a little moisture. Anyway—doesn't seem like moisture is happening anytime soon." He waved his beer up high, and sure enough, Morgan could see baby blue stretched across the Kentucky sky.

After the family had had it out with Amber, coming down hard on her to finally, for once and for all, drop the deadweight that was Grant Maycomb, Amber had said she wanted to take a shower and have a little time to herself.

Morgan wanted to talk to Amber alone, though. It had been years since they'd had one-on-one time. *Real* one-on-one time, where they could speak in girlish whispers and giggle and dive deep down into the heart of matters normally reserved for such special nights as the rare sleepover.

Here they were, two cousins who once considered each other the closest of friends. Living in the same house, working on the same project half the time, and still, Morgan felt as far away from Amber as she ever had.

Morgan's mom swung past them with a platter of raw burger patties. "Emmett, you want to do the honors?"

* * *

Going downstairs to the basement was challenging for Morgan. She had to take a step at a time, relying heavily upon the railing to twist her body so that pain didn't shoot up into her hip. It was funny, the aftermath of a gunshot wound. Julia suspected the majority of Morgan's pain was in her head, which pissed Morgan off even if she didn't disagree.

Morgan could hear the shower running when she let herself in to Amber's basement apartment.

Once she arrived at the bottom of the stairs, Morgan found the door unlocked. She pushed it open and called out. "Amber? It's me!"

The sound of something or someone echoed to Morgan's left, startling her. "Amber?" No answer came and Morgan was certain the shower was still running.

Straight ahead of her was a kitchen area, complete with one of the oldest stoves Morgan had ever seen. It was the original stove from when great-grandma Nelson lived there, inherited from her own mother-in-law. To the right sat a simple wooden kitchen table with four matching chairs. Currently, a puzzle was splayed across the tabletop. Framing the other side of the table was a short wall along which spread a small set of cabinets and the sink. The design of the area made the kitchen feel like it was its own separate space.

To the left of the kitchen was the living room area, complete with a rustic leather love seat and a matching ottoman. A small television with a built-in VCR sat on top of a dresser across from the love seat.

Opposite the living room and to Morgan's right was the bedroom and en suite bathroom. A door opened into the bathroom just off of the kitchen, and Morgan headed for it with a plan to knock and announce her presence.

As she took a step right, movement caught the corner of Morgan's eye. She swiveled around toward the living room. "Hello? Amber?"

A flash of gray bolted from behind the sofa to the dresser. "Julep." Morgan laughed. "Here kitty, kitty," she purred, distracted only momentarily by one of Amber and Grant's two cats. "Where's your little buddy?" She lifted her chin and looked beyond the living room toward the exterior door which Morgan only now realized was ajar. "Uh-oh. Did Mint escape?"

The cats weren't allowed outside, but they were industrious enough to find their ways out there if only the screen door was closed, and the wooden door was open. Which it was. Probably to let in cool air on such a warm day, but it was foolish of Amber to get in the shower with the cats having easy access outside.

"Mint?" Morgan made her way past the tidy living room—though Grant had a slovenly overall character, Amber was notorious for keeping the basement apartment neat, her workstation neat, anywhere neat. It was one of those things about some people—a surprising feature of their personality and habits.

As Morgan passed Julep, she gave the precious kitty a scrub beneath the chin and cooed again, "Mi-*int*, sweetie."

Morgan arrived at the screen door, which edged open about half an inch thanks to a faulty hinge. Morgan pushed it the rest of the way, slowly, careful not to let Julep out, too.

"Hey!" a voice and its accompanying body jumped out from behind the corner outside the door. A rush of heat zinged up through Morgan, and she froze and fell back into the screen door, crashing it closed. "Oh, my!" She pressed her hand to her heart.

"What're you doing here?"

Morgan swallowed and stilled herself for a moment before taking him in. "Grant. I'm sorry—I was looking for—"

"You all ain't supposed to come down from the main floor from the inside." He referenced the agreement the family had in place once they'd settled living arrangements. Part of that agreement, though, was the understanding that Amber and Grant would simply keep the interior door locked and mainly use the exterior. The illusion of separation had been more important to Grant than Amber. Before, Morgan had figured this was on account of their romance and the fact that though Amber was family, Grant was not. Now, it occurred to her there may be other reasons for such a rule.

"I'm so sorry." The apology was a perfunctory response to

getting *caught*, but Morgan wasn't sorry, of course. "I needed to talk to Amber."

Grant, who was usually boring and plain enough to be quiet and unremarkable, seemed edgy. Then the smell hit Morgan as soon as she saw a cigarette in his fingers.

"What's going on?" he grunted between drags.

Morgan stammered, "Oh. Uh—um, nothing. Just about..." She wondered if he knew. *Had he and Amber already spoken? Had she already broken up with him, maybe?* "Did Amber talk to you?" This was *so* not Morgan's place. *And yet... wasn't it?* Was it not her place to do what was best for her cousin? Or was Morgan falling into the trap of being the well-meaning but super inappropriate cousin who meddled?

"About what?" Grant didn't appear suspicious.

"Oh, nothing." Should Morgan invite him to the cookout? Surely Grant was well informed of it. He'd come to every single one. "You heading up to the cookout?" This was a test.

"Yeah. Gotta eat where the eatin's good." Grant grinned lazily at Morgan then dropped his cigarette onto the cement slab that functioned like a front porch. He drove his heel into it but didn't bother picking it up.

Morgan had never once seen a cigarette butt on the property. Not a recent one, at least. She'd come across ancient packs of Marlboros out in the tobacco field here or there, but that was it. Amber must pick up after Grant. This tiny realization nettled at Morgan like a corkscrew, twisting into her side and hurting her so much that she lost control over her brain and mouth for a moment.

"You cheated on her."

It fell out. Like a slippery frog sliding from the top of a smooth wet rock down to the ground, plunking into mud. Amber's new secret. Or rather, more appropriately, *Grant's* secret.

Grant's face burst into an angry tomato red. His fists balled up at his sides. "What!" he spat.

"What's going on out here?" Amber's voice emerged from the door behind Morgan. As she came out, Mint dashed from the grass beyond and into the house. Maybe the cat knew she shouldn't be out there. Maybe the cat had been a party to such conflicts before. Morgan wondered what else went on between Grant and her cousin that no one knew about. *Was he really the soft-spoken, easy-going guy everyone had thought he was?*

And more than that, what had Amber ever seen in this man?

Nausea formed in Morgan's stomach. She knew exactly what Amber had seen in Grant. It was the same thing she'd once seen in her ex-boyfriend, Nick.

In Grant, Amber saw what she *thought* she deserved.

CHAPTER NINE

1992

Bill

It was Saturday, and the standing family tradition on Saturday nights was a full country supper, drinks on the porch, and, if it was warm out, the women might go for a walk or the kids would chase fireflies and trap 'em in mason jars.

Over the summer months, they'd usually get to barbecuing out on the back lawn. Bill wasn't much for grilling, but Essie knew her way around just about every cooking contraption one could think up. She would end up manning the grill, flipping burger patties and tube steaks while the other women flitted around sipping on their teas and nagging about this, that, or th'other.

It explained, though, why Hank was lingering out there with Bill. What with no other men around—no thanks to Bill's cousins who were hit or miss on Saturdays—Hank had two choices: listen to the women talk about hair and nails or join Bill out in the barn.

Maybe Hank didn't much care to hear about wine, after all. Maybe this was just the lesser of two evils to him, Bill figured, though at least Hank preferred the company of a man who made wine to a flock of silly-headed women. It was a check mark in the right box, so far as Bill was concerned.

"Well, what do you want to know?" Bill scratched his head. He had a lot more writing to do. And then again there was the tractor and the Gator. If there was anything the old man was good at, it was finding something to tinker on or fiddle with.

Hank acted like he had nowhere to be and nothing to do. He probably didn't neither. "So, how does this all begin? I mean, I've seen your farm—do you harvest your own grapes? Or do you buy in bulk from a warehouse somewhere?"

Bill laughed, but he wasn't trying to be cruel. "Well, I'll just show you."

They bypassed the Saturday evening events, which nowadays included fussin' over two new babies, little girls who'd one day go on to become one of the women. Bill was proud of his daughters, Barb and CarlaMay, for having babies. He was sure he'd be proud of them babies one day, too. But while he loved 'em, he had to be in the right mood to tolerate a baby. Today he wasn't in that mood, and even less so what with Hank botherin' him.

Hank didn't seem to mind they'd be late to supper, which encouraged Bill on down past the fence and into the heart of the farm.

"I always thought your family were tobacco farmers."

"They was, Essie's folks. Bootleggers when they had to be, too."

"Were your parents farmers?" Hank asked.

"Ever'body 'round here was farmers. Corn, wheat, and ginseng. Soybeans, too. All over these parts." He looked over his glasses at Hank as he passed through an opening in the fence. "You're not from here?"

"I'm a Loo-vul boy. Wildcats. Class of 1990."

Bill knew this somewhere deep down. Essie had probably told him, and Barb had probably told her. The reminder did nothing for him, though. "You ever been in one of these?" He waved his arm toward the vines and fruit trees that had been planted here long, long ago.

"In an orchard? Oh, sure. Yeah. Well, I haven't actually been *in* one, but I *did* see the film *The Vineyard*." Hank's eyes lit up. "It's a horror, directed by James Hong and..." He snapped his fingers a few times and Bill was growing so bored he might fall asleep standing up. "William—Rice? Rice, yeah. William Rice." Hank beamed with pride.

"Ain't never heard of it."

"It was a cult classic. Limited release. A little on the, uh, *sexy* side..." Hank winked at Bill, and he all but recoiled.

"I don't know what could be horror and sexy about vineyards, but, well." He stopped mid-thought. "Anyway, here we are. They got all kinds of berries from wine grapes to other varieties, I s'pose. I use these ones here. Shamberchin, or somethin', Essie's dad told me." He held up a heavy bunch of nearly black grapes. "They're great for wine, I guess." He moved through a row of vines. "Here we got some flowers and trees to help lure away the bugs and critters. Lemon and pear and orange." Bill pointed on down the rows of trees. "There's a strawberry vine down there." He pointed back up the other way. "Blueberries." He pointed over. "Blackberries."

"Wow. You've got a self-sufficient farm here."

Bill laughed. "Well, that's what a farm *is*."

"You know, Mr. Coyle." Hank gave his shaggy head a shake. "Sorry, *Bill*, you really ought to document all this."

"Document?" *So it was this hippie who'd put Barb up to the notebook gift.* Bill felt an itch to burn the thing. "I'm writing down recipes to pass along to the grandchildren." He meant the two babies. Bill couldn't exactly picture them two babies one day being real live adults. Just as he never pictured his own children growing up into something resembling himself and Essie. Then again, there they'd done it. And one was married, too. To this hippie right here.

"Well, document, sure." Hank used his hand to move his hair from his face, and Bill could see it getting stuck on the sweat of the kids' forehead under the blazing Kentucky sun. "As in record. You could write down your process or—"

"I already *am* writing it down. Barb said it was a good idea." Bill huffed and pretended to inspect a nearby bunch of grapes that hung up high, as if it might float up into the air like a group of them helium balloons they'd taken to the hospital when each granddaughter was born.

"That's awesome," Hank remarked, and he seemed to be excitable over it, Bill estimated.

"Well, thank ya. I'll see about it. Takes a lot of work to write all them recipes down. Can't imagine much more detail than just the ingredients and steps and whatnot."

"Have you ever considered a different medium?"

Bill scratched his head. "Ah'*what?*"

"Instead of writing down how to make your wine, what if you filmed it?"

At that, Bill guffawed louder than a mare in labor. "I know you's from Louie-vull, so you don't know this, but we ain't got Hollywood people down here in the holler." Bill found Hank to be a real jokester or a real idiot. Wasn't sure which.

"No—I know that." Hank was smiling like an idiot. "They make home-video recorders. You could videotape all of this yourself."

"No I cain't." Bill was getting real agitated now. Who did Hank take him for? A fool? "Writing it down is the way."

"I have a home-video recorder," Hank replied. "I could help?"

CHAPTER TEN

PRESENT DAY

Amber

Amber knew exactly what was going on outside the big house; Morgan Jo was standing up for her. Grant didn't see it that way, though. He pointed a thick finger at Amber's cousin. "She's sayin' stories!"

"No, she isn't, Grant."

"Yes, she is! She's accusin' me of being a lyin' cheat!"

Amber, her hair wrapped up in a towel and nothing on but her ratty old robe, propped her hands on her hips. With Morgan Jo there, she felt bold enough to fight back. At least, a little bit. "We saw what you did today. Everybody saw it."

"Saw *what?*" He'd fallen back a step, and Amber was smart enough to see Grant's easy facade turn greasy and brittle like a thin sliver of overcooked bacon.

A different, sharper voice came in reply. Tiffany hissed, "Saw you kissin' Crystal Finnegan." Tiffany and Travis had appeared out of nowhere. They stood behind Grant, trappin' him like a rabid raccoon. "Look here, you fool." Tiffany wielded her phone, pressing play for Grant to watch himself in the clandestine show of infidelity.

"I already told you to pack your things, Grant," Travis said, cracking his right knuckles against his left palm. "It's time you listened." Travis wasn't always good for much, but he had the redneck intimidation factor down pat. The only question was whether pathetic ol' Grant would bend to it now.

Amber had seen what a cornered rat could do, and it wasn't just worm away into the bluegrass. Usually, they fought back, harder.

Grant looked at Amber, desperate sweat fogging up his glasses. "Amber, come on. Kissing? Who counts *kissing*?"

"I do," Morgan Jo replied.

Amber glanced at her then took a step forward, closing in on Grant. "Grant, it's over."

"Like hell. Kissin' doesn't count. I'm going into *my* house." He started for the door.

It was laughable, everything about Grant. His false bravado and his choice of words and the stupid lies he believed. Like he was entitled to something. To Amber and the big house and the family, and everything good Amber had.

Amber moved in front of him but facing him churned up a deep repulsion in her loins. Weakening enough to shuffle to the side, Amber begged, "Grant, *stop*. Don't go in there."

"I *live* here," he shot back and pushed forward. But Morgan Jo was blocking the door.

"Grant, get the hell out of here," Travis hollered.

Tiffany added, "We'll call the police!"

"You can't call the police," Grant snorted, "they'll side with *me*."

He lunged at Morgan Jo and grabbed her left shoulder with his left hand, tearing her out of his way.

Amber was horrified to watch Morgan stumble onto her right side, her *bad* side, and fall to the ground like an oak tree that had been severed at the bottom. Amber, Travis, and Tiffany all fell forward to try and catch her, but like they were moving in slow motion, they were all too late.

"I'm going in there after him," Amber promised Morgan Jo, who was fine but shaken up. Just as Amber reached for the door, though, she was met with Grant's back, which was coming at her.

She looked up to see Emmett, sexy ol' Emmett Dawson, who'd come from inside of the basement and thrust back through the door with one hand gripping the front of Grant's shirt as he shoved him back outside and past everyone. "That's reasonable self-defense. And I can promise you one thing, Grant Maycomb," Emmett said, "Kentucky law doesn't look too favorably upon men who rough up women."

* * *

Amber sat in a wooden lawn chair with a sweet iced tea gripped in both hands. Her sister and cousin sat on either side of her. Emmett and Travis were finishing in the basement, helping Grant pack so well that he wouldn't ever have to come back to Moonshine Creek again.

"How ya feeling, Amber?" Morgan Jo asked through a mouthful of burger. Morgan Jo was lucky; she had the height to withstand chowing down on burgers or anything else she wanted. Her body seemed to absorb food in all the right places. Amber didn't realize how being cheated on and then breaking up with someone could make a person feel so low down and so aware of the good in others. And the bad in herself.

"I'm feeling pretty low down." Amber sighed and took a slug of her drink. It tasted good. It tasted so good that Amber wondered when the last time was that she'd enjoyed Aunt Carla's sweet tea so much. *Must have been a while, but why?*

Amber was always around for Saturday supper. "This tastes different." She held up her glass.

Morgan smiled. "I know what you mean."

"Did Aunt Carla spike it with whiskey?" Tiffany asked. She was leagues behind them, yet. "I did that once and nobody noticed." Or maybe she was leagues ahead of them. A wildcard, that's what Tiffany was.

"No, I don't mean like *that*, I mean… like everything about my life is different now." Amber didn't often wax thoughtful, but when the urge struck, she knew better than to ignore it. "He's still down there." She twisted in her seat and looked down toward the basement door that led out onto their short concrete porch. The door was closed, and Amber wondered at the conversations unfurling inside. *Was Emmett giving Grant another talking to? Maybe describing the sort of cases he saw in court where a man and his fiancée had a spat over this or that? And what about Travis? What would Travis say to his once future brother-in-law?*

Then there were the cats to worry over. Amber asked her brother to put them in their carriers while everything was going on. *What if Grant kidnapped them?*

"Do you think Mint and Julep are okay? Should I bring them out here?"

"They'll be okay. Last thing in the world Grant wants to deal with are the cats, I assure you. I don't think I ever once saw him give an ounce of attention to those girls."

Morgan was right, and Amber forced herself to let out a breath. She set her drink on the arm of her chair and made a face at it. "I don't think I can stand to drink that."

Morgan Jo downed the last of her own tea. "I felt the exact same when I came back home. Like everything was different around me. Not that it was *me* who changed."

Tiffany, once again off in her own world, scrunched up her

face. "I don't know about you two, but I'm gon' go get me some of that lemon pie I spied on the table."

After she left, Morgan Jo reached for Amber's hand. "At first, when I was home, I didn't even want to drink the tea. It felt like some sort of betrayal to my new world, what I'd chosen."

"Well, that makes sense seeing all you went through before." Amber meant every word. Even though things were rocky between her and Morgan Jo not too terribly long ago, she'd never stopped thinking about how dang sorry she felt for what had happened to her cousin.

Morgan gave her a small smile and squeezed Amber's hand. Then she let it go and reached for her burger again. Amber followed suit, even if the beef might wind up in all the wrong places on her apple body. "You know," Morgan went on, "after I'd been home a while, I just decided to take a drink of some dang tea. Okay, I'm exaggerating. It wasn't a long while. I only waited half an hour." She laughed. Amber laughed, too.

"Who can resist sweet tea?"

"Right? Anyway, then things changed for me, and I sort of had this weird drifting away in my mind, about Nick, I mean."

"The hot cowboy from Tucson?"

"He was no cowboy." Morgan's smile fell off and, in its place, kinked up a knowing smirk. "He was probably the *opposite* of a cowboy."

"Emmett could be a cowboy if he wanted to." Amber loved Emmett, and not just because he was so sexy, but actually because he was as much a brother to her as Travis was. Not that she saw him altogether much, but as kids, they were close. He was kind. He teased Amber in a sweet way, which made her feel good about herself even when others made her feel rotten about herself. That was the sort of man Emmett was. A cowboy.

"I don't know if he's a cowboy, but Emmett is a gentleman."

A gentleman. There was one other man in Amber's life she thought of as a gentleman. Someone kind-hearted and slow to anger. Someone who opened doors for ladies and listened quietly to his elders. Someone who loved Amber's mother *almost* as Amber loved her.

Amber's very own daddy.

For being a gentleman, though, Hank Taylor wasn't in the picture. Could it be that there was more to being a good man than having good manners like Amber's daddy and Emmett Dawson?

If so, then Amber had a lot to learn about picking a good man.

Anyway, she couldn't talk about her dad. Not to Morgan Jo.

After all, Morgan Jo didn't have a daddy. At least, not one that anyone knew about. So, Amber kept quiet on the subject. And instead, she sat and thought about what had gone so wrong in her parents' marriage that being a gentleman wasn't enough to save it.

CHAPTER ELEVEN

PRESENT DAY

Morgan Jo

April and her showers washed over the farm like a just-tapped well. Just as Morgan had predicted, this was a bad thing. Very bad, in fact.

On a farm, the seasons were God's way of bringing new life to His creation. The ice and snow of December on through February cleaned the land. March's wind threw seeds across the earth, scattering them far and wide. April brought forth the rain to water the seeds, and soon enough May bloomed to color with buds and sprays of green leaves.

But in a vineyard, too much water was no good. And that April, they'd endured several downpours of rain.

Still, come late May, there was hope. Emmett had kept a careful eye on the crops, and it was looking like they'd have good strawberries, blackberries, raspberries, and even at least one row of grapes that'd come through.

There was no telling if the fruit would be any good, but just the fact that the early signs all pointed to *yes* had gotten Morgan and her little team riled up.

Before May could turn over to June, she knew that they'd better start working on other aspects of the grand opening. Time was of the essence. While people were reminding Morgan that *it's okay if you can't open this year*, she knew better. Emmett and Julia had jobs. Full-time incomes. Amber, too, raked in decent wages. Meanwhile, Morgan felt like she was living like a princess off of family land, and it wasn't good enough. She couldn't do that. She didn't feel right about it. This business had to work.

Morgan also knew better than to rush, though. Especially when it came to growing wine grapes and turning juice into the nectar of the gods. You couldn't rush it.

Even so, Morgan was rushing. Blame it on her natural-born impatience or her urges to get going, all the time—something passed down from generations of Coyles. Always be starting something, doing something, finishing something, getting somewhere. It was just who Morgan was. She couldn't sit there and pray for a good crop. Prayers got you started but *doing* was the only thing that could make it happen.

That, of course, was before May came to a screeching, frigid stop.

It all began on a Saturday in late May. Emmett had worked the fields that morning, studying the berries that had started to appear, and then he helped the rest of the day in the barn.

Meanwhile, Morgan had done a walk-through of the hangar —an old back building that had been off-limits to her as a girl, but that her grandmother had had big plans for. Memaw had once told Morgan she'd like to see something nice become of the space. Something to take away from that bad thing that had happened inside of it.

Decades and decades ago, Memaw's twin sister, Dottie, had died in the hangar. Since then, Morgan had thought of the structure like a tomb. It wasn't safe to use anymore, and it needed to come down and be replaced, but Morgan didn't have the heart to do it. Or the stomach, maybe. Especially since that tragedy wasn't the only one the Nelson-Coyle clan had ever seen. Oh, no. Over five years ago, Morgan had a life-threatening accident – one that she was still feeling the physical effects of. Even though she'd forgiven her grandmother and continued to work on healing, there was no forgetting what had happened.

The presence of the hangar didn't help. After all, it was what had happened in there that sparked whatever was deep down in Essie Nelson that would one day impact every other decision in her life. From who she married, to how she raised her children, on down to how she would handle that fateful argument with the man she loved so much but sometimes couldn't stand to be around.

Ideas about what to do with the structure had floated around—tearing it down and starting over. Using its wood. Going in and restoring it, using the basic framing.

That morning, she walked the dusty cavern devoid of inspiration. The back-right corner was boarded up tight, and if Morgan had more energy, she might pull the boards back to inspect the strangely shut-off corner.

Instead, she closed it up and decided to focus on the barn. Especially since she had Amber there that day. With no appointments at the salon, Amber was eager to dive into the family project. She'd shown up in the kitchen bright and early, wearing denim overalls, a straw hat, and work boots.

Morgan marveled at who Amber was fast becoming now that she was free from Grant. A change had set in. She'd let her highlights grow out then did an at-home treatment to subdue the yellowed ends, claiming it was Grant who'd always wanted her to be a blond, and that she herself had no such aspirations. Other things felt different about Amber, too. She was around more than ever, spending her evenings with Morgan as they finished staining the outside of the barn, and her Sundays walking the farm picking weeds.

Morgan liked it, Amber's being around so much. It came to feel comfortable. Like old times, when they were kids.

That particular Saturday, the team of four were going to set about finishing the barn for good. All it needed to function at an operational level now was a slab of concrete and a good sanitization. All the boxes, tools, and machinery of Grandad's had been stowed at the far back. Emmett and Travis built a beautiful set of barnyard doors that rolled along the middle of the space, separating Grandad's hoard from the present. Separating the past from Morgan and her team.

"Have you ever done this before?" she asked Emmett as he mixed water into cement in a wheelbarrow.

"Sure I have. I set concrete at my parents' house up in Bardstown when I was just a kid."

"That was a long time ago," Amber pointed out.

For whatever reason—maybe exhaustion—this struck Morgan as hilarious. She started laughing and couldn't stop. Julia laughed, too, and soon enough Amber was doubled over laughing at the lame little joke about Emmett being older than the back hills of Kentucky.

"But for real, Emmett," Morgan caught her breath. "It's got to be level and, well, *good*. We could hire someone to come out here."

"You've already hired someone." Emmett fastened knee pads over his pants and dragged the wheelbarrow to the first sectioned-off square—rebar and nylon rope cut a perfect grid from one side of their winemaking space to the other. "You hired *me*, remember?" This was meant as another joke, but the laughter had come and gone.

Morgan, Julia, and Amber were doing nothing more than watching now, each with different degrees of anxiety. Morgan rubbed her hip with one hand and worried her lip with her teeth. She glanced right to see Julia, bored, chewing a nail. On

Morgan's left, Amber stared intently at Emmett, her hands folded over her chest.

"Slow down," Amber called out.

This was a first. Morgan had yet to see Amber take any kind of a leadership position, and with regards to *concrete*?

"You don't have to rush," Amber added.

Emmett kept his focus on the wheelbarrow and the fall of the mixture, but he gave a slow nod to show he'd heard her.

Morgan whispered to Amber, "Have you done this before or something?"

Amber replied, her eyes fixed on Emmett. "I watched Grandad and Geddy pour a slab for each of the bunkhouses. We even got to draw our initials into it before it dried."

"I think we should all put our hands on one of the squares," Julia announced.

Morgan loved the idea.

Julia went first, bracing herself in the wet cement and pulling her hands out only to pretend to claw at Amber with the gray mud. Amber dropped down next, pressing her hands in and lifting them out before dragging her initials into the wet gray slate.

"Your turn, MoJo," Emmett said. He leaned back, his butt on his heels.

An avalanche of emotion rose up inside of Morgan. Overpowering tears stung her eyes. "Morgan Jo?" Amber's guiltless, open features betrayed her innocence. Something crossed Amber's face. Worry. "You okay, cuz?"

Morgan sniffed away the bizarre sadness, rubbed her tired eyes and nodded. "I'm just exhausted." She offered a smile as proof she was *fine*. "There's Orange Glo on the mudroom sink." She looked at Julia, who continued holding up gray-caked hands. "You two go on and wash up. After this, we ought to eat supper."

. . .

Once they'd left, Morgan lowered herself to the ground with Emmett's help. He didn't usually handle her with kid gloves. Emmett, like Julia, was hard on Morgan, holding her to a higher standard than she held herself. But although Emmett might push Morgan to finish a long walk around the farm with him or to climb a ladder and replace a light bulb all on her own, he'd never compromise her safety or her *need* to feel safe. "I got ya," he whispered, reaching over her back so he could hold her waist as she leaned forward and pressed her hand in the middle of Amber's and Julia's.

She drew her initials beneath the palm print: M. J. C. Studying them for a moment, Morgan couldn't help but to wonder if they'd always stay like that.

Emmett must have had the same thought. "M. J. C.," he read aloud and eased her back onto her heels. It felt good, the stretch on her thighs in this position.

"M. J. C.," Morgan repeated and looked at him. A dare.

Emmett accepted the dare and tucked a wild strand of her hair behind her ear, running his thumb along the side of Morgan's face. "Don't get too comfortable with those initials."

She smiled, the sadness bursting through in a fresh peel of tears. Morgan didn't deserve him, but that didn't stop her from needing him.

Emmett's face turned serious, and he wiped her face with his thumbs. She could feel streaks of dry cement turning wet on her cheeks.

"You're going to turn me to stone," she said, laughing through the tears.

"Seriously, MoJo. Are you okay?"

"Okay?" She sniffed one last time. "Yes. I'm just—overwhelmed. Are we going to be able to do this?"

Emmett held her face in his hands and looked her right in the eye. "Of course we are."

"What if it doesn't work out?"

"I won't quit my day job. Don't worry," he joked.

"What about me? What will I do?" Morgan protested.

He seemed to consider this for a moment, then planted a kiss on her lips. "Have you ever considered being a stay-at-home mom?"

She wanted to smile. Hell, she *needed* to smile. She needed to say yes. Of course she had. *What woman hadn't?* Morgan swallowed her truth, though. "What if..." She looked down and shook her head, but he pulled her face back to his.

"Morgan, I was joking. The vineyard will work. The winery will work. It'll just take time. And we've got time. Right?"

"I don't know?"

She did know, though. They did not have time. Especially not if having children was still on the table. If Morgan's body could have children then she absolutely didn't have time to put that off. The biological clock was a very real thing, and Morgan was fairly sure that she didn't need one more strike against her fertility.

If she was one day going to have any hopes of growing a little life inside of her, then she'd better get this vineyard going *soon*.

The best thing to do now was to change the subject. Morgan wrapped her hands around Emmett's wrists and laced her fingers through his.

Morgan could feel her tears dry up in the concrete dust on her cheeks. Her resolve returned, and her sadness sealed itself back up in her heart. She squeezed Emmett's hands and lifted her tone. "Anyway, it's your turn, *E. L. D.*" She tried to pull his hands to the cement.

He resisted gently. "Naw. This is your girls' thing. I'm just a grunt."

"You're part of this, Emmett. Heck, you've done most of the work."

"I don't need my initials in this floor. It was your grandad's, anyway. Not sure how Bill Coyle would feel about his grand-daughter's boyfriend marking his territory in here."

"I doubt Grandad would have been too keen about any of what we're doing." A memory struck her then. They were seventeen. Emmett, a sinewy teenager with sun-kissed skin from his head to toes. Morgan, freckled with windblown hair. They wove through the orchards until he pulled her up against a peach tree and scrawled their initials into the bark.

Morgan's eyes lit up and she poked Emmett in the arm. "Anyway, you already marked your territory on this farm. Remember?"

"Hm." Emmett tapped a dusty gray finger on his chin, smudging dry cement over his cleft. She could eat that boy right up, right now, Morgan could. "You might have to *remind* me."

When Morgan was distracted enough, she forgot entirely about her bad hip and the spell of sadness. It was like the injury had never even happened. She pushed up from the dirt patch where she was kneeling and grabbed both of Emmett's hands, dragging him to his feet. "I'll *show* you."

CHAPTER TWELVE

1992

Bill

The summer had passed on like a riverboat floating down the Ohio. And what's more, you could bet that if summer was a riverboat, filled to the gills with tourists and freewheeling happy folk, then, well, autumn was a barge. On a farm, autumn time meant business, not play, and that's just what Bill was about to get into.

October was closing on out, and Essie had a mind to host a full-on Halloween party at the farm that afternoon.

Just as soon as Bill learned about the plan, he worked on a new one.

"Essie," he grumbled while she was doing dishes the day of the party, "I been checkin' on the vines, and it's all about time now."

"Time for what, sweetheart?"

"Well, it's time to *harvest* the grapes, Essie."

"Now? Cain't you wait until tomorr-y?"

"I was jes' out there this morn', Essie, and they got to be picked now. Probably not later than sundown."

"What about the party, Billy?" Essie had dried her last dish and was looking at him with big wet doe eyes.

Bill pressed his mouth tight together then bared his teeth a bit and replied, "The party ain't 'til tonight. I'll be 'round for that."

"The party is at lunchtime, Billy. The babies go to bed before sundown. We're just havin' a little lunch and some candy to celebrate. And a game or two is all. Cain't you pick the berries after?"

"Well, it might take me a while."

CarlaMay appeared in the kitchen, setting about warming a bottle of milk on the stovetop. "It's okay, Mom. Dad can do the harvest today."

Essie gave Bill a funny look before she turned to their daughter. "But he's gon' want to see the babies in their get-up, CarlaMay."

"I know, but I'm pretty sure Hank would love to help Dad. He's coming, too."

Bill scratched his head. Now he was really stuck. Either watch two babies drool or let his hippie son-in-law take movie footage of him pulling bunches off the vines. He grumbled something to himself and trudged away, hoping God might intervene on his behalf.

As soon as the so-called party got going, Bill mumbled something about being back real soon. He ambled off alone into the barn, where he tinkered for a minute with tools, wipin' them down in oil to stave off rust. After five or ten minutes had passed and no one had come after him, he figured he might be safe to go and check the grapes again. If they tasted just right, he'd have a mind to harvest 'em right then and there during the party. Wasn't any reason not to, 'sides from Essie's warning.

Just as he took off, passing from the barn to the orchards and vineyard, he heard Essie's voice holler after him. "Billy! Bill!"

Bill fussed and swore under his breath. He shook his head and turned to see her moving his way. "What is it, Essie?"

"We had an idea. How about you rustle up half-a-dozen apples from the orchard and bring 'em up."

"Up where?"

"Over to the party, Bill!" She smiled big, her hands tucked into the pockets of her white apron.

He grumbled, "What're they even for? You've got more food than any one of ya is gon' eat."

"We're gon' have the babies bob for apples!" She beamed in a real goofy way, but Bill just frowned.

"How the hell's a baby gon' bob for a damn apple, Essie?" But try as he might, Bill loved Essie enough to push down a bad mood. He laughed after all. Just the thought of such a sight was ridiculous enough to fit right into a circus.

But then Essie's mood closed up like elevator doors sliding together. Her face went straight as a sheet of metal. "Billy, just get the damn apples."

He could feel heat splotch over his face. Essie probably saw that heat, because her lips curled up and she looked down at her apron. "Thank you, honey."

Bill was raking his gnarled hands through an apple tree when a voice hollered up from behind.

"Mr. Coyle!" The voice was familiar, and it grated on Bill. "Bill, I mean!"

Bill twisted around to see the hippie there at the fence, heading his way into the orchard. "Oh. Hello. The party's back at the house." If only Hank had come for his daughter's Halloween party.

Hank didn't leave, though. Instead, he lifted a black box into the air. Well, it wasn't so much a box as a case of some kind.

Bill pointed at it, his brows low and his mouth in a deep frown. "What in the wide world is *that* thing?"

Hank shook his long hair back, set the case down, and pulled out a black machine. He held the device against his face and squinted before he replied in a goofy-as-all-get-out voice, "And we're *rolling!*"

"What in the *hell* does that mean?" Bill just laughed, and Hank seemed to think it was all a joke, too.

"I'm here to film you, Bill. To document your process. Remember?"

"Oh." Bill plucked another dry leaf off the vine. "Well, yeah. All right, well... the whole thing, it don't start right here, you know."

"Oh, sure. There's prep work in the barn first, or...?" Hank put the camera back to his eye.

"Put that thing down. It ain't time for it, yet. If we're gon' start right, then we start talking about raisin' a crop."

"Oh, sure." Hank looked like Bill had let him down. Bill hated to disappoint the try-hard kid.

"Well, I mean, I can just talk through that part."

"Great!" Hank was too eager. Naive and immature. Bill figured he was the type to get himself in trouble a lot.

"You work down at the video store, then?"

"Sure do. I'm the manager. Got a promotion last year."

"You good at watching movies?"

Hank laughed. "I guess. I'm just, like, *really* into the process."

"Which? Winemaking?"

"And filmmaking. Sometimes I wonder why I didn't move out to Hollywood when I had a chance."

Bill gave him a harder stare. "When you had the chance." He grumbled something under his breath.

Hank's eyes flashed up, all panicked like he'd just confessed something bad. Real bad. "I don't mean—sir, I *love* your daughter. And my daughter!" He laughed, nervous. "I just—things happened, and it got a little crazy."

"You're talking about Barb gettin' pregnant before you all was married." He said it, didn't ask. It wasn't a question, after all.

Hank's eyes fell to the dirt floor of the orchard. His camera hung in his hand, and he looked about as hurt as a puppy dog, and Bill didn't have time for that.

"Oh, hell, I don't care. You married is all. What's right is right. Now, turn that thing on and let's change the topic before someone hears us and makes a fuss out of nothing."

CHAPTER THIRTEEN

PRESENT DAY

Amber

Amber let Julia wash up first. Then Aunt Carla hollered at the girls to come in and help set the table.

Amber sent Julia in, then washed her hands with the gritty orange detergent, taking care to clear the cement from beneath her fingernails. After washing, she reached for the shop towels on the windowsill, but movement flickered through the mudroom window.

Morgan Jo and Emmett. Hand-in-hand, her pulling him along and him pretending like he didn't want to follow that girl to the ends of the earth.

Amber watched with a prurient interest. They looped around the barn but didn't head toward the big house, instead veering back toward the orchard. Before they got to the dip in the grass that led up the hill to the fence line, Morgan Jo's body jerked back. Amber squinted through the window, her breath appearing on the pane beneath her view out. Emmett tugged her to him and wrapped his arms around her middle. He pulled her in and pressed his mouth to hers.

Amber swiveled away. She had no interest in watching *that*.

After a beat, she turned her head carefully over her shoulder and looked again to see them fading into the distance like wisps from Grandad's cigars. It was rare to catch Grandad with a cigar, but when she did, Amber found herself entranced by the fragrant, masculine smoke curling into heaven like a spirit.

Envy spasmed inside of Amber. It wasn't that she harbored outright jealousy toward her cousin. Amber knew better than to carry envy in her heart, but how could it be helped? Even if it was the silliest thing the world, it was still just the way Amber felt, and you couldn't exactly change the way you felt about something, now, could you?

Anyone could see plain as day Morgan Jo and Emmett were mad in love and meant to be. How could a fair person be jealous over that? Amber's mom had always taught her that if you were going to be jealous of something, it'd better be something you can't ever have. Not something you *can* have, because if you *can* have it, well, then why waste time being jealous instead of going on out and getting that something?

The logic was undeniable, even to a simple girl like Amber.

Still, having a good man such as Emmett felt far out of her reach. Amber couldn't picture herself with a kind, handsome gentleman. Not now. Not ever. Maybe she was meant to be more like Aunt Carla, a sweet little woman who didn't have one lick of interest in dating. Not after such a burn as Carla incurred. Funny now that Amber thought about it. She'd shared that with her aunt, too: the burn of heartache and infidelity and all the horrible things that you had to swallow down when the person you thought you'd loved ruined everything for the two of you. It must be like having your insides set on fire.

Amber wondered if Aunt Carla still bore such pain in her heart. She wondered a lot about her aunt, in fact. Of everyone in Amber's family, she often felt the closest to CarlaMay, whose path in life wasn't so straight as that of others. Well, sure enough, Aunt Dana hadn't walked a straight road, either. Come to think of it, Amber had come from a broken line of people.

Was the whole family broken? Was Amber a shattered woman because she was destined to be so? Because every woman in her family who'd come before her... well... they'd been broken. All of them.

No wonder jealousy zipped up Amber's spine like a natural reflex. She was born into a life where happiness never stuck around. It hitched a ride in the suitcase of the man who got you pregnant. Amber left the mudroom thinking hard about her own dad and his failed marriage with her mother, and she wondered why in the world the Coyle women were so unlucky in love.

Maybe it demanded more than thinking on.

Maybe Amber had better ask about it. Get some answers. Settle her troubled, worrisome mind.

She entered the kitchen, full of the vim and vigor that spiked up in a girl who was in between worlds and floating so far away that she needed to toss a hook onto someone and rip herself back to earth. "Aunt Carla," Amber said this with a sharpness in her tone that felt unfamiliar, even to herself.

It must also have struck Aunt Carla and Julia as unfamiliar, because they stopped what they were doing—Carla basting the chicken and Julia setting out silverware. They both pinched their eyebrows together and stared at Amber.

"Everything okay, Amber Lee?" Aunt Carla wiped her hands on her apron, and she looked like Memaw, standing there in an apron with an extra dish towel slung over one shoulder. Even Aunt Carla's wild brown hair had started to show streaks of gray at her temples and in little strips throughout the loose waves. Amber secretly thought her aunt looked kind of cool with the gray streaks, almost like a witch. A wild woman, to be sure. So wild she was almost part animal. It was all very exotic, Carla's natural look, that was certain.

"Yes, everything's fine." But Amber gave her head a shake and recalled her mission. "Actually, I have a question."

"Shoot away, hon," Carla went back to basting and Julia to setting the table.

Amber blurted out, "Do you know why my parents divorced?"

CHAPTER FOURTEEN

1992

Bill

"Okay, we're *rolling*."

"Hello."

"Wait! Rolling means the camera is on, but—just..." The hippie cleared his throat and pushed his hand through his hair which was longer now than ever. "Can we try again? Wait until I say *action*."

Bill huffed. "Fine."

"Okay, we're *rolling*. Three, two, one, and... *action!*"

"Hello. I s'pose you know who I am, but if you don't, I'm Bill and this here's the farm." Bill waved his arm around behind him. He'd dressed up for today—a brown-and-green flannel shirt complete with his good suspenders. His hair was combed into place and he'd applied wax to it to keep it that way, and he'd cleaned his glasses with alcohol and a kerchief this morning.

For this first part of the video, Hank stood in the gap between fences so they could easily walk into the orchard and then the vineyard beyond.

Hank gave him a thumbs up but kept his eye behind the suction cup of the camera lens. Bill had learned all about video-taping thanks to Hank.

Bill took the thumbs up to mean that he should keep going, and so he did. "This farm, let's see..." He scratched the side of his face. "Well, this farm belonged to my wife's parents, the Nelsons of Brambleberry Crick. And before that it was in her dad's father's family. There's a lot of history there, y'see. Boot-legging and tobacco growing, mostly." He coughed into his fist then lifted both hands and let them fall again. "Well, I could keep on talking more about the history or..."

Hank leaned away from the camera and spoke in a way that made it impossible to hear him. Bill cupped a hand around his ear and leaned forward. "What'd you say?"

"You can keep talking!" Hank replied, now loudly and clearly. He didn't seem aggravated with Bill, but Bill felt a little like he was being aggravating which made him nervous.

"Well, all right. I don't know a hell of a lot. You'll have to ask Essie about what her parents' parents did with the farm back then." Bill turned and looked behind him. "All these plants and flow'rs, well, they been here since the beginning of time, I reckon." He scratched the back of his head.

Hank lowered the camera and the red light faded away. "That was *great*, Bill. Let's talk a little more about what you know of Essie's parents. Like when you first came to the farm?"

"Well, okay."

"How about we do that shot in front of the big house. Gives it clear context. The setting is super important even in docu-mentaries. I'd argue *especially* in documentaries. We need a sense of where we are and its relation to everything else."

"Well, okay." Bill followed Hank as they made their way to the front of the house. Bill didn't much care who knew about the videotaping, but the funny thing was that none of the women much cared. In fact, when Barb drove up with Hank—

who rode along in the passenger seat for some reason—she stayed in the car and asked for Essie and CarlaMay to come out to her. Then, the women loaded up and headed out. For all Bill knew, they hadn't the faintest what in the world Hank was doing with the funny black case. Bill didn't care if the women figured the pair were up to something weird, but he was disappointed they hadn't really asked.

Maybe one day they would.

After another round of filming Bill as he went on and on about the family history and the history of the house, and the history of this, that, and th'other, the two decided it was time for a drink.

Bill brought out a bottle of Jack Daniels and two glasses he'd rinsed in the sink. Hank lit up a pair of cigars, and they lowered into a set of iron-backed chairs on the back porch just in time for the sun to fall down on the farm.

"You've got something to be proud of here, Bill," Hank remarked.

"Thank ya." Bill hated to receive compliments. He didn't know what in the hell to do with them. "Well, it's not mine."

"It's yours now." Hank puffed like a chimney. He was so easy and carefree and just so damn happy. *Who in this world had a right to be so happy?*

"It'll be someone else's someday."

"Mortality. *Classic.*" Hank laughed and threw back his drink.

Bill didn't get it. He just sipped at his whiskey and looked real hard at the cigar. "Where'd you get this?"

"Oh, right." Hank looked at his, too. "My dad gave me two cigars to celebrate the birth of my firstborn child."

"I hate to tell you this, Hank, but she was already born." Bill cracked a grin.

Hank, though, didn't find it funny. "I know."

A strange sort of silence swallowed up the air between

them. Bill felt like he was sitting on rocks all a' sudden. Bill couldn't just sit through the silence. "Well, how come you didn't smoke 'em back then?" The least the hippy could do was spit it out. Bill wasn't trying to do a little dance with the boy.

"Well, one was for my dad. These cigars I mean." Hank was just lookin' real hard at his stogie again, like it might answer him with something smart.

Bill realized the kid had mentioned his dad, and Bill didn't know a thing about the guy other than what he'd heard in passing here or there. A business-type. Not much around was all Bill knew. Couldn't come to the wedding because of the short notice and something else. It was fine, because Bill didn't much care to make a new friend in some *in-law*, anyway.

"Okay, then." Bill took a puff of his own. The thing tasted like paper and tar to him, but he didn't mind it. Could be fun to light one up from time to time. He used to smoke cigars up until Essie read a report about cancer. They both quit, then.

"You don't know?" Hank asked.

Bill looked at the boy and saw his eyes were all glassy like he was higher than a kite or drunker than a sailor or something. "What's wrong?"

"He died."

"Died? Who? Your dad?"

Hank looked at Bill real funny. "Yes, my dad *died*. Last winter. I thought Barb told you."

Bill got huffy at all this. He wasn't the type to forget somebody's *death. And hell, what about a funeral?* Bill was good when it came to funerals. He knew just how to act and be. They were the easiest sorts of affairs a quiet man like Bill could go to. He liked them, even. "I don't remember no funeral," he answered.

"There wasn't one." Hank was smoking the stogie again and playing with the glass. Bill worried he'd drop it and it'd hit a pebble and break, but he tried not to say anything about that. Hank added, "Not here, anyway."

"How come?"

"He didn't live here. Anyway, they had him cremated and sprinkled out across the water."

"But you're from Louie-vull." Bill didn't feel much like bickering, but the kid wasn't telling the whole story, here. "Your folks up and move?"

"My mom and I live in Loo-vul, yeah. But my dad moved away when I was kid. We lost touch for a long while, but I tracked him down. I sent him letters. When he found out about Baby Amber, he sent me cigars by mail." Hank's eyes went from watery to twinkly. "I always figured he'd be the one traveling out here to see me and meet Barb, you all, and Baby Amber. Turned out it was the other way around."

Maybe the losing touch part explained why Barb hadn't made a stink over things. She probably didn't even know the guy.

Bill scratched his head. Barb ain't said nothing about Hank's dad dying and even less about them driving somewhere for some funeral.

"Where did he live that you all couldn't go? China?" Bill wanted to laugh real bad but he didn't.

Hank's eyes got a little glassy like again. He took a long puff and replied as he stared out at the last edges of the warm orange sun. "Cali."

CHAPTER FIFTEEN

PRESENT DAY

Morgan Jo

Morgan Jo dragged Emmett playfully across the farm and to the fence. Every few feet he pulled her back and planted a kiss on her in a new place. Her forehead, her cheek, the hollow of her neck.

The arrived at the fence gap and she pressed her hands into his chest. "Okay, enough of that. Do you *really* not remember this?" She referred to the first time they'd made their mark on the farm. A physical mark. Not the initials by the bunkhouses—which Morgan was strangely sad over. Not the palm prints in the new slab in the barn. This was a different sort of mark. The mark of young love.

"Remember *what*?" he was teasing her. *Surely, he was teasing her.*

"You really forgot that your initials are already carved into the farm." She lifted an eyebrow, daring him to continue the lie.

Emmett's mouth broke into a grin so delicious she could lean in and taste him right then and there, even after a long day of work. Maybe especially after. There was something about a sweaty man that just *did* it for Morgan, and especially when that salty man was Emmett. She started to lean in and ravish him, but Emmett beat her to the punch, wrapping a dry, cement-crusted hand up under her ponytail and pulling her face to his. He kissed her and moved his mouth to her ear where he whispered, "I thought this was supposed to be a secret."

It was, too. Their secret moment in the orchard when they were teenagers. Emmett and his pocketknife and Morgan and her questions about what would happen to that particular peach tree.

Morgan spun in his arms and fanned a hand around them. "No one can hear us. We're alone out here."

"Hm, well. In *that* case." He swooped a hand under her thighs and swung Morgan into the air, ducking through the fence gap and deep into the orchard. Her worries vanished. Gone was the edginess she'd felt toward him. Gone was her jealousy over her family working on the bunkhouses and scrawling their initials. Gone was every bad thing. Instead, Morgan allowed herself to be carried—body and mind—through the rows of vines and valleys of flowers and to the far side of the orchard, where their peach tree lived on.

Emmett eased her to the soft grassy earth, and Morgan reclined, her hands falling to the ground by her ears. Her heart pounded in her chest. Emmett braced his hands on either side of her. She let her eyes drift closed, but instead of feeling the heat of his body lower to hers or the brush of his lips on her face, a cool wind wicked over her.

She looked up. Emmett was studying the tree, one hand still on her side and the other reaching to feel the trunk where he'd etched their initials so long ago.

"Wow," he whispered. Morgan wanted to grab him by the shirt and tug him back to her but the moment had passed. Edgy all over again, she sat up and stared with mild interest at the scarred trunk of the tree.

It had lived after all, that peach tree. Back when he'd carved into it, she had been worried maybe they'd kill it. Maybe trees couldn't withstand even shallow flesh wounds.

But if a tree couldn't withstand a shallow nick, how in the world had *she*, Morgan Jo Coyle, withstood all that she had? Surely she was weaker than a tree?

"Feel it, Mo," Emmett urged, taking her hand and pressing it to the faded bumps. The tree hadn't just survived their careless teenage lark. It had healed, even. Now, the decades-old letters resembled veins, like they were the thing that brought the tree life. Not something that could have cut off its blood supply.

"It's still there," she murmured. "It didn't go away."

Emmett pulled Morgan into his lap and tucked his chin into her neck. "Of course, it's still there. Just like us."

Then, out of the clear blue, the sun blinked away from above their heads, and when Morgan looked up, heavy gray clouds had begun to creep overhead, casting thick shadows over Moonshine Creek.

CHAPTER SIXTEEN

PRESENT DAY

Amber

Aunt Carla had brushed off Amber's question quickly and easily. "Your parents divorced because they weren't meant to be. Simple as that." She lifted the tray of chicken. "Open the oven for me, would you?"

Amber reached for the door of the oven and tugged it down. "If they weren't meant to be, then why did they agree to go out on a date?"

"You're talking about last month?" Carla slid the tray of basted chicken wings onto the top rack and set the time. "Oh, hon." She gave Amber sad eyes.

"What?"

"I think your momma did that for you, baby girl."

"Why? Why would she do that for me? If she wanted to do something for me, she could have *not* divorced Dad twenty years ago."

But Aunt Carla didn't have the answers, and Julia didn't have the interest. "Amber," Julia asked, maybe as a diversion, "is Geddy comin' to supper tonight?"

Amber shrugged. "Heck if I know. He and Travis went fishing this morning. For all I know they got drunk on Bud Light and fell asleep in their camping chairs."

Morgan Jo and Emmett burst through the front door, their faces aglow; a great big grin spread over Emmett's mouth. It did nothing but fuel Amber's bad mood.

But Morgan wasn't as happy. "Storm's coming."

"Storm?" Amber looked out the window, only barely interested.

"We need to pray it passes quick," Morgan added.

"Is Tiffany coming?" Aunt Carla asked.

"No, she's on a date. And my mom is staying home tonight, too, so it'll just be us, I guess. Assuming the boys aren't coming," Amber replied.

"Well, good." Morgan Jo sat heavily along the bench that spread on the window side of the table. "We need to talk business, and we need to talk it *now*." She drove a finger into the table then reached for a fresh glass of sweet tea and took a long gulp.

"I hope you wash your hands before you dig into the appetizer," Amber pointed out, grumpily. As she said it, she sat in her usual spot adjacent to Morgan Jo and dished herself a heaped serving of tossed salad then perched a buttery roll on the side of her plate.

"Chicken'll be about fifteen minutes," said CarlaMay. "I'll come back out when it's ready. Meantime, I need to get a shower."

"Why now?" Morgan Jo called after her mom. "You could wait 'til after supper."

Aunt Carla was already striding out of the room as she hollered back, "Tiffany isn't the only one with a date tonight!"

This bombshell of a nugget stung Amber nearly as sharp as it had Morgan Jo, whose face went still as stone. Amber noticed it had a gray hue to it, too, now, as Amber studied her.

"Did you know about this?" Amber hooked her thumb over her shoulder.

Morgan pushed up from the table, nearly knocking her tea over. "Mom, what did you just say?" She stormed out of the dining room, following her mother.

That left Amber, Julia, and Emmett alone at the table.

Emmett seemed to hardly notice the unfolding drama. Typical man. So Amber only had Julia with whom to confer. "What was all that about?"

"I didn't know Miss Carla was dating," Julia said, her big blue eyes wide as she bit into her roll and tore a piece off with the side of her teeth. "It didn't look like MoJo knew, either."

"What's up with everyone around here falling in love anyway?" Amber figured she could count on Julia, who was *permanently single*, to commiserate with her.

Julia didn't seem to be on Amber's side, though. Not that Amber was on a different side than people who wanted to fall in love but Amber was certainly in a different world. She was in the post-break-up world, which was one of crumbling facades and heartache and losing bets. It was sort of a dark side, she supposed. Julia said, "It's springtime, Amber Lee. Of course everyone's falling in love."

Her appetite ebbed, and Amber pushed her food around the plate. Everyone *else* was falling in love. Meanwhile, Amber was simply falling.

CHAPTER SEVENTEEN

PRESENT DAY

Morgan Jo

Not once in Morgan's life had her mother made a date with someone. She'd never accepted any dates. She'd never talked about a desire to date. She'd never so much as *revealed the name* of Morgan Jo's father. As far as anyone in the family—or the world—knew, CarlaMay Coyle was a romantic. Her heart, a sealed coffin, six feet under. Long since dead. And indeed, the woman had only ever assured Morgan that her whole world revolved around family. She couldn't care two pennies worth about tolerating a man.

Their private chat in Memaw's old bedroom revealed a flip side to the coin. CarlaMay admitted she was up and down and left and right about dating.

Morgan was surprised to find that she didn't feel too weird about this. If she was mad, it was only because her mom held out the secret and hadn't shared it. They could have been spending last weekend shopping for a date-night outfit and the day fixing her hair and makeup. Instead, CarlaMay had carried on as usual and was rushing in between prepping their meal to get ready.

Regardless, Morgan's excitement for her mother pushed through any fleeting or playful anger that they hadn't shared the build up to it. "Mom, don't worry about our dinner. What time is this guy picking you up?"

CarlaMay was showering as Morgan leaned against the sink. "He's not picking me up. We're meeting. At six. What time is it now, Morgan Jo?"

Morgan Jo glanced at her watch. "Four thirty. You're good on time. Want me to fix you up a cocktail or a glass of wine? Calm the nerves?" Morgan smiled to herself. It was fun to be on the other side of this conversation. Up to now, it was usually CarlaMay prepping Morgan Jo for big evenings out on the town with Emmett. She was the sort of mom to help pick out the right jewelry and do last-minute checks for any stray hairs flying about Morgan's face or errant lipstick smeared over her front two teeth.

"I already had a glass," her mother trilled through the blasting water. "I don't want to be a lush!"

"You're not a lush!" Morgan kicked her legs against the cabinets behind her feet like a little girl. "So, who is he?"

The shower cut off and her mom pulled the cream-colored cloth curtain aside, reaching for a blue terry-cloth towel that hung nearby. "Nobody." She said this quickly, her voice high, before she ducked back behind the curtain and emerged again with the towel fastened around her torso.

Morgan lifted an eyebrow. "Nobody, huh?"

CarlaMay set about flossing and brushing her teeth and combing out her hair, effectively ignoring the question.

"Mom, if this were a *nobody*, then how did everything take shape?"

"What does that mean?"

"Where did you meet this person?"

"Oh, um. Just out and about."

"So, he's a stranger?"

CarlaMay patted Morgan's thigh. "I need to use the counter."

Morgan hopped off and leaned against the far wall of the small bathroom. "Out and about? Okay, like, where? At the market?"

"No, well, I've seen him at the market, though."

"Oh, so you *know* him."

CarlaMay stopped working on her hair and set the amber-colored comb at the side of the sink. She grabbed a dress that hung on the back of the door. "How's this?"

It was a gingham-printed, white-and-blue sundress, sleeve-less. When CarlaMay held it up to herself, it hung squarely at her knees. "It reminds me of Dorothy Gale," replied Morgan Jo.

"In a bad way?" Panic streaked over her face, and she pulled the dress away from herself, studying it with new eyes.

Morgan considered the dress again. "It really depends on who this guy is? Like, is he that creepy cashier at the service station?"

"No." CarlaMay rolled her eyes.

Morgan shrugged. "He'd probably like it. Or, if it were the manager at the movie theatre—it's that guy named Lindsey. He's been manager there since I was a kid, I swear. See, I think he'd like it, too. Both for different reasons of course, but—"

"Morgan..." her mother warned.

"Where did you even get this dress?"

"It was Mom's."

The answer struck both of them. Morgan didn't expect it, and maybe CarlaMay felt ashamed to say it. Or like she was making an accusation. The underlying current was that Morgan was making fun of the dress, and how did each of them feel now that it was out in the open that the dress was more than just a would-be movie costume. It was an heirloom.

"It's beautiful," Morgan whispered at last. "You should definitely wear it."

CarlaMay hung the dress against her body again and looked in the mirror. "Maybe it won't fit."

"It'll fit."

"Maybe he'll think it looks... silly."

Morgan looked at the floor for a moment, then pushed off from the wall and stood behind her mother and propped her chin on the woman's bony shoulder. "If he thinks it looks silly, then you ditch him."

CarlaMay smiled at Morgan's reflection in the mirror. "I love you."

"I love you, too, Mom."

In the sliver of a window that hung high on the bathroom wall, a streak of lightning flashed. Then the house shook with the boom of thunder.

CHAPTER EIGHTEEN

PRESENT DAY

Amber

Morgan Jo returned to the table without her mom.

"Everything okay with Aunt Carla?" Amber asked, rolling a swish of tea in her mouth and acting cool even if her brain itched to know the drama behind this whole *date* thing.

"Everything's great. She's going out on the town with somebody she knows, and she's going to keep her phone on. Just in case." Morgan Jo walked past the table and stood at the window that looked out on the back fields.

Amber followed her gaze to see the sky had turned from blue to gray.

Morgan Jo asked, "Did you hear that thunder?"

"Saw the lightning, too," Julia answered. "But don't worry about it, Morgan."

Morgan seemed distracted but she returned to her seat. "I am worried. The crops," she said weakly.

Emmett cleared his throat and changed the topic. "Who's the lucky guy?" he asked.

"You mean for Mom? She wants to keep it discreet."

Morgan Jo pursed her lips like she knew the answer and was keeping it a secret, which was a different thing than discretion.

Amber swallowed her annoyance. If only her own mother were motivated to go out, maybe then it would be easier for Barb and Hank to reunite. Even so, she let the line of inquiry die off.

"I'm starving." Morgan Jo sat down and dove into her salad just as the oven beeped.

"I've got it." Julia got up to tend to the chicken.

Amber had barely eaten her salad and had only nibbled at her roll. Her tea was half full still and her stomach felt as empty as a dry holler.

"Okay, so." Morgan Jo settled into her chair and tucked a paper towel over her lap. "If this storm doesn't totally wipe us out, I'm thinking we plan opening weekend for October. Early October."

"This October?" Emmett choked on his drink briefly. "Like, this year?"

"Well, yes. We've already agreed to open this year," Morgan bristled.

Julia chimed in, "We might want a backup plan."

"Backup plan?" Amber asked. "You mean in case we don't have a good harvest?"

"We can harvest some fruits early. I was out there today. The pears are close. Really close. Maybe we even start with a summer perry. Or!" Morgan snapped her fingers as Amber used the tongs to pass out chicken pieces to each plate. "I know. Strawberry wine. We harvest strawberries earlier. We can do the same with any of the berries except for the grapes. Almost every bush and vine has good-looking fruit." She spoke through a mouthful. "I tasted a peach today. It was divine."

"But then we won't have any grape wine. I think that's a risk for the business's opening. We want to have a full offering. There's a lot to be said about branding and creating a tradition,

Morgan," Julia said this softly. "I know you're anxious to get started, but it's better to take our time and make sure everything is just right."

Amber was confused. "If we aren't opening *this* year, then why've been working our hides off, anyway?"

Morgan Jo gave her an appreciative glance. "We've been working our hides off so that we *can* open this year. And we will. The business won't only be about grape wine. And besides, remember Grandad's recipe book?"

The others nodded, each in turn. Amber the most enthusiastically. She'd cherished that notebook. Something about it spoke to her. It represented the man she'd loved so dearly, even if the information it contained was scant. So scant, in fact, that Amber was worried they didn't have enough information to work with when it came time to actually make the wine.

Feeling a little better now that she'd relaxed for a bit, Amber tried to look on the bright side. "Grandad's recipe book had lots of alternative wine recipes. He even had a citrus wine, which I bet you would fly off the shelves."

Morgan Jo smiled at her, and Amber realized this was just what she needed. An alliance with Morgan Jo. She beamed under her cousin's approval.

Morgan Jo said, "Exactly. Plus, since our branding extends beyond the vineyard to a winery, we can play around with recipes."

"Speaking of recipes," Amber went on. "Have you all tested them out yet?"

"What? You mean from Grandad's book?" Morgan Jo asked her.

Amber assumed that they had, or else she wouldn't have asked.

"Yes?" she replied, wincing inwardly.

"Well, no. We need the fruit first." Morgan took a long drink of her tea, and behind her Amber watched as a lightning bolt sliced across the window in a jagged flash. Thunder came at once, and after it the sky opened up. It wasn't rain that came down, though.

Oh no.

It was hail.

CHAPTER NINETEEEN

1992

Bill

"Anddddd... *action.*"

"Well, here we are. It's, uh, October now. Early October. The third, I believe. Anyway, here we are in the vineyard, and today I'll show ya how to harvest the berries, and that'll be grape berries, on account of single grapes bein' called berries. We'll have to do the other fruit another day."

Bill stepped up to the first vine, which was heavy with bunches and bunches of rich purple-black grapes. "These here are probably *vitis vin farrah* or whatnot, but I don't know. I just know what Essie's dad told me which was that they had wine grapes, and that it's Italian for wine. Anyway, you take the bunch and pop a berry, this is how I do it, anyway. You take a bunch and pop off a berry and you put it in your mouth like this." He plucked a grape berry and pushed it between his lips before biting down. It had a sharp flavor, not so sweet as what they sold at the A and P. "Tastes right." He swallowed the berry. "Well, it tastes right to me, but I don't know what a professional would say is right. I bet they have thermometers and needles and run tests." He laughed. "Once you decide the fruit tastes right—which is when it'll be sweet but not so sweet it might turn into a raisin." He laughed again.

"You can use prunin' shears, but I just..." he grabbed the base of the bunch and snapped it in two, "crack it off like that." He eased the bunch into the woven basket he'd brought out.

"You go on and on until you have what you want to press or ferment."

Hank cut in from behind the camera. "How much would make a barrel of wine?"

"Well..." Bill shoved his hands into the pockets of his overalls and whistled long and low. "I guess it depends. I mean, I'll bring in all the grapes that are ripe. If you let 'em go on too long they go to rot anyway." Bill scratched his head. Something else came to mind that he'd better add while he was at it. "While I'm at it I'd better tell ya that if you taste a berry from a bunch and it's sour or under-ripe tastin', then you just leave the bunch and try again the next day or week, even. I dunno, but that's what's sensible, anyhow."

He shrugged and went to the next bunch and on and on until he had about ten bunches of dark-colored grapes all piled neatly into the woven basket he'd found in the sewing room upstairs. It used to be the boys' bedroom when they was just kids, but now Essie used it to keep her machine and supplies, and the basket was empty anyhow. She wouldn't notice it gone, he hoped.

"Once you got the basket full or however many grapes you pick, you take 'em in and start on your first batch. I suppose we'll talk about that next." Her gave a forced smile for the camera and a salute. "Goodbye."

Hank lowered the camera. "That was really great, Bill. Nice job!" He shot a thumbs up and moved the camera to his side, where it hung from its handle. "Want to take a break now? Or...?"

"I don't need a break but if you want one, we could go into the house there. Essie'll fix us up something, I'm sure. Or Barb will."

They went in to find the women gossiping at the table. Essie, Barb Jean, and CarlaMay. The two babies weren't really babies no more. They were toddlin' about around the house, liable to get into something. Maybe even break something. Essie knew better'n to let the grandchildren loose about the house. Meanwhile, the women were working their way through one of Bill's own bottles of wine.

Could be coincidence or they could have found out about Hank and Bill's production. Bill didn't want to talk about it, but maybe Hank had already spilled the beans. "Essie, where are the kids?" He asked, his tone frosty with concern.

"Oh, they're around. Come on in, you all. We been wonderin' where you went off to?"

Bill raised an eyebrow at Hank, who'd stowed the camera in the trunk of his Toyota—another symbol of how Hank was so different from Bill. He drove a Toyota.

Hank, for his part, didn't say much. "Enjoying the farm. Your family sure has it all."

There was a kink in the boy's voice, but Bill didn't pay it no never mind.

"Whatcha drinkin'?" Bill asked as he peeked around corners looking for a three-year-old and a two-year-old, each with blond ringlets and a preference for playing with family heirlooms, real antiques. Anything glass.

"Well, CarlaMay and I are working on a bottle of your red," Essie announced with a great puff of pride. She jiggled the bottle. "Come on over and taste this, Hank. Bet you didn't know your father-in-law brewed wine."

Bill frowned at Hank. At the start of things, Bill hadn't wanted anyone to know about what happened in the barn. An unspoken secret formed between him and Hank. It was fine if

Essie knew that Bill sometimes made wine—everyone knew. It wasn't fine if the women found out they were *filming* the wine-makin'. That'd be embarrassing.

Anyway, maybe it'd amount to nothing. Maybe the tapes would ruin or maybe they'd be dumb to look at.

Maybe, deep down, the tapes Bill and Hank made together would one day be a gift to his children and grandchildren. But that was a real sentimental idea and it didn't bear no thinking on.

Thankfully, Hank played along. "I might've heard that rumor."

Bill followed behind the shaggy-haired boy who'd put on a little paunch in the two short years Bill had known him. His hair was shorter today, which was a change. Barb had given him a cut at home.

"This here, Billy made about five years ago. I remember, because it was for Barb's high school graduation. It was going to be her gift, but then he made so many, they became a party favor!" Essie was all delight and smiles over her own little thrills, like that. She wasn't lying. They'd put together a patch of about a dozen bottles. Felt like it took forever, too.

"Anyhow," Bill added, "it ain't a sweet wine. Which is why you probably didn't like it then and maybe why you ain't drinkin' it now." He pointed a crooked finger to his oldest daughter who was instead sipping on fresh lemonade. Fresh because Essie had made it ahead of their visit. Of course, then, if Essie had made fresh lemonade for the family visit, why wasn't she drinking that? Essie only ever drank wine at night. One glass with a bowl of popcorn while they watched the news together, Essie's feet on Bill's lap. He'd give them a good rub in between his own handfuls of popcorn. Wasn't no food in the world Bill Coyle loved quite as much as popcorn. There was something magical about it, he figured. How a corn kernel could explode into a tasty morsel you swallowed with just a bite or two. Bill hadn't ever much been one for foods that weren't a part of a meal, but popcorn was the exception.

"That's not why she's not drinking it now, Billy." Essie said this with her mouth in a great big grin and her eyes dancing behind her glasses. He saw now that her lipstick was even a little smudged, and her blouse was untucked. She looked more like her old self, the farm girl he'd met so long ago. Less like her new self, who got her hair all did up and put her face on and worried about things like belts matching with shoes and handbags and pearl necklaces. She looked happy Bill reckoned.

And so a smile filled up his mouth, too. "Oh. All right." He didn't want any surprises, and one was surely coming, but if it had a thing to do with Essie, then that was all right by him.

Bill looked around the table, and every face was wide open, waiting for him. Even Hank, who now stood behind Barb with his hands on her shoulders and his haircut looking goofy as all get out.

"Okay." Bill scratched his head and propped a hand on Essie's seatback, leaning her way and rubbing a sore spot on the lower left side of his back.

"Dad," Barb spoke up from her seat, one hand on her lemonade and the other gripping Hank's hand on her shoulder. "Hank and I have some news to tell you."

"Uh-oh," Bill looked at CarlaMay then at Essie. "Somebody died?" his rough voice let forth a low cackle. Bill thought funeral jokes were some of the funniest ones. "Lemme guess—your pet monkey?"

Essie swatted him. "Billy, hush. Let 'em say it."

Hank laughed a little, too, then said, "Quite the opposite, Bill. Barb and I are happy to tell you that Amber's getting a little brother or sister."

This reminded Bill that he hadn't seen the babies, still, and no one else seemed to care too much. He glanced around and grumbled again about them.

"Mr. Coyle." Hank cleared his throat obnoxiously. *"Bill."*

Bill looked over the top of his glasses at Hank, waiting for the kid to spit it out, whatever *it* was.

Hank grinned all big. *"We're pregnant."*

A great booming laugh crawled right out of Bill's mouth, but it was as much one of joy as anything. He pointed at Hank and said, "Let's see your belly, then, Mommy!" He guffawed and guffawed, and Hank took it fine enough, but Barb did not.

She burst into tears. "Why do you gotta be so damn *mean*, Dad?"

This struck Bill. Ain't nobody had called him mean. Not once in his life. Sure, he liked to make jokes, and sure he could get caught up in a bad mood just the same as anybody else. But he wasn't a mean person.

Was he?

Bill felt himself drifting away from the table as the women cooed and cawed over Barb and Hank joined them, rubbing her shoulders and urging her to take a drink and calm down. Hank bent down next to her and Bill watched him cup her torso, which did look a little bigger than normal.

All in all, Bill was on the outside of this. He'd done something wrong and bad, and it made him feel itchy and annoyed.

He'd drifted so far back from the table, he found himself at the door in the mudroom, which led out to the back of the farm. It was open but the screen door was closed most the way. Not all the way, though.

Hrm.

Bill pulled the door and studied the hinges. They were too tight, probably. Now this was a problem Bill could solve. Something easy and simple, black and white. Might take a little oil and work, but it wasn't a matter of the heart, which made it all the more manageable to a man like Bill. Normally, he might holler in to Essie that he was heading out to the barn.

Instead, though, he just left for it. All he'd need was grease and a screwdriver, probably.

Once there, he put together a small assortment of other tools, anyway. Hammer, two screwdrivers—one flathead and one Phillips, drill, drill bits, nails, screws of varying sizes, a coupla' wooden shims, and several other odds 'n' ends filled a medium metal pail.

He turned to leave the barn, and something felt wrong.

Why in God's name was the mudroom door open? They never left that door open on account of the critters that wondered up. The screen had been wacky for weeks, and Bill didn't trust raccoons, skunks, or the like not to sneak in.

Essie hadn't been out. Made no sense that she'd gone through it. Of course, CarlaMay wasn't so dependable. But then, see, that was the other thing all together. Ever since Morgan Jo was born, they all been extra careful about the back door on account of its faster access to the more dangerous parts of the farm.

Nobody had ever answered him inside. Could...

Bill stood just outside the barn door, set the pail down, stayed real still, and just *listened*.

In the distance, he could just make out the sound of quiet screaming.

CHAPTER TWENTY

PRESENT DAY

Morgan Jo

Morgan had turned in her seat and stared out the window. Just as soon as the hail had started, it had stopped, like a flash hailstorm.

She sent up a silent prayer and turned back.

"Let's hope that's it."

Emmett gave her a look that was surely meant to calm Morgan Jo's anxiety, but it didn't. Not after Amber's unintentionally explosive inquiry.

Had they ever tried to make Grandad's wine?

What kind of a question was that?

A really, really good one.

Morgan Jo hated to make embarrassing admissions, especially this late in the game. But it wasn't a secret. She answered Amber. "No. I haven't. I've just tasted it."

"Have you ever made wine *at all?*" Julia asked, her pretty face twisting into worry.

Morgan Jo looked at Emmett for help. He could be trusted.

"I have. I made it with my folks when I lived at home. My dad made it all the time," he stated smoothly.

"See?" Morgan shifted in her seat and devoured the last of her chicken wings. She wiped her hands on her paper towel and regarded Julia and Amber honestly. "We've got winemaking experience. We've got a vineyard and ripe fruit. We've got some grapes that will hopefully hit the harvesting mark. And we have other berries which we can harvest *now*. We've got the barn for the winery and the hangar for whatever we need it to be, too." Morgan flashed a quick, warm smile at Julia. "I think we're good."

Amber—easy-to-convince Amber—didn't look so convinced. Determination shaped her face, lowering her eyebrows and tugging her mouth down in a frown that was reminiscent of their grandfather.

"Well, that's not quite the same," Amber protested.

"What's not the same?" Morgan shot back.

"Tasting Grandad's wine and having the right set up is different than making it." Amber looked from Morgan to Emmett to Julia and back to Morgan. "Morgan Jo, we could try *tonight*, you know."

"Try what tonight?"

"We could set about making some of his wine."

* * *

The four of them found themselves, full-bellied and renewed, heading together to the barn. The short walk over thick Kentucky bluegrass felt like a trek to Morgan. The air swelled with moisture and dark clouds continued threatening the late-afternoon sunlight.

"Jeez." Morgan pointed to the ground, where hailstones peppered the grass like crystal marbles. "Do you think we're in the clear?"

"I don't know," Julia replied. She withdrew her phone and tapped for a moment as they walked. "Eighty percent chance of rain tonight. One hundred percent tomorrow morning."

Emmett took up Morgan's hand and gave it a squeeze. "We could use the moisture."

"As long as there's no more hail," Morgan said.

"It'll be fine."

Amber opened the barn door, and Emmett switched on the new overhead fluorescents he'd installed. The space lit up brighter than Morgan had ever seen it. Barns were supposed to enjoy natural light. The false illumination added an aberration to the space.

Julia stretched her hands out from her body then twisted her head from side to side. "Where do we start?"

CHAPTER TWENTY-ONE

PRESENT DAY

Amber

They were all set. Once the sky had quieted for a solid ten minutes, Emmett and Morgan Jo braved the outdoors to head to the vineyard to fill a great big bucket of strawberries. Had to be at least ten pounds, which wouldn't make for much wine, but it'd give them a good idea.

It wasn't long before the couple had returned, joining Julia and Amber in the barn, where the two girls had cleared the workspace and set up the tools and supplies just so. Everything was already sanitized and prepped because Emmett had been particular about having things ready to go just as soon as a crop presented ripe.

"No thunder or lightning so far," Morgan remarked, holding up crossed fingers.

Now that they were all four together, Amber settled onto the three-legged stool.

Julia was stationed at the left of the workbench, Morgan Jo in the middle, and Emmett to the right. Amber teetered on the stool, one of Grandad's old antiques. It used to be that they weren't allowed to sit on the stool. Amber could distinctly remember being barked at for even looking at it once.

After his death, Memaw had passed the stool on to Travis for fishin', but he said it ought to stay indoors. That he'd only wreck it. It was one of the few times in his life that Travis had showed maturity.

Once it was established that Morgan Jo and the rest of them would open a business, Travis bequeathed the item to the operation, citing it as the sort of thing that belonged in a family winemaking business.

The stool was unstable at best, which gave Amber's legs a good workout, and she rather liked that. It reminded her of the one time she joined the gym on a free trial and woke up feeling tight and accomplished all over. Maybe she'd get back into exercising one of these days.

Amber now referred to Grandad's notebook, her finger tracing his words as she read them aloud for the others. "Okay, step one," she spoke slowly and clearly, like a teacher. Grandad's words weren't precise, but she felt the vibrations of his voice ringing through her as she repeated what he'd written, word for word. "'Put the grapes in there in the crock.'" She glanced up to see Emmett dump the bucket of strawberries into the five-gallon bucket.

He turned and gave Amber a thumbs up.

"All right, then. The next thing Grandad says is, 'Cover 'em with water, then push 'em down and let 'em set.'"

Morgan Jo poured from the gallon jugs they'd acquired. "Does it say how long? I know the timing is critical, right?"

Amber looked back over Grandad's words, a twinge of panic percolating inside of her. This was *her* idea to try things tonight. She hadn't realized that there might be critical information missing or that Morgan Jo wouldn't know the ins and outs of this whole thing.

She read aloud, "'Then you let 'em go for awhile.'"

Morgan Jo whipped her head at Amber. "A while? That's all it says? I thought he'd put down a time frame."

Amber confirmed by reading it again and nodding. "It just says 'awhile.' One word."

"How long is *awhile?*"

Emmett held out his phone screen to Morgan Jo, a Wiki how-to page glowing at her. "Just a day or two. Strawberries are quick."

"We don't add yeast or sugars at this point?" Morgan Jo indicated the row of ingredients they'd compiled on the countertop. Amber turned hot from within. She hadn't done her job very well. There were steps missing. She was the one in charge of confirming Grandad's information and having everything ready, but she'd passed off ingredients on Julia and had just figured all the right information would be there.

Frantically, she read ahead in Grandad's notes. "Um, oh look, here." She pointed for her own benefit. "You add sugar in later. After it's fermented."

"That doesn't sound right," Morgan Jo fretted. "Are you reading it right, Amber?" Her face was pinched and annoyed, and this made Amber turn hotter on the inside.

Emmett broke in. "It's okay. If we're doing this Grandad Bill's way, then let's do what he wrote down. It's just a test. No pressure." He was speaking directly to Morgan Jo, but his words lifted the tension from Amber's shoulders. "So, we'll come back tomorrow afternoon and give it a smell, go from there."

"Give it a smell?" Julia made a face. Amber couldn't help but crack a laugh at that.

"You can smell when fruit has turned. That's the goal, here. Right?" Emmett asked.

"Right," Julia acknowledged. "Does that mean I can go home and get to sleep?" She checked her phone, maybe for the time. Maybe for the weather again.

"Right." Emmett had taken over. "Julia, maybe you should

stay over the night. What with the potential for a storm and all." He covered the tub with a plastic lid and hefted it onto the workbench.

Julia again looked at her phone. "Rain doesn't start until later. I can make it fine." Her face gave away relief.

"What's wrong, Jules?" Morgan Jo asked her friend.

"I'm wiped out, you guys. I'm sorry, I'm just—I'm tired."

"Take tomorrow off," Emmett told her. "You deserve it."

Morgan Jo let out a little huff, and Amber felt irritation set back in. Morgan Jo wasn't quick to anger or anything like that, but she was an only child. At least that's how Amber's mom had always excused her behavior.

Amber realized she had a little power here. "Go on home, Julia. We can check on this tomorrow, Morgan Jo and me." Anyway, they hadn't had much one-on-one time, Amber and Morgan Jo. Maybe there was an opportunity there for Amber to turn a corner, of sorts.

"How about that, Morgan Jo? You and me can take over tomorrow?"

Morgan Jo unfolded her arms and smoothed her hands down her jeans. She smiled at Amber. "Just you and me?"

Amber felt her insides turn all hot again. She smiled a cheesy smile back at her cousin. Like a little plea.

Morgan Jo shook her head and clicked her tongue then crossed to Amber and looped her arm around her neck and said, "I'd love that. It'll be like when we were little, and it was just you and me, girl."

CHAPTER TWENTY-TWO

1992

Bill

Bill left his bucket of tools at the barn door and moved several paces away, listening with each footstep.

At first, he figured the screamin' was an animal. Could be a calf being born at the back of the farm. They had a few heifers who were due soon. But a quick glance out at the back fields revealed no obvious signs of that.

Besides, the scream didn't sound like an animal. It sounded like a human scream. Bill did some quick calculations in his head. *Who lived nearby the farm, still?* There was the Foster family cabin just north of the back field, beyond the pond. That was a ways off, though, and he was pretty sure no one lived there year round. It was more like a retreat than a home.

He continued to move in the direction of the sound, and just as soon as he was halfway through the back field, past the hangar and close to the fence, he could make out that the sound was not only comin' from a person, but it was comin' from a *child.*

A reflex kicked into Bill and he bolted, fast as a Derby horse, through the gap in the far back of the fence and to the pond.

At the edge nearest him, stood little Morgan Jo, her blond curls matted around her ruddy, swollen face as she screamed and cried and pointed a small grubby finger at the water.

He threw his body into the shallow water, thrashing his arms at the surface and below hoping to God he hit a smaller body. The body of Morgan Jo's little cousin, the youngest grandchild, Baby Amber.

Other screams came from the houses, and somewhere in the back of his mind, Bill assigned these to the women who must have realized the girls had wandered off, but he ignored them in his search for Amber.

He was halfway across the pond, his arms hitting nothing more than the muddy bottom of the pond when he squinted across the pond to see a small figure in a brown heap on the opposite shore.

Five great big lunges took him to the wet body of his youngest granddaughter. He grabbed her up and carried her to dry grass on the far side of the pond but not before calling over her shoulder for Morgan Jo to, "Stay back! Stay out of the water, Morgan Jo!"

He lay Amber's quiet, unmoving body on the grass and did the only thing he could think to do, which was CPR. Bill was not an educated man, but he was a smart enough man to understand the human body and what you ought to do if water got in the lungs. He pumped Amber's chubby legs up to her chest, and on the second pump, water sputtered out of the baby's mouth. Her eyes fluttered open.

It was a miracle was what it was. Bill knew this as much as he knew Jesus Christ was his Lord and Savior.

The rest of the others crowded around him, but Bill was only focused on Baby Amber, who was now wailing like a banshee, which was a good thing. He picked her up and patted her back and something deep down inside of Bill turned to mush.

There'd been many times in life when Bill had helped someone or someone had helped Bill, even. He'd witnessed ambulances flying down the street only to follow and help peel a guy off the middle of the road. He'd been at the hospital for a routine operation when someone came in with half their blood spilling out on the gurney. He'd held his wife's hand when she'd given birth to their kids, and he'd mopped up puke and dunked a child into a cold shower to bring a scarily high fever down.

But never in Bill's life had he felt such a fear as he did when he saw the pond and heard the wails of his granddaughter. What was more was that all logic told him he ought to be pointing fingers and fussin' at the women for losing track of the girls. Instead, though, a maddening rage came over him. Not at the women or at Baby Amber for wandering off. Not at himself for not running faster.

No. Instead, Bill was angry with the one person in the world who was in charge of protecting his own children. The person who should have sensed danger sooner, run faster, gotten there *first*.

Bill patted that baby girl's back and rocked her and hushed her wails and stared daggers at that damn fool. Amber's daddy.

Hank Taylor.

CHAPTER TWENTY-THREE

PRESENT DAY

Morgan Jo

The morning after Morgan and the others set the strawberries in water, she woke up late, stretching beneath her lace duvet in her iron-framed double bed that creaked.

She'd dreamt of her wedding. No, she didn't have a wedding in the works, but it was one of those dreams that felt so real she had to sit for minute and try to recall if somewhere along the way Emmett had proposed. When she was disappointed to realize that he hadn't, and that he hadn't even stayed over the night before, she lay back down and thought of her dream. In it, she wore a simple sheath dress, ivory. It fell like cream over her body, accentuating her hips. With thin, rope-like straps that showed off her freckled shoulders, she felt free in the dress, free in the dream. She walked down the aisle, which was none other than the green grass in her very backyard. Also featuring in the dream were her mother, Amber, and Julia. That was it, though. No one else. Amber was the flower girl, and Julia walked Morgan down the aisle. Her mother acted as the officiant, reciting beautiful gibberish until Emmett leaned in to kiss Morgan. Then she woke up.

The smell of weekend breakfast wafted up to the second floor of the big house and into Morgan's room.

She rolled from the bed and pulled on a pair of sweatpants over her underwear. On top, she wore the shirt she'd fallen asleep in. It was her mother's from when CarlaMay was young and had started college at the University of Kentucky. CarlaMay hadn't graduated. She'd gotten pregnant in school there. But during her freshman year, she'd become immediately involved in the Catholic church on campus, the Newman Center. So involved, apparently, that she'd earned a shirt from the parish.

This was the shirt Morgan wore now: a pale-blue crew neck with a small insignia that read *UK Newman Center* with the image of a cross peeling off of the top-left breast area.

Morgan loved the shirt. It was comfortable and it smelled like her mother and like Morgan's childhood. She wore it to bed most nights, and sometimes even during a casual day out.

Now, she pulled it off, folding the threadbare fabric into a neat square and tucking it beneath her pillow. Then, Morgan tugged on a different T-shirt and left her room, following the heady smell of apple-smoked bacon into the kitchen to find not CarlaMay at the stove, but Amber.

"Hey. Where's Mom?"

Amber moved a sheet of sizzling bacon from the cast-iron pan onto a plate lined in paper towels. She wiped her hands on a dish towel that hung over one shoulder. "She went to church."

Morgan rubbed her eyes and studied the clock on the stove. "Is it that late?"

"You slept in." Amber pointed at her with the bacon tongs. "But I did, too. It's on account of the gray skies."

"Oh, right." Morgan pushed herself against the window that

hung over the sink, peering outside with a purpose. "It's not raining now. But it's still cloudy."

"It only sprinkled last night, from what I can tell," Amber replied.

"Thank God." She swiveled. "Speaking of which—we have to remember to check on the strawberries today."

"How could we forget? It's just about the only thing on my calendar."

There was a freshness about Amber that morning. A happiness, too. She'd set the table for two. A bowl of scrambled eggs, yellow and fluffy, sat like a centerpiece. Coffee was poured. Creamer and sugar set neatly adjacent to the salt and pepper shakers. It looked like the scene of a date.

"This is amazing." Morgan settled into her chair and draped a dish towel over her lap. Amber joined her and they tucked into breakfast together. "Thanks for cooking, Amber."

"My pleasure. I don't have anyone to eat with in the mornings anymore, so I guess you're stuck with me."

Morgan swallowed a slug of coffee and looked up. "When are you going to start dating again?"

"Dating? Never." Amber snorted. "I need a break from men."

"I get it."

"Really?"

"Well, sure," Morgan replied, shrugging. "I mean, I know—I moved from Nick to Emmett in, like, record time, but... there's something to be said for lying low and just worrying about yourself."

Amber didn't respond.

Morgan worried she'd said the wrong thing. "I don't mean you have anything to worry about, you know."

Again, silence.

Morgan reached for a third slice of bacon. "I just meant that it's nice not to have to worry about being with someone. Like, even though I love Emmett, it's sort of a job, being in a relationship."

"It didn't feel like a job with Grant," Amber replied, then looked thoughtful. "How does it feel like a job with Emmett? I mean, you two are, like, *perfect*."

She wasn't sure, truth be told. "Being with Emmett is easy and comfortable. I think about him all the time. But... I guess it's not *too* comfortable. Does that make sense?"

"Grant and I were too comfortable." Amber seemed to say this just as she had the realization. "How can that be a bad thing, though? Do you really want to be uneasy around the love of your life?"

Morgan was going about this all wrong. "I don't mean I'm uneasy with Emmett. I mean... there's still a level of wonder there. Of discovery, maybe? Like I don't know everything about him. For example," Morgan went on, brightly, "I don't know what he's doing right at this minute."

Amber gave another snort. "I didn't know what Grant was up to every minute of the day. *Obviously*."

Again, the wrong step.

"You and Grant were practically married from the get-go. Right? I mean, he moved in, and he—"

"Mooched off of me."

"I'm not saying that, but, well, yeah. I mean, he seemed to think this was a safety net."

"You're saying it's not that I was comfortable with Grant. You're saying he was too comfortable with me? Like, he wasn't ever stressed?"

"That's it." Morgan sat up straighter. "Like, with Emmett, I feel like he still cares about his image with me. And I do with him, too."

Amber seemed to consider this point. "Grant didn't really care what I thought of him. He just... we were just... doing our thang."

Morgan took a deep breath. "When I was with Nick, the guy back in Tucson? Remember?"

Amber nodded.

"He had high expectations of certain things. I always felt like I needed to have my hair done and my makeup on. But then, when it came to other things, his standards for me were low."

"How could it be both?"

"Okay, for example, when it came to my hip," Morgan rested her hand on the scar hidden beneath her sweatpants, "he treated me with kid gloves. Never wanted me to push it too hard. Never wanted me to tax myself."

"But he wanted you to look perfect?" Amber made a dubious face.

"Right, yeah. It was like, backwards. He'd hate to see me with tears streaming down my face in physical therapy, but he was happy to tuck me into bed with my hair splayed out in perfect curls and lipstick still neatly painted on my mouth."

Amber's face opened. "Like Sleeping Beauty."

"Sleeping Beauty, sure."

"Grant never cared if I wore makeup or not."

"And he never cared if you did hair the rest of your life or not."

"There's nothing wrong with doing hair," Amber retorted.

"No. If that's what you *want* to do." Morgan looked at her cousin with a steely resolve. "Is hair what you want to do?"

"It's what I do." Amber looked thoughtful. "But I'm also interested in this family business thing, obviously."

"And maybe you'll soar."

"Grant didn't think it was a good idea, you know."

"What, the winery?"

"Yeah. He thought it'd be too big a deal. The public would be coming here, to our property. There goes our privacy, he'd say. He wasn't wrong."

"He was selfish, probably. But that's true. It's going to change our lives, this business." Morgan thought for a moment. "Remember when we were kids? How you always wanted to own a restaurant? You were always baking food and coming up with new drink ideas? Remember that?"

Amber nodded and a small smile formed on her lips. "I wore Memaw's apron and I'd go 'round and take you all's orders."

"You'd put extra sugar on everything. Even sweet stuff!"

"That's the secret to southern cooking," Amber pointed out. "Heck, it's probably the secret to winemaking, too."

Morgan reached for Amber's hand. "Don't quit doing hair if you love it but promise me something."

"Okay."

"That you'll push yourself harder than Grant ever pushed you."

Amber's face went cloudy like something important had struck her mind. "Do you remember the pond?"

"What, when I almost fell in, and Emmett pulled me out?" How could Morgan forget? If there was one moment into which she could stick a pin that nailed down the start of her love for Emmett, that moment was it. Even now, so long after, she still felt the rush of attraction and the thrill of infatuation just by thinking about the pair of them as young teenagers. They'd just met. She'd only barely slipped, but she'd slipped fast. Despite its shallow depth, the pond could suck a person right down. Emmett had been fast and strong, and his quick thinking and acting hadn't necessarily saved Morgan's life—that'd be dramatic—but it had saved something else. Her heart. Probably.

Amber wasn't smiling over such a pretty memory though. Her face, cloudy moments before, was now dark and somber. "No. When *I* fell in." She turned her face to Morgan, who felt sick at the very thought.

Technically, *no*. Morgan did not remember that day. Not

from her own brain. Of course, the whole event had been one of those things that becomes a memory just because of how big a deal is made about it to you by others. There weren't photos, but the whole scene stuck like a stubborn photograph in the corner of a mirror, right up in Morgan's head.

"I thought that was supposed to be a family secret," Morgan whispered.

The incident from long, long ago was like a creeping shadow over the cousins' lives. As they'd grown up and away from the day that Amber Lee Taylor nearly lost her life to the little family pond, their distance to one another had ebbed and flowed. The cousins' friendship drifted like the gentle tide of a lake on a breezy day. More often than not, Morgan figured there was only one thing that had ever been a real wedge between Amber and herself, and it was that single moment in their lives, when Morgan, a three-and-a-half-year-old had let Amber, a two-year-old, totter into the pond.

Nobody had ever accused Morgan of doing it on purpose. Blame had only ever rested squarely on the shoulders of the adults who hadn't been watching well enough. That was where the little wedge had formed, though. Aunt Barb blamed Carla-May. CarlaMay blamed Memaw. Memaw blamed nobody and said it was just one of those things that happen to kids on a farm.

Ultimately, the whole ordeal was resolved handily, with Grandad saving the day and keeping his thoughts about it to himself, which had been uncharacteristic.

"It's still a secret," Amber acknowledged. "I just think about it sometimes and how little things like that maybe changed the course of our lives."

"Amber," Morgan's tone narrowed to a point, "we were toddlers. You ended up fine."

"I ended up repeating the third grade."

"That had nothing to do with you fallin' into the pond."

"You pushed me."

"I was three! It wasn't my fault!" Morgan broke out in a sweat. She took a deep breath. It wasn't right or just of her to begrudge Amber her feelings on the topic. "Let's go out to the barn and smell the strawberries. Okay? Forget about all this? Jeez, Am, why'd you even bring it up?"

Amber's face had cleared of the darkness. "Yeah. Sorry."

CHAPTER TWENTY-FOUR

PRESENT DAY

Amber

Amber was no grudge-holder, but she couldn't help that sometimes she thought about that fateful day of her early childhood. It was a day that did not live in Amber's head in any tangible way. More like it was a historic event that older people had talked about all her life. Like the assassination of JFK or the day Amber's mother got to see Dolly Parton live in concert.

Barb Taylor referenced the Dolly Parton concert any time she needed a story. If it were a funny story, Barb would tell about how she won the tickets to the concert in a radio contest while working at the service station. She'd almost gotten fired. If it were a sad story that needed telling, Barb would tell about how she invited her sisters to the concert but none of them could go. She ended up taking her dad. That one could actually double as a funny story. If it was a story about a time you met a famous person, Barb was happy to claim that Dolly pointed at her in the middle of "Jolene".

Anyway, that's what falling into the pond was like for

Amber. It may have happened to her, but it wasn't her story. It belonged to the family, and it was more precious than a pile of gold. Secrets usually were precious, after all.

Amber didn't care that the toddler version of Morgan Jo had just *let* her go in. Not *really*. In fact, she had no recollection of the event, whatsoever. However, Amber knew for a fact that it was a big deal, even if they weren't supposed to discuss it outside of the family, or else people might cast harsh judgment over Memaw, CarlaMay and Barb.

Together, they left the big house through the mudroom, but as soon as Amber stepped outside, the heavy smell of rain filled her nose. The air was colder than she expected, and the cotton jumper she'd selected for the day was a poor choice.

"Oh my gosh." Morgan looked at Amber, and a shiver shook the taller girl's body. "It's freezing cold out here."

Amber stepped out farther, onto the grass, and held up her hands as if she could take the temperature of the atmosphere with her palms. She said, "It's cold, but it's not freezing." This was a fib, though. While the air itself was cool, yes, it wasn't that which gave away the truth of the weather. Instead, it was the frostbitten ground, hard beneath Amber's flip-flop. A late season freeze.

"The crops." Morgan Jo raced away from Amber fast as she could, and the sight of her was pitiful. Morgan Jo's sprint was an uneven jog that looked harder than it had to be.

Amber hurried after her. "Wait for me!"

They stood, huddled together, at the stretch of grapes that had begun to ripen.

The leaves were thawing before their eyes, dew sliding away from frosty green edges.

Morgan Jo plucked a grape from the vine and snapped it free. She passed it to Amber. It was cold. Bitter cold.

Amber looked around them. "We'll harvest everything we can today. Right?"

Morgan Jo was despondently quiet. "I was wrong."

"Wrong about what?" Amber asked.

"It wasn't going to work. We can't do this in a year. I was crazy to think so."

"Morgan Jo, we'll harvest what we can. Okay? We'll have enough in strawberries and fruit to have *something*."

"It won't be enough. Who was I kidding, Amber?" Morgan Jo shook her head. "Nothing will grow now. It's all going to die."

"But we have everything that's ripe. We pull everything now. We go from there."

Morgan Jo looked at Amber, hope absent from her gaze. "Even if we do, what if the batch we made last night tastes like crap?"

"What if it doesn't?" Amber returned. "If it doesn't, then we know that we have a start. Right? We can pull the fruit and make more. We'll replant what we can. We'll do what we *can*."

Amber gave Morgan Jo a shake on her shoulder. It was their moment to shine. They had to look beyond their failures— Grant and his affair and Morgan Jo and her rushed experiment —and they had to *do* something with it.

Amber could hear Memaw in her head. *Waste not, want not.*

"Morgan Jo. Let's go get buckets and pull all this in. Then we'll take a look at the wine we made last night. Morgan Jo," Amber insisted. "God is giving us lemons right now."

Morgan Jo let a little smile form on her lips. She glanced over her shoulder, her teeth chattering more from stress than cold, as the day was warming up fast. Amber followed her gaze to a lemon tree in the orchard beyond them.

"Amber, we have *frozen* lemons."

"Okay, well God has given us frozen lemons. We can let them fall to the ground and rot—"

Morgan Jo turned back to Amber and grinned wider now. "Or we can make frozen daiquiris."

CHAPTER TWENTY-FIVE

PRESENT DAY

Amber

Morgan's disappointment at losing the crops overwhelmed Amber. And yet, there was something in it that freed them a little. It freed them to be flexible. To think outside of the box. That's how Amber tried to spin it, at least.

After calling up Emmett and Julia to share the crushing news, Morgan and Amber returned to the barn for tubs in which to carry back the frozen, soon-to-die produce. Only two trips and they'd gotten everything they could, from the one vine of grapes that were still too under-ripe and tart to the sweet strawberries, blackberries, and blueberries, some premature tangerines, lemons, a handful of those early season peaches, and a few other random fruits. The harvest was paltry by vineyard standards. But it was all Morgan and Amber had. For now, at least.

Without having set up a freezer or fridge in the barn quite yet, they were left to stuff as much as they could in the fridge. But that would have to wait. Both of them were too anxious to follow Amber's advice and test out their sample product.

Sun poured into the barn from the eastern-facing windows, but even so—they'd need to be able to treat the concoction like a science experiment. Morgan flipped on the overhead fluorescents Emmett had installed just a week prior.

"Here we go," Morgan Jo muttered as she peeled back the plastic lid on the tub.

Amber wasn't sure what to expect. It'd been less than a day. *Were they really gonna smell something? Would they see anything? Would the strawberries be soggy and mush? Could mold have grown? Had they missed a step?*

The lid came off, and Amber and Morgan Jo peered inside together.

The strawberries floated atop the water like they'd been dropped in half an hour ago. "Do you smell anything?" Amber asked.

Morgan sniffed. "It does smell a little sweeter than you'd think."

"They smell like strawberries to me."

Each woman leaned away from the tub. They shared a blank expression. Morgan Jo set her mouth in a line. "Should we go to the next step in Grandad's notebook?"

Amber had brought it along. She opened it up to where they'd left off and read aloud. "'Then you put 'em in a flo'r sack after it's fermented, then you squeeze it and the leftovers and seeds and such you don't keep. But you've already let it set so long it ferments.'"

"'Set so long it ferments?'" Morgan Jo asked, puzzlement raising her voice high. "Emmett said it could be a coupla days. That doesn't sound like a coupla days. 'Set so long it ferments' sounds like weeks, hearing it now."

They had the benefit of hindsight at this point. Once again, it would appear Morgan was rushing them.

"Grandad certainly wasn't specific," Amber admitted.

"I googled it last night. It can take anywhere from twenty-four hours to two months for a wine to properly ferment. There are millions of articles on the subject. You're supposed to stick to one recipe and see it through. And here we are, with half a recipe at best. I don't know. I guess we could technically pick an article and just do it that way, but then what's the point?" Morgan's tone burned like acid.

Amber felt she was at fault in some way. "What do you mean what's the point?"

"We're making Grandad's wine. *Coyle* wine. Moonshine wine. Right? If we rip off someone from online, can we even sell it? I mean, where is the line between organic boutique wine and *search engine wine*?"

"For starters, it's in the fruit," Amber tried. "We're using our own fruit from our own family farm. That's something."

"It's not enough!" Morgan cried.

"Maybe we need to give it time, Morgan Jo. One day is crazy. We should wait. Close it up and wait."

"How long, then? A week? Then we check again and it's still not fermented. So we give it five weeks, say. Five weeks, and it's gone bad. Where's the science in all this? How did he forget the *specifics*?" She snapped the lid back on and threw her arms across each other. "I feel like we're missing a whole chunk of his notes or something." Morgan Jo was flailing around the barn like a crazed woman.

"Maybe you're right," Amber agreed. "Maybe there's another book. We could look around harder."

Morgan Jo fell into a rickety wooden chair at the workbench. The height of the workbench was such that she could lay her head back on it like it was a headrest. "Don't you think I've looked. While Julia and I have been cleaning this dump, we've looked at everything." Morgan lifted her head up. "I was positive we'd find a store of his wine, in fact. I thought maybe we'd find a whole box of it, and we could use that to... I don't know... reverse-engineer our produce or at least display it as a decoration when we open."

An idea struck Amber. "How about I call up Travis?"

"Travis?" Morgan Jo made a face. "How would he help?"

"He made liquor in his bedroom when we were growing up. Under his bed. Sold it to kids at school. Remember? He got caught and suspended for a week. Mom was fit to be *tied*."

Laughter erupted between the two of them, not because of this one incident but because it was one of so many similar incidents that Morgan Jo quite obviously did *not* remember it.

Even so, she agreed readily that Travis might be the next best thing to Grandad's notes. And he *had* to be better than the internet.

* * *

"Okay, so here we go." Travis stood like a captain at the helm of his ship in the barn. He was surprisingly organized, with a milk crate full of supplies. Amber wondered if he was still moonshining in his bunkhouse, come to think of it.

He gripped each item with a thick fist as he named it. "You got your juice—in case you ain't got enough. I brought red grape juice. Easy. We'll use the jug, too, which is just half a gallon. More'n enough for a practice batch. You got your sugar. You got your airlock—these are dirt cheap. Buy a lot. You'll need 'em every time. You got your yeast, which you can buy in bulk or in packets—whatever's cheap. And you got your vodka."

"Trav, no offense," Morgan Jo replied. "But your set up is nothing like ours. Or even what Grandad did."

"Sure it is," Trav argued. "Who do you think I learned this from anyway? Besides, winemaking is just about juice, sugar, and yeast. I mean, technically, it's just about sugar. Well," he scratched his redneck beard, a patchy blond thing etched jaggedly over his cheeks and chin, "technically, all you need is some fruit juice. You'll eventually get wine. Sugar ferments. It's chemistry. Okay?"

Even Amber wasn't convinced.

"Go on, Trav." Amber was already annoyed enough with her brother. He could just hurry this right along so they could get to the making part and see just how well things would go for this whole operation. If it worked, they could at least make a limited number of bottles for a soft opening in the fall. That was the tentative plan for now.

He fell quiet and set about work, first by studying their strawberry juice then pointing out that it wasn't strawberry juice, but rather a weak effort at strawberry stew. He told them if they were going that route then the next time they'd want to do it the Grandad way and let it set for a few days.

Morgan snorted. "Yeah, well, *the Grandad way* hasn't been as well-recorded as we'd hoped."

Instead of using their strawberries, Travis simply worked with the store-bought juice, adding sugar, shaking it up, adding yeast, uncapping it and recapping it with the airlock. Less than thirty minutes later, he was finished. The whole thing looked like something out of a fifth-grade science fair project.

"When'll it be done?" Amber asked him, studying the ruby-red solution.

"We put it in a lot of sugar, so I'd give it five to seven days. Once you let air in, it'll change things. You'll want to do your taste test whenever you open the jug. Write down how many days you let it set. Write down *everything*. You'll be able to tell how alcoholic it is just by tasting it, but if you want specific figures, you'll get a special meter for that. Whatever you did, you make tweaks to that based on what you want the drink to taste like."

"Right." Morgan Jo was taking fastidious notes.

Amber was in awe of her brother. This was not the Trav she knew. "Do you have any of your own wine in the bunkhouses?"

"Naw," he replied readily. "I stopped brewing once I got hired on at Malley's out in Hickory Grove." Travis worked the line at the diner across the river. "No time and no need."

"You made more money selling it under the table in high school."

"Yeah, well. That was high school." He rubbed the back of his head. "Any other questions? I gotta report for my shift in an hour."

Amber looked at Morgan, and together they shook their heads. They shared an understanding, and the understanding was that maybe this was enough. Maybe things were going to work out, after all.

CHAPTER TWENTY-SIX

PRESENT DAY

Morgan Jo

Travis was a huge help to get started, but it remained to be seen if his idea would prove out, and the only way to see was to wait.

So that's what they did. The week unraveled slowly. Everyone had jobs except for Morgan Jo. Julia went to the hospital. Emmett to his law firm. Even Amber to her salon. She had fewer appointments and was around more than the other two, but mostly, it was just Morgan Jo, alone at the farm and unsure how to keep herself busy in such an awkward time.

Mostly, she wandered aimlessly, through the vines and orchard, tasting the different fruits and finding nothing ripe. Nothing good enough to make a new test of, save for the strawberries. She harvested every single berry that came from a ripe vine, sliced the green off, stowed it in a tub with the others of its sort and shoved the whole thing in the freezer. It was the best she could do for now.

As the week creaked along, she found herself waiting for Amber to get home. Once they were reunited, they'd eat snacks and sip tea together, mostly. Sometimes catch a sitcom on TV in the living room.

On Thursday, Amber decided to pull out all the stops. "We've got one more day 'til we taste the strawberries," she said after she'd gotten home from a short morning of haircuts. "What if we try some other things out?"

"What do you mean?"

"Well, we can't just serve wine in the tasting room. Haven't you been to a wine tasting before? We need charcuterie boards. Sides. Desserts, even."

"That takes a whole different license. If we're serving food, we'll need a kitchen." Morgan crumpled onto the table as Amber whipped up fried chicken and creamy mac 'n' cheese. Amber was most comfortable in the kitchen. "I'm overwhelmed," Morgan murmured from the crook of her arm, where her head rested.

"Oh, come on, Morgan Jo. A food service license has to be easier to get than a liquor license. Plus, more income. Right? Isn't that your goal?"

"I don't know what my goal is anymore."

"Your goal is to run a vineyard, make wine, and serve it in a tasting-room experience."

Where had this girl come from? Morgan didn't recognize her cousin.

"Fine. Yes. That's true, but what if we have bum batches? What if we can't make it work?"

"We're gonna make it work." Amber was unfazed.

"We need a backup plan," Morgan Jo realized. "We'll just have to put Emmett to the task of making a plan B. Right?"

Amber stood at the butcher-block island and carefully chopped vegetables for a salad. Since Grant's departure, Morgan had noticed small changes in her cousin. For one, her hair. Amber had cut it, herself. A shoulder-length blunt cut. No curls. She wore it thrown in a quick part to the side, straight.

Her highlights had long since grown all the way and the left-overs were cut off, so just the chestnut brown was there. Her face belied that of a hair stylist. Just mascara and a peachy blush on her ample apple cheeks. Her eyebrows were neat but not drawn in like they used to be.

It occurred to Morgan that Amber looked great.

For some reason, this made Morgan feel worse about herself. She couldn't remember the last time she'd had a haircut or bought a new outfit. Every ounce of her energy was poured into the vineyard, even on the days when she had nothing to do, it was all she could think about.

Was this complacency? Was Morgan too content? And if so, had Emmett noticed? Was his attraction at risk of fading?

Morgan blurted out, "Can you cut my hair?"

"Right now?" Amber cocked her head.

"Tomorrow?"

"Sure. Um. Okay, yeah. We'll go into the shop. My schedule is pretty light, since I wanted to save time for our first test of the juice." Amber was so calm, collected, and even.

Morgan shook her long wild waves back and took up the wooden ladle to stir the mac. She chewed thoughtfully then wondered aloud, "What if the juice is terrible? What if we're way, *way* off? We have to have a backup plan." She repeated this as if it were a plain truth. Everyone had a backup plan. Especially first-time entrepreneurs and business owners. She'd just have to figure out what that was. Maybe they could simply order wine from a local winery. Right?

Amber threw the vegetables into a wooden bowl and took two wooden salad servers and mixed it together. Lastly, she drizzled a tablespoon of Thousand Island dressing over the top and then mixed again. "Actually, I once heard a motivational speaker on a TED Talk say that you should not have a backup plan."

"What?" Morgan tapped a wooden ladle against the pot of

mac she'd just finished stirring. She brought the dish over and set it on a thick trivet.

Meanwhile, Amber carried the fried chicken from the stove. It would be just the two of them for dinner. Morgan's mom had to go to a work dinner.

CarlaMay had started a new job just the week before. She'd moved from secretarial and receptionist work at the small law firm on Main Street in Brambleberry to a new gig up in Louisville. Now, she worked as a secretary for St. Augustine's in Louisville. It was a longer commute, sure. *But a work dinner?*

Morgan suspected her mother had a second date, because the excuse was so out of the blue for the woman. Not once in Morgan's life had her mother had to *work* late, and when had she *ever* gone to a work *dinner?* Never.

Even at her new job, they didn't exactly wine and dine clients or pour over financials at five-star restaurants. CarlaMay wore cardigans and sensible shoes, and she filed things, just like at the law firm. She answered angry parent phone calls and scheduled group confessions for the fifth graders. At least, that's what she'd reported after her first week of work.

Morgan checked the clock. It was just after six. Her mother was probably right now sitting down to a meal with this so-called mystery man. A thought occurred. *What if the mystery man coincided with the new job? What if Mom knew him from interviewing?* That didn't sound like her mother. She wasn't one to mix business and pleasure. Heck, she wasn't one to really seek pleasure at all.

Morgan stowed the thought and returned her attention to Amber's TED Talk reference.

"You should always have a backup plan." Morgan said this in defiant response to Amber, who was plain wrong. "You should *always* have a backup plan." It bore repeating.

"That's not what the TED Talk guy said."

"Why wouldn't we want a backup plan?" Morgan argued. "What if none of this works? Then, what? We just... give up?"

"Well, the TED Talk guy said if you have a backup plan, then you don't work as hard on your first plan."

"I'm working my butt off!" Morgan was indignant.

"I know, Morgan Jo." Amber squeezed her shoulder. "My point is just that we have a good plan in place. I know we do."

"It's one thing if it were just a restaurant. Or just a tasting room. But it's an altogether different thing having the operation start and end *here*. We need to break it down more."

"We got too excited," Amber said low.

"What?"

"We found Grandad's notebook, and we thought we had the answers to the universe."

Morgan smiled mirthlessly. "Too bad he didn't leave a YouTube tutorial."

CHAPTER TWENTY-SEVEN

1992

Bill

After his granddaughter nearly drowned to death, Bill grew hard feelings about Hank Taylor. No, it wasn't Hank's fault that the women weren't watching after the kids. But shouldn't it be Hank's conscience that burned like a furnace?

Instead, the hippie showed up the very next day asking if they could go on with filming.

Bill was in the barn tinkering at the time.

Hank came into the barn as if nothin' ever happened. "Heya, Bill. Ready to shoot?" He pointed his fingers like a gun at Bill and added, "Don't tell me you already fermented them grapes!"

"A person don't ferment grapes. It's time that does that," Bill answered grumpily.

"Right." Hank set down his camera case and clapped his hands together. "*Right.*" He pushed a hand through his long hair.

Bill couldn't believe the guy hadn't mentioned Baby Amber. He forced himself to ask. "How's the baby?"

"Mom didn't tell you?"

Bill cringed. Hank had lately taken to calling Essie *Mom*. It was the damnedest thing he could do. "You mean Essie? Well, no. The appointment was today?" Of course Bill was up to date on things, as much as was possible. He knew that after the near-drowning just the day before, Hank and Barb took Amber to the urgent-care facility in town, a small clinic at the westernmost edge of Brambleberry. They'd given her the okay to go home with strict orders to follow up with a specialist up in Louisville the day after the *incident*. Bill was gettin' tired of *incidents* in this life. Couldn't he just have things go on easy and borin'?

"You know we took her into the doctor up in the city this morning. They checked her lungs and all that. She's healthy as a little horse."

"Good." Bill felt his blood pressure slow, almost like his veins turned from gushing waterfalls into gentle streams. Funny how good news could soothe a man like that. "Well, anyway." Bill straightened and gestured to the crock in which the grapes sat, waitin'. "This can wait. Bet you want to be home with her."

"They're in the house, Amber and Barb." Hank got a funny look on his face. "They're okay. I know we need to move quickly getting the grapes into the crock, right?"

Bill figured something was wrong but he couldn't quite put a finger on it. Was it that the grapes had set a day earlier? They might be ruined now. Too late to get a good crock going. Or was it something else? Something about that damned hippie and his long hair and his easy way with the *incident*? Bill couldn't be sure.

One thing he did know, though, and that was *waste* not, *want* not. And he had ten bunches of grapes setting in the crock about ready to go bad on him. And that would be a damn sin.

"Yeah, okay. Let's go on."

CHAPTER TWENTY-EIGHT

PRESENT DAY

Amber

Morgan Jo went to bed early, but Amber wasn't tired. Maybe she wasn't working hard enough or maybe her mind couldn't shut off, but instead of heading down into the basement to while away the night in front of the glow of the television, she stayed in the kitchen and read and reread Grandad's notebook until she'd practically memorized his half-baked recipes.

Sometime long after dark had fallen across the farm, a soft, low growl slipped inside of Amber's sleep-quiet mind. She'd succumbed to a deep sleep on the kitchen table, but the quiet noise wasn't enough on its own to wake Amber.

It took the added sensation of something tickling her leg to stir Amber. She unpeeled the skin of her cheek from the skin of her arm and looked down to see little Mint, fluffy and white, curled around her ankle. Amber groped the table for her glasses, which had slid from her face as she'd slept. She adjusted them onto her nose and squinted at the grandfather clock that ticked in a heavy drum at the far end of the hall. It was nearly midnight.

"Hey, little girl," she cooed to Mint, collecting the furball and heading for the basement to return her down there. "Where's your sister?"

Groggy, she maneuvered to the stairs that would carry her down from the bathroom off the kitchen and into her own little living corners below.

"Julep!" Amber hissed into the dark below. She next to never left her door open to the basement. Otherwise, the cats could come up into the big house, where doors were left open or people were moving in and out. The cats really shouldn't be outside. It wasn't safe for them—what with predators stalking the nearby woods.

Of course, calling for her cats was a futile effort. Amber searched the usual spots: the sofa, the television bureau, behind the TV, under the dresser, in the bathtub.

It was time to give up the search and fall into her bed when Amber blinked her sleep-bleary eyes at the exterior door. She'd never come downstairs to lock up for the night. She'd never closed and bolted the door.

"Not again," she muttered to herself. Probably, Julep was fine. Probably, she was having the time of her life, hunting mice and lizards and feasting like a tigress. Even if Julep *was* fine and *was* having the time of her life, Amber wouldn't sleep knowing one of her two babies was outside, wandering the farm in the dead of night.

Amber admonished Mint for not taking better care of her sister and stepped out into the darkness, closing the door firmly behind her.

"Here, Julep." Amber clicked her tongue and used her phone's flashlight. "Here, girl." Click, click. She wandered around the house to the front porch, checking behind planters and chairs, beneath the porch swing.

She turned from the front of the house to head across the driveway, where she expected to see three vehicles: her car,

Travis's truck, and Aunt Carla's van. All three were accounted for.

Plus a fourth one: an old-fashioned orange Bronco, boxy and foreign. Amber figured it belonged to one of Travis's or Geddy's friends and dismissed the question of its ownership. She dropped to the gravel drive and shone her light beneath each of the four vehicles.

Nothing.

Nearly defeated, Amber moved beyond the gravel drive and past the big house to the back, shining her light across the grass. There were any number of spare buildings where Julep could be, and Amber was getting crankier by the minute. Maybe she would give up and go to bed. In just a few hours, the darned cat would be meowing at the door to be let in.

Amber angled her phone's light across the wide-open spaces one last time. It caught something. A glimmer at the barn. She moved closer, taking slow paces and clicking her tongue as she treaded carefully over the dew-damp grass. Her eyes narrowed on a gap in the barn door. Another oversight. Maybe Morgan Jo's, maybe Amber's. Although Amber was certain they'd closed the barn door when they'd left earlier. She could picture Morgan Jo pulling the silver metal hook into place over its bracket.

Stopping just a few yards off, Amber stilled herself and clicked her tongue a few times, waiting for the emergence of Julep in her pink collar with its little heart-shaped name tag. But nothing appeared in the narrow gap of the barn door.

The sound of something—laughter—tore Amber's attention from the barn back to the big house.

A spooky feeling descended from the starless sky. Amber took a deep breath. The air wet her lungs, and it occurred to her that the storm that was due never had materialized. It had just hung around all week in the form of dark clouds, threatening

Brambleberry with a downpour but holding out. Teasing and taunting.

Amber looked closer at the big house and saw a light on where it shouldn't be. In the kitchen. Amber had *just* been in the kitchen. She'd been alone. Asleep. *Had Morgan Jo come down for water? Or Aunt Carla for a glass of milk?*

Nothing was evident in the small box of the kitchen window, and neither could Amber see anything in the strip of picture windows that rolled across the back of the dining room table. If somebody was in there, laughing or getting milk or anything, Amber couldn't see a hint of them. Maybe they were in the sitting area beyond the kitchen. Or the living room. But then...

And just like it had never happened, the kitchen light went out. The big houses fell back into the shadows of the night. No further laughter. No voices or sounds at all. Not even the faint mewing of Mint or Julep. Not the chirp of crickets.

Nothing.

Amber shook the scared feeling. Whatever she'd seen or heard was rational. The Bronco belonged to a friend of the boys. The light was Morgan Jo or Aunt Carla. The laughter was her imagination getting the better of her.

Amber forced herself to shine her light back on the barn door. It still sat just cracked open.

She went to it and slid the heavy wood across its track, opening the space wide. As soon as she was in, she flipped on the lights.

The sound of something scattering was readily familiar. "I got you now, you little Houdini," Amber said to Julep, who she was *positive* had been the source of the sound, the open door, and probably Amber's general feeling of unease. "Where'd you go?" Amber spun around and closed the door behind her so the cat couldn't escape once more.

Now that she was in the well-lit barn and *positive* she was about to find Julep ducking behind old whiskey barrels, Amber set her phone down and let out the breath she'd been holding. She called out for the kitty and poked around the winemaking space they'd set up. It was devoid of any living creature, unless you counted fermenting grape juice. Amber went to the double sliding barn doors Emmett had installed to separate the wine-making space from the old part of the barn. Those doors, too, were cracked. Amber ignored the nagging truth that neither she nor Morgan Jo had opened them when they were in here and pushed the doors open wide enough for the fluorescent light to illuminate the back of the barn.

The area back there was a wide, shallow hall, effectively. More like a storeroom that included the open rafters above, two platforms at each corner and then boxes and crates stacked in piles on the floor.

"Psst. *Julep*." Amber clicked her tongue again and from the corner of her eye she saw a gray shape blur from one stack of boxes to another. "There you are." Amber inched her way to the back right corner, following the direction of the gray blur.

Once she was all the way to the back, she saw her, Julep, staring back at Amber from between two towers of boxes, piled neatly but precariously in high columns.

"Come here, you little scoundrel."

Julep just watched Amber cloyingly, like she dared her mistress to come and grab her.

"You're trouble." Amber tried to make herself skinny and prayed the two columns of boxes were steady as she reached through them toward Julep, down on the ground below.

There were two problems, however. One, the boxes were not steady. Two, Amber was not skinny. She managed to wrap her hand and forearm in an awkward hook around her dastardly pet but when she pulled back, Julep freaked out and braced all four legs against the towers. The combined force of Julep pushing and Amber pulling was enough to tip Amber off balance and send her flying into the column of boxes on the right. Four cardboard cubes, each full of ancient heirlooms and historic junk, toppled like a poorly built Jenga tower, falling awkwardly on top of Amber, who braced for impact as she lay on her stomach on the ground-floor box.

Amber let a few select curses sail from her mouth before she assessed her situation.

One, Julep hadn't even scrambled off. She was just two towers to Amber's right, staring at Amber with the mockery that only a cat can muster.

Amber wanted to curse her out, too, but she was too busy for that. Luckily, Amber didn't feel any emergent pain. Mostly, she was just sort of stuck under a mess of crap. Two of the boxes —probably the topmost ones—had rolled over to the wall and remained taped and intact.

The other box, probably the second from the bottom, had burst open and its contents erupted over Amber's body like lava.

It took her just a moment to realize what had exploded out of the box and now lay in a shambles on and around Amber and the rest of the nearby hoard.

Video cassette tapes.

Over a dozen *video* tapes.

CHAPTER TWENTY-NINE

PRESENT DAY

Morgan Jo

Morgan's alarm rang to life at five, a good hour before she usually got up.

Today was important because Travis's wine should be ready to taste and hopefully good. If it were, then she knew she had enough information to run with, and her wine recipe would still firmly be scratched from family sources, rather than online ones. This was important to Morgan. Even if the world never knew, *she* would know. As would Amber, Julia, and Emmett.

She sprung from her bed, pulled her nightgown off, and shrugged into a pair of jean shorts and a T-shirt with a saguaro cactus on it. After all, the Tucson desert still had a place in her heart, even if was fast becoming a distant memory. One thing that was nice about Tucson was that her hip was less sore there. No steps or stairs to maneuver. No regular humidity to kink up the bolts in her hip. Nothing hard to deal with.

Back in Brambleberry there were plenty of obstacles to Morgan's comfort. Maybe one day, though, the obstacle course that was her forever home would pay off.

Maybe one day her path would be even and smooth and gentle.

She raked her fingers through her hair and slathered sunscreen onto her face—another good thing she'd gotten from her brief time in Arizona. Then, Morgan grabbed her phone from its charger, yanking the cord and shooting a quick text to Emmett: *Rise and shine! It's winemaking time!*

She shoved the device down deep into her back pocket and emerged from her bedroom, fresh and ready to conquer the day.

As soon as Morgan arrived at the top of the staircase, something felt different. The house was quiet. Yes, most homes were quiet at five in the morning. Not the big house at Moonshine Creek, though.

CarlaMay was a notoriously poor sleeper, for one. Normally, she was up at three or four, the coffee maker percolating and pages of a magazine swishing. By five, she usually moved to the living room and turned the TV on, very low. Even so, Morgan could always hear the murmur of the news and weather forecasts as a dull background to her morning routine.

Morgan's mom wasn't the only source of morning business, however. It was highly unusual to not hear the mewing of Amber's cats, who'd lately taken to scratching from the inside of the basement door in the hopes that CarlaMay would let them into the big house and feed them. Granted, this had only ever happened *once*, but Mint and Julep were smart enough—or silly enough—to keep at it.

The cats weren't mewing either this morning.

Morgan double-checked her wristwatch for the time. Had she forgotten about springing forward or falling back? No. It was the dead of summer. Or, at least, the start of summer. Her watch read five after five.

Morgan crept down the stairs, relying heavily upon the bannister as she leaned over and peered into both the living room and kitchen to see nothing. No one.

Surely her footsteps on the creaking wood would alert the cats, however.

But Morgan set the coffee and checked her phone to see Emmett's response—*"Be there in half an hour"*—before she went all the way down to the basement door to listen in.

No sound came. Not cats or Amber shuffling around in her little kitchen, which Morgan was certain she usually did.

Morgan returned to the kitchen and started on eggs— Emmett liked them sunny side up just like Morgan—and bacon. As soon as the butter began to sizzle in the griddle, a sound finally emerged.

Craning her neck around the fridge, she tried to listen both in the direction of the basement and her mother's downstairs bedroom. At only five fifteen now, it'd be totally rude to holler out and wake them if they were still asleep, but then...

There it was again. The sound. *Crying? Soft weeping? Was Mom having a hard night in her room? Or Amber downstairs?*

Morgan moved out from the kitchen a few paces and listened harder.

There it was *again*. Definitely *not* crying. It was laughter. Soft and sugary. It was CarlaMay's laughter.

"Mom?" Morgan turned down the short hall just around the corner from the kitchen. "Are you up?"

But as soon as Morgan was at her mother's door, the laughter died away.

"Mom?" Morgan rapped her knuckles lightly on the white-painted door and rested her hand on the antique glass knob, ready to twist and open it. There wasn't much privacy between mother and daughter. After all, they'd lived together as veritable sisters most of Morgan's life, save for the brief spells she attempted to try her hand at living somewhere else.

A gentle turn of the knob revealed it was locked. The heat of panic zinged up Morgan's spine. She twisted harder and rattled the knob. "Mom!?" Frantic knocking gave way to a hurried voice on the other side of the door.

"I'm fine! Morgan Jo! I'll be right out!"

Morgan released a breath so big it had inflated her body like a balloon. She released the doorknob and backed away, crossing her arms over her chest. "Okay," she answered, more for her own benefit than her mother's

A moment later, the door opened quarter of the way and CarlaMay emerged, squeezing through it and closing it behind her.

"You have makeup on." Morgan pointed this out plainly. "And your hair. It's curled."

CarlaMay tied a silk kimono about her waist. "So?"

"What are you wearing?" Morgan pointed to the lace poking out from the hem of the robe.

"A nightgown."

"That's lingerie."

CarlaMay sputtered a short laugh. "Morgan Jo, what's gotten into you?" She reached for her daughter's shoulder and pushed her down the hall and toward the kitchen. "Come on. Have you got coffee made?"

"Mom, what's going on?" Morgan stole a look back at the closed bedroom door, but before she could tear away and do something ruthless and indecent and *nosy*, the sound of heavy footsteps on stairs pulled Morgan's attention from her strangely behaving mother.

Now at the top of the stairs to the basement stood Amber, her arms laden with a heavy-looking box. "Look," Amber said, her eyes shadowy and face drawn. She seemed tired and somber, and neither of those things often described Morgan's otherwise buoyant younger cousin.

"What is it?" Morgan glanced back once more at her mother and beyond, as if a secret lingered. CarlaMay appeared docile and unfazed, though. More interested in whatever it was Amber had brought up from downstairs.

Amber set the box down on the bench at the table and lifted the first of what would be many VHS tapes from the cardboard void. "It's Grandad." She held the tape horizontally so that Morgan and her mom could study the neatly etched label along the spine.

In black ink on a faded white sticker read the words: BILL COYLE, Fall '92, Vol 1.

Morgan's brain whirred through decades of recollections, stopping briefly here and there, wondering if she could remember seeing a camcorder or the like emerge somewhere, anywhere. But nothing came up.

"That isn't Dad's handwriting," CarlaMay pointed out, tapping a red-painted fingernail along the label.

Amber flipped the tape around so she could see. "That's what I thought."

"Wait, what's it say there? On the back?" Morgan asked. She took the tape from Amber and flipped it to the other side, where a similar label was printed, equally neatly, on the edge of the cassette box. On that side, scant but critical extra information was added: WINE DOC.

CHAPTER THIRTY

PRESENT DAY

Amber

"I already tried. I've been fussin' with these for the past two hours. I haven't got a lick of sleep, but this could be *it*, Morgan Jo," Amber insisted.

Morgan Jo turned the tape over in her hands and then pulled it from its box, inspecting it anew. She passed it to her mom.

"Here. Look." Amber braced her hands on either side of the box and peered inside herself. "There are tons. And they span a couple of years." Amber pulled the last tape from the box. The one that read the year of her parents' divorce: 1995. Just a few years after Amber was born.

"Did you watch them?" Morgan asked.

Amber shook her head. "Well, I tried to, but they wouldn't play on my old VCR. It's built into the TV, the VCR I mean. It usually works just fine. I watched *Dirty Dancing* last weekend. It was fine then." Amber could give many other examples. Yes, she appreciated that VHS tapes were a thing of the past, as were DVDs. But that didn't change how she enjoyed some of her favorite films and television shows. Plus, she could get copies of some of her best-loved shows for less than five bucks at Bargain Bessie south of town.

"Girls. If you'll excuse me. I just have something to finish up in my room. I'll be out in a bit?"

Without waiting for their responses, CarlaMay left Amber and Morgan Jo alone with the box of videos.

"Isn't she curious about this? It's... *her dad*." Amber jerked a thumb in the direction of CarlaMay's private quarters.

Morgan Jo stared after her mother. Something thick lingered in the air between the mother and daughter. Amber knew a family conflict when she felt one, and there was a conflict brewing there. "What is it, Morgan Jo?"

But Morgan Jo tore her gaze from the hall and smiled blankly at Amber. "Nothing." Her eyes widened with the word and she clapped the plastic VHS case against her palm. "This is *huge*. Come on." Morgan Jo waved the tape she held in the air, then strode with purpose to the television that sat atop an antique buffet that served as an entertainment center.

There at the VHS-DVD player that was newer than Amber's TV set but still dated, Morgan Jo dropped down to the floor, favoring her left side as she leaned in, gave a quick blow to the innards of the VHS player then slid the tape inside.

"Here goes nothing," Morgan Jo whispered. She turned the TV on, then hit the power to the VCR player. After fiddling with the remote for a moment, she changed the source on the TV to EXT, then pushed PLAY.

Gray static crackled on the screen.

"I feel like it's 1998 again."

"Yeah." Morgan Jo fiddled with the remote, the TV, and the VHS player again and again she pressed PLAY. *Again*, static.

"Did you try them all?"

Amber nodded and joined her, ejecting the tape. A heavy sigh sank her chest. "Yes. Every single one. Like, five times. I fiddled with my tape player. I fiddled with the tapes themselves. I cleaned them. They were caked in dust. I used my hair dryer. I used cotton swabs and alcohol. I googled how to restore VHS tapes. I've been up at this for hours."

"Did any of them *seem* to work? Like, *almost* work?"

"Nope. Not a single one. There are like, twenty."

"It's probably time. They're so old."

"What do you think is on them?" Amber wondered aloud. "I mean, do you think he, like, reads his recipes or something? Like LeVar Burton on *Reading Rainbow*, kind of?"

"LeVar Burton never read any recipes. He just sort of reported on books. Right?"

Amber yawned and rubbed her eyes with the heels of her hands. She dropped to the floor and inched over next to Morgan Jo. "I don't know what's on there, but I want to see it." She chewed the inside of her cheek. "Let me try again." Amber studied the tape again and tightened the film tape with her pinky finger. She inserted it until the cassette clicked into place. The TV blinked black, and a breath caught in Amber's throat.

Morgan Jo glanced her way.

The screen went fuzzy and the static roared back.

"Dang it."

Morgan Jo slapped her hands on the tops of her thighs. "You know what? It doesn't matter. We've got Trav's recipe. Speaking of which, we need to go taste it. You comin'?" Morgan Jo gripped the edge of the bureau and hauled herself to her feet uneasily.

"True." Amber hated to give up so soon but she did want to find out what Travis had made for them. "Yeah, okay. Let me get these downstairs. I'll be right out there."

Maybe Trav's recipe would be enough.

But even if it was, were they really going to just... abandon this newfound treasure?

No. At least, Amber wouldn't.

CHAPTER THIRTY-ONE

1992

Bill

"After you pick the grapes, you get 'em straight into the crock. Well, first you pull off the vines and prickers. Some folk leave it I guess, but I say you just get the grapes clean off the bunch and then put the berries into the crock."

Bill was sitting on his three-legged stool, shucking the grapes berries off the vine and tossin' them into the crock as Hank watched from behind his black machine.

Hank poked his head to the side. "Do you leave the skin on?"

"Well, I do. I guess you could skin 'em, but we'll strain 'em anyhow, so there ain't no point in that." Bill finished up and carried the vines and prickers to a metal trash can he kept at the corner of the barn.

When he returned, Hank had lowered the camera. He was checking a second, much smaller black device at his hip. "It's Barb calling." He looked up, alarm swelling his eyes to the size of prize-winning peaches. "She paged me. Emergency. Do you have a phone out here?"

But before Bill stopped to explain why he didn't have a phone in the barn, they were both out the door, across the grass and into the big house, barking at Essie about Barb and an emergency.

Before Bill knew it, Hank was in the door behind him swinging the plastic dial around the rotary phone and tapping his foot like a drummer.

Essie's neck was streaked over in red, which was exactly how Bill knew this was no laughing matter. "Do you know where she is right now?"

"She was at home. With the baby. Ever'thang was jest *fine*. The doctor said Amber's lungs were clear as the day is long. Not a thing wrong with that girl."

Bill grabbed up Essie and gave her a firm squeeze. He felt like a helpless fool watching his son-in-law hem and haw on the phone, saying *um-hm* this and *oh, wow* that.

What really took everyone by surprise was when Hank said one last thing into the line, "Awesome."

Bill was about ready to whip that boy for talkin' stupid when Hank returned the receiver to its cradle. Urgency had flown from the boy's demeanor, but his face looked white as a sheet after a bleachin'.

"Hank?" Essie reached for him but not before Bill took a big step forward and caught Hank in his arms. The boy had passed out cold, and Bill and Essie hadn't a clue as to where their daughter and granddaughter were or how they were doing.

CHAPTER THIRTY-TWO

PRESENT DAY

Morgan Jo

Before Morgan left the big house to meet Amber in the barn, she had one other thing to attend to.

She waited until she heard the basement door close at the bottom of the steps then peeked down, glancing around the kitchen wall to ensure Amber was gone.

Satisfied, Morgan shuffled silently across the kitchen, past the living room, and down the short hall toward her mother's room.

With each careful step she took, she listened for something —anything. Her mother's voice. The sounds of the radio. *Something else?*

As she neared the door, it came. A distinct, clear commotion. Her mother's voice was half of it, cut up with a second sound. Deeper. A voice. A second voice. A man's voice.

When it occurred to Morgan that her mother had a man in her bedroom, she gasped. She felt all of five years old. A memory gripped her. Something uncomfortable and strange.

She was five. Maybe six. Old enough to have a memory but too young to make much sense of anything, back then or even now, decades on.

It was a family Christmas party, and Morgan remembered the Christmas elements more crisply than the heart of the incident itself. This was likely on account of her girlish heart's love of the holiday. A girl's adoration for Christmas overcame many things. Not this one thing, though: this family secret.

Bing Crosby crooned "White Christmas" from Grandad's record player. A full Douglas fir tree shimmied to life with tinsel, glass bulbs, and multicolored lights. The smell of a great big Christmas roast overwhelmed the house, warming the house with the promise of a succulent supper. Fresh-baked rolls piled in high pillowy mounds framed a long metal table Memaw and Grandad had dragged out of the hangar and hosed off that very morning. Morgan remembered that detail because she had been out there with a rag, wiping it down before they brought it inside.

She could remember standing, her chin level with the tabletop, as CarlaMay and Memaw each took the corner of a heavy cream-colored cloth. It might have been an heirloom or it might have been a rummage sale find, Morgan didn't know now. A sudden burning need to know arrested her. It halted the memory—this need to tear through the house—probably like Amber had torn through those VHS tapes. The need to take an inventory of every last thing left in Memaw's wake. *What was real—what was the family's from long ago? What was false—a cheap find?*

The family secret returned to her mind as she pressed her head harder against the door, trying to make out words. Carla-May's voice fell softer. The man's voice was entirely absent now. Again, the little secret from Morgan's childhood Christmas stirred back up.

She could trace the memory like a dot-to-dot. Her mother and grandmother filled the dining room with that pretty table-cloth like a party parachute under which children would run and squeal in glee. They laid the soft fabric over that rusty-edged metal table. Morgan could see the ropy veins of Memaw's hands as she smoothed it down. CarlaMay transferred the rolls and a platter of cut vegetables. Then came accoutrements. A bowl of sugar—always sugar with the Coyles. A pitcher of sweet tea, soon to be refilled, no doubt. A stack of paper napkins, the cheap kinds: scratchy and quick to disintegrate with one good wipe of a runny nose.

Morgan could picture her younger self reaching eagerly for a roll, only for her small hand to be swatted away. "Wait 'til supper."

The younger Morgan skipped away, looking for something more interesting. Little Amber, Morgan's best friend in the world, was down for a nap in the playpen set up in the basement.

This left Morgan to wander the house, which always felt a bit less familiar during parties. It was cleaner, for starters. That in itself was a Christmas miracle, because the big house was *always* clean. But for parties? Well, you could lick gravy right off the bathroom floor if you had cause to.

Then there were the smells. Typically, the big house smelled like Memaw. Like her lotions—old lady stuff, mostly. Her perfume—something purchased in bulk at the wholesaler up in Louisville. And her cooking—wholesome, practical dishes that combined leftovers with an artless flair. Memaw didn't believe in waste, and neither did Grandad. They made food last to the bitter end. For breakfast, it wasn't uncommon for Morgan to eat last night's rice served up with a fried egg. Instead of jam or butter for toast, she'd often have the dregs of the maple syrup bottle that had sat upside down for so long, little Morgan figured that's just how it sat.

The food was always tasty, though. Even when it was just hours away from going bad.

Still, this is exactly how the magic of Christmas came together. Instead of thawed chicken breast, a fresh oven-roasted prime rib, complete with hot *au jus* and sprigs of herbs from Memaw's little window box.

That Christmas, that fateful Christmas that Morgan came to know the facts of life long before any little girl should, she walked through the rooms of the house like she was visiting a museum for the first time. She saw artifacts of Grandad's she'd never seen before. She ran her hand over sofa cushions that were normally draped over an afghan for protection. Morgan peeked her head into each room, marveling at just how much *work* had gone into the celebration of Jesus's birth.

She started downstairs, peering into Memaw and Grandad's bedroom, her nose lifted to sniff the distinct smell of Murphy Oil on the floors. The bed was made up extra pretty with a second lace coverlet secured over the foot of the bed. Shoes and coats were out of sight. The wardrobe door was closed.

Closing the door, disappointed not to find something a little more dramatic, little Morgan Jo ran her hand along the floral wallpaper of the hall and turned toward the staircase. She grabbed the bannister and swung herself up onto the wooden steps, hopping like a miniature Easter bunny: up, up, up, counting as she went.

One, two, three... all the way up to seventeen. There sure were a lot of stairs.

Morgan started with her own bedroom. The door was closed—it was never closed. She cracked it open and looked inside to see her bed made. It was usually made. Memaw had hand-sewn the pink comforter, and it fit the bed so perfectly that the mattress pretty much tucked the blanket into place naturally. Her floor was picked up, which it usually was. It smelled like dusting oil, and the big white rug was vacuumed anew. Morgan could tell because of those pretty vacuum lines the Oreck made.

She left that room. There were three more upstairs. The next one down was Memaw's sewing room, which had no reason to be any different, even on Christmas Eve.

Morgan skipped that and went on to the next, which was a bedroom once assigned to Aunt DanaSue, who was the baby of the family and still sometimes stayed the night when she didn't have anything going on in her regular life. Morgan still wasn't sure what Aunt DanaSue's regular life really was, and this made her bedroom *extra* interesting.

Little Morgan Jo *technically* wasn't allowed in Aunt Dana-Sue's bedroom on account of things she didn't understand, like the fact that it bothered her relatively young aunt for anyone to go in there and "mess with her stuff."

That's why the kindergartener crept along the wall on the balls of her feet, like a ballerina-spy or something *very* quiet and sneaky. Like a mouse. Maybe even a snake. That's how Morgan could remember thinking of herself, like something that she *wasn't*. Maybe the disassociation helped the little girl remove herself from the bounds of her daily rules and do something a tad dangerous.

As Morgan neared the door to Aunt DanaSue's bedroom, she frowned. It should be empty, Aunt Dana's room. But the little girl could hear sounds coming from within. Happy sounds, she decided. The happy sounds made the moment far, far less scary. Not that she was scared, Little Morgan.

The door was closed shut, but the little girl could open just about any door in the house except for the hangar door which was always locked when not in use.

She twisted the glass knob now and slowly pushed her little body into the door. It creaked against her slight form.

That's when Morgan saw them.

Her Aunt Barb sitting on the edge of the bed, wearing a swimsuit—which was strange, because they didn't have a pool there at the farm. She was smiling and laughing and kicking her feet against the edge of the bed and across from her stood Uncle Hank, who looked taller than ever, and he didn't have any shirt on. Like maybe he was going swimming, too.

Then came the part that really worried Morgan.

Uncle Hank *attacked* Aunt Barb. Right there, on Aunt DanaSue's bed. It was like watching her other uncles—Uncle Garold and Uncle Billy—when they played ball in the yard. They attacked each other like that, one swooping in and crashing into the other, and everyone else hollering and screaming in glee.

And that was the part that didn't make any sense to little Morgan. Aunt Barb didn't holler or yelp. She laughed!

That was when it hit Morgan, that young, naïve girl. It hit her that what she was seeing could get her into trouble.

With DanaSue.

Barb and Hank shouldn't be in there playing their game on DanaSue's bed, that was true.

But neither should Morgan, snooping her life away.

So she kept it a secret.

* * *

There was a secret going on behind her mom's bedroom door now, too. Of that much, Morgan was positive. Would it be right to interfere? Would it be right to barge in on her mother and, apparently, her mother's date?

No.

It wouldn't be.

And so Morgan decided that she could keep that a secret,

too. That she could play along with her mother that she wasn't awake, dressed, and made-up with a man in her bedroom in the wee hours of the morning. Morgan could do that.

Because her mother deserved at least *some* happiness.

CHAPTER THIRTY-THREE

PRESENT DAY

Amber

Amber stepped up to the barn doors with high hopes. She'd splashed water on her face, downed an ice-cold glass of water, and changed into fresh jeans and a T-shirt. Now, here she was, tugging open the heavy sliding door and expecting to see Morgan Jo inside, stirring Trav's mixture like it was potion.

Instead, the barn was dark and quiet.

"Hey."

Amber swiveled around to see Morgan Jo coming along over the grass, her face squinting into the sun. Amber hollered back. "Hi-ya!"

"Let's see what we've got." Morgan Jo joined Amber at the door, reached around her and flipped on the lights.

"I have an idea." Amber didn't often have ideas, or ideas you shared at least, but she figured Morgan Jo might appreciate this.

They had a rack of wine glasses hanging in the barn, clean

and ready to drink from. As Morgan opened the jug and tipped it beneath her nose to smell, Amber grabbed two glasses. "How does it smell?"

"Good? I think? A bit... *tart*? I'm not sure."

"Come here." Amber handed over the two wine glasses, capped the jug for Morgan Jo and collected it up in one hand.

They walked together out the far side of the barn where Amber had cleared a space on the workbench and added a vase of fresh flowers. It was supposed to be a little tasting corner, a small contribution Amber had come up with one afternoon.

"Time to Taste Brambleberry." Amber glowed with self-satisfaction at the name. "You like that?"

"It's an idea." Morgan Jo tipped her glass to Amber. "Fill 'er up. Let's see what we've got."

Amber dipped a plastic ladle into the jug and poured them each a modest sample.

"Here's to Travis." Amber raised her glass.

Morgan Jo clinked it.

They each took a whiff of the drink then tilted their glasses and sipped.

Their reactions were instant and conclusive.

Amber didn't have to swish the burgundy liquid in her mouth or take a second drink to know.

Morgan Jo let her sip dribble back into the glass. "Oh my Lord," she murmured, her face pinched and twisted.

Amber nodded in agreement. "It's bad."

"Really bad." Morgan Jo's face fell into her hands. A muffled sob came.

"Are you seriously crying?" Amber took Morgan Jo's glass and rinsed it in the sink, returning the cap to the jug and wiping down the counter errantly.

Morgan Jo dragged her hands down her face, and her skin turned to putty. She released her jowls and her freckles pinged back to life as she propped her chin in her palms. "Amber, I don't know what we're going to do."

"It's literally fine, Morgan Jo. We'll buy a kit. Follow directions online. It's what we should have done all along."

"You said no plan B." Morgan Jo pointed this out miserably, in an accusatory tone. Like it was all Amber's fault.

Amber took a deep breath. "You're right."

"I'm right that you said that?"

"No." Amber studied the jug of too-bitter, too-acidic, too-sweet, too-everything homemade wine that Travis tried to fool them with. "I mean I said that we shouldn't have a backup plan."

"Okay, then what do we do? It's not like we can serve this." Morgan pulled her hair out from the sides of her head. She could be a cartoon character if she weren't so pretty. "Amber. We are *months* away from the grand opening. My mom has told everyone in her church. I made a Facebook post teasing my '*Big News*.'" She curled her long fingers around the words, turning into a billboard. But Facebook wasn't a billboard and St. Mary's wasn't Town Hall.

Amber rustled up a weak smile. "That's no big deal. We could wait, Morgan Jo. Give it another year. Prove out the crops. We could practice the recipes. Get a few down pat. You know what they say, don't you?"

Morgan Jo raised an eyebrow, skeptical and aggravated.

Amber chose her words with care, but even as they came out, they landed coarsely. Crudely. "Good things come to those who wait." Instead of wisdom, it rang like an *I-Told-You-So.* Unhelpful at best. Rude at worst. Amber winced and braced for a slap in the face.

Instead, Morgan Jo gave a sharp shake of her head. "No. It's happening. *This* year." She pushed the tip of her index finger into the waxen wood of the bar top. "I'm done *trying* things. I tried college. I tried architecture. Design. Real estate. I tried waitressing somewhere in there. I tried do *nothing*. I'm done *trying*, Amber." Her voice strained; her eyes pled.

Amber shrugged. There was just one thing left to say. "Then, I guess we'd better start *doing*."

CHAPTER THIRTY-FOUR

1992

Bill

Bill barked another series of orders at Essie as Hank lay prone flat on the floor in the farmhouse kitchen. "Check his mouth. Make sure it's clear. Listen for his heart, Essie."

Once upon a time, Bill himself had been brought back from passing out with smellin' salts. He'd drunk too much at a cousin's house up in Louisville back when he was just a kid, and his cousin waved something awful beneath Bill's nose. He felt like he wouldn't be rid of the smell for a hundred years, but it went away with time, as did the hangover that came next.

Here at the farm, they didn't have smelling salts. In fact, Bill wondered where you got smellin' salts. If it was something that the A and P sold on a shelf next to deodorant and mouthwash or what.

Anyway, they may not have the real deal there, on the farm, but they *did* have pure ammonia. Bill raced to the cabinet beneath the sink and pulled the bottle out. "*Flatter*, Essie. Get 'im flat on his back."

She lifted Hank's head in her hand, and Bill uncapped the

chemical. The fumes were noxious enough to put Bill right out, and sure enough, all he had to do was lower the bottle near to Hank and give him a good hard rub on his sternum, and Hank zipped right back to life, coughing and fake choking like a movie actor or something.

Yes. That's just what this scene amounted to: something out of a movie, Bill figured. He also figured Hank might like to know that, so he said, "You passed out like one of 'em ladies in the movies Essie watches where they wear those big skirts and tight corsets!" Bill roared with laughter, but Hank wasn't laughing. He was as bewildered as a hog to butcher.

"Where am I?"

"Oh, for heaven's sake." Essie had even less patience than Bill. She grabbed him hard by his shoulders and gave the kid a rough shake. "Where is Barb? What's going on? Was that her on the phone? Were you talkin' to her? Is she okay? Is Amber okay?" The concern over Barb getting word to Hank's pager that there was an emergency and to come quick, well, it had only inflated even bigger since Hank passed out. Whatever information he took in on the phone hadn't clarified anything, and the fact that it preceded Hank's own passin' out just added to the drama and fear.

Hank frowned, but the confusion passed soon enough. "Right. Right. Um..." He licked his lips and looked first at Bill. "She's okay. Amber is *fine*. She's with Barb." Hank coughed and winced. "They're at the hospital."

Bill hardly waited for the hippie to go on, but Essie was smarter. "Which hospital?"

"Louisville! St. Joe's."

Bill was fast of mind when it came to this sort of thing, and so was Essie. They could be a good team when they had to be.

Essie grabbed the truck keys from the hutch. Bill yanked Hank to his feet, and together the three of them made for the road. The details of why Barb and Amber were there and what had been said on the phone were nothing now. It didn't matter why she was there. She was okay. They just had to get her home.

Determination washed over Bill like a slug of smooth whiskey.

As long as his family was safe, nothing else mattered.

* * *

St. Joe's was deader than a doornail. The three of them rushed the front desk.

Hank, surprisingly, took back control of the situation just as soon as they landed at a big-haired lady in a bright-blue top with claws for nails. She didn't look up from the phone she yabbered into.

"Taylor. Barb Taylor. What room?" Hank didn't wait for her to end the call, didn't say please or thank ya, and he spoke with the firmness of a real man. Bill smirked. At least the kid could pull it together in the face of real action. The whole car ride over, Hank hadn't uttered a word. Bill figured it was shock that had grabbed hold of the guy, but no matter what or how they asked, Hank just stared ahead, pale as a sheet.

The big-haired woman in the blueberry shirt stopped talkin' and dragged her eyes to them.

Essie added, "And what's *wrong* with her? Is she hurt?"

The woman took one of her claws and scratched it over a clipboard. She ignored Essie but gave them a room number. "Fourth floor. Room number three."

They didn't hang around no longer than hearing the number before rushing off to the elevators. Once inside, Essie signed the cross and pulled a rosary out of her shirt pocket and started in on it.

"Where in the hell'd'ya get that?" Bill pointed.

"I started carrying it around just as soon as Barb told me she was pregnant again. Every mother needs Mother Mary when a baby's involved."

"The baby ain't involved," Bill scoffed. "That baby ain't due for two months."

The doors clanged apart and a different smell hit Bill square in the face. It wasn't as he expected. Every time Bill had ever been to a hospital in his fifty-some years, all he smelled was sickness and death and antiseptic.

In this moment, though, he smelled... well, *not* death.

The piercing screech of a baby's cry sent splinters down into Bill's ears. He peeled back into the elevator and watched as Essie and Hank stepped through the doors onto what could only be the maternity floor.

He knew Barb was pregnant, but only what? *Six? Seven months? Couldn't be that she had the baby, yet. Or if she did...*

Bill reminded himself that Hank said she was fine. Amber was fine. *Where was Baby Amber?*

By now, Essie had already clued in, because she turned to Bill and gave him a big hopeful grin, showing her teeth and widening her eyes. "Billy, this is *it*."

"What d'you mean? She had the baby? Early? Is it alive?"

Hank gave him a hard look, but now they were moving through a big wide door and the scent of baby powder and rash cream and bandages.

Bill remained in the doorway and just watched as Essie flew to the bedside, where Amber was tucked into the crook of her mother's arm.

Hank went to the other side of Barb, running his hand around the side of her face and leaning in and kissin' on her. He scooped up Amber and tickled her, and then Hank kissed Barb again and then he started cryin'. *Oh for heaven's sake.*

Barb was propped up in bed, smilin' and cryin', too, her hair in a pile on her head and her face tired and drawn but still happy as a clam. The scene didn't make no sense to Bill. Where was the all the fuss?

What in the *hell* had happened that was an emergency?

"'Scuse me, sir! We've got a *delivery* comin' on through!" A shrill voice chimed behind Bill and he turned to see a nurse pushing a medical device in through the door.

He dodged out of the way, which was toward the foot of the bed.

The nurse set about hooking Barb up to the machine and when she was done, she asked Hank. "Are you ready?"

He nodded, and Essie asked to come along, but Bill was still confused.

"Come on, Billy." Essie took up his hand and pulled him behind her, and they left the hospital room and walked down a short hall then came to stop before a window.

So, the baby *had* come. Early. "Is he okay? The baby?" Bill felt worry creep up from somewhere deep in his heart. He felt detached from everyone. Like they knew what was going on, but he wasn't piecing it together. Like he was stupid or something.

It was only when a kindly faced, plump nurse on the other side of the mirror pointed down at *two* little plastic bassinets did Bill put everything together.

Barb didn't just have the *one* baby.

She'd had two.

Essie said the word on a breath. "Twins." She clasped her hands together and looked at Hank. Bill followed her gaze.

It was funny, moments like that. Bill could remember his own days seeing his own babies in the hospital, sometime after they'd been born. It'd made him happy. Of course it had. Then again, back then having babies wasn't anything much special. More like it was a natural progression in life. With each baby born, Bill counted up the number of farmhands he'd have one day. There weren't no baby showers, not for Essie. There weren't any special parties 'cept for when the babies got older and birthday parties fell on an odd weekend and Essie pulled together a few extra dollars to buy balloons and ribbons and put together a little something.

Now, as Bill studied Hank who still held Amber, her little chubby cheek pressed against his chest as she nearly dozed off, safe in her daddy's arms, there was something similar Bill noticed. Between him and Hank, that was. Hank looked through the glass with eyes full of love. Not just fatherly love, but with a deep love that wouldn't ever change. Even if those three kids—*three, wow. And twins!* Even if those kids didn't turn up to become helpers in the house or on the property. But Bill saw the love there. Even without the silly party and baby shower—which Barb hadn't gotten this time around on account of having just had one less than two years earlier—there was a little thrill in the air.

Bill turned to look at the two babies. One wore pink booties and mittens, and the other blue. Tubes ran in and out of their bassinets, and the babies looked so tiny that if the nurse picked one up, she could practically hold it in her hand. Another person behind the glass came up and grabbed their plastic tubs and wheeled the babies off.

Hank ran his finger beneath each eye. "They're premature, of course."

"Two months early," Essie whispered.

"They're okay?" Bill asked.

"Barb said they're jaundiced. They'll have to sit under a light. Stay in here for a while. Maybe a couple of weeks."

"But they're okay?" Bill asked again, getting aggravated at not having the answer yet.

Hank nodded and propped his chin on top of Amber's head. Amber slept now, worn out, no doubt from all the excitement. "They're okay, Bill."

"Then I guess I have to get something." Bill hadn't had this idea any earlier, and if he had then he'd have kept the dang things on hand. "I'll be back."

He left without a word, heading for the elevator and taking it down to the ground floor, wandering around until he found the little shop that hospitals had inside. The kind of shop that had a small selection of flowers and even some balloons, stuffed bears, and cards. All the things you might need if you were comin' to see someone who might kick the bucket soon. Or someone who'd almost kicked the bucket but hadn't. Not yet, anyway.

He went up to the counter, found what he was looking for, paid, and left, heading back to the elevators.

The doors whooshed open, and he got inside, riding back up to the maternity floor where he ambled out and down to Barb's room.

Inside, he found Amber asleep on the bed with her momma, Essie fussing in her purse at a chair, and Hank standing like a guard near the door.

"Hey, Bill," Hank whispered.

"I got you something," Bill replied, passing one to Hank.

Hank looked at it, twirling the brown-paper cylinder in his hand. "You can't do that in here. We'll have to smoke them outside, but I figured it was the right thing to get." Bill revealed the second one, the one he'd gotten himself more out of tradition than personal interest.

Hank shook his hair off his forehead. His eyes turned wet again like he might bawl, but instead he held up the cigar Bill had just purchased and said, "This means more to me than you'll ever know. *Thank* you, Bill."

Bill got itchy and nervous. It wasn't often people thanked him for nothin'. He thought up a great joke in reply. He cracked a smile and held his cigar up, too. "Just keep doin' what yer doin', and we'll call it even."

CHAPTER THIRTY-FIVE

PRESENT DAY

Morgan Jo

The plan was set. Morgan Jo was tasked with Emmett and Julia —putting them on research. Amber, meanwhile, would start interviewing people to find out all she could about Grandad's winemaking days.

Morgan had the less interesting task, to be sure, but it was more important. She had to lay a foundation for success. Period. Bottom line.

To do this, she began with Emmett, leaving Moonshine Creek and Brambleberry to head up to Bardstown.

Emmett would still be at the office by the time she made it up there, but maybe they could grab lunch and talk? Then Morgan Jo could hunt down Julia and steal her away for a fifteen-minute break. Every moment counted to Morgan Jo if she was really going to *do*, as Amber had said.

And she was.

She had to.

Not one more year could pass with Morgan just *trying*. No more backup plans. Only forward motion from this point on.

I-65 was never a pleasure to drive, but it wasn't so bad late in the morning. Morgan had managed to dodge the morning rush and settle into a comfortable brunchtime cruise just in time to get to her exit, the Bluegrass Parkway. This would take her to 31E and straight into town, along what became Stephen Foster Avenue.

Minutes later, Morgan arrived at the western tip of the heart of Bardstown.

She eased down Stephen Foster Avenue toward Bardstown Square, admiring the quaint beauty of the colorful street. Brick-trimmed sidewalks that gave way to varied storefronts, some of which dated back to Kentucky's earliest days.

At the end of the pretty strip was the old courthouse, which sat within a grassy roundabout. The structure, red and white and steepled like a cathedral, reminded Morgan not only of earlier trips to Mammy's Kitchen or Spalding's, but also of her own education, when she studied the beauty of buildings such as this.

There was a reason Bardstown was nationally considered the most beautiful small town in America, and the old courthouse sat at the center of that reason.

She entered the roundabout, passing by the historic Talbott Tavern and coasting onto S. Third Street, a shady arm of Bardstown Square on which Emmett's father had long ago bought a five-bedroom family home for the sole purpose of housing the family law offices.

The brick home still looked like an apron-clad mother might be hanging laundry across a line in the front, calling her children over from the neighbor's lawned front yard.

A short driveway wrapped its way from the street to the backyard, which now played parking lot to the few employees. Emmett, his uncle who worked very part-time, and two paralegals. Indeed, Morgan saw at least two vehicles peeking from the back of the property. She pulled her car down to the right side of the road where a space was open outside another brick-faced home.

Morgan crossed the street with care, as even this branch of the square flowed with heavy traffic at all hours.

Up the way, closer to the old courthouse, Morgan could hear the distinct twang of a banjo. As a little girl, it seemed as if there was always a lone man sitting in the grass somewhere in Bardstown, strumming his banjo. The warmth of the memory filled her and fortified Morgan in her greater mission: to pull to life the history of her family's farm even if she had to sprinkle a little modernity on it, with the help of Emmett and his wizardly internet ways.

She turned into the cobblestone path that led up to the brick house and its white-columned front porch. Two rocking chairs sat motionless on either side of the white front door. A heavy iron bell hung to the right of the door, but Morgan didn't pull it.

Instead, she opened the door and poked her head in, peering around inside.

Emmett's office was a relic of a bygone era, all waxen, curled bannisters and white-painted walls. If you stuck a knife into the wall, you'd be able to chip off no less than ten layers of paint and perhaps two of wallpaper.

"Hi, Miss Shonda!" Morgan said brightly to the woman at the desk.

Shonda Carney looked up from her computer. Emmett could not have hired a better woman to welcome clients into the business. At once friendly *and* fierce, Shonda ran the law offices with sharp diligence and also buoyant affability. She accented her hourglass figure with a raspberry-red wrap dress. Her dark hair was pulled meticulously and fashionably in a neat, sleek bun on top of her head. Heavy gold hoops hung low on her ears, stunning but still unable to draw attention away from her full red lips. Shonda was the epitome of professional perfection.

A bright white smile filled Shonda's wide, heart-shaped face. "Morgan Jo Coyle! Why, bless my soul!"

She pushed up from her desk and pulled Morgan into a tight hug across the desktop.

The smell of apples and honey entombed Morgan as she hugged back.

Shonda pushed her away, squeezing her shoulders and lowering back to her seat. "Baby, I was beginning to wonder if Emmett had done somethin' wrong." She laughed and returned to the screen, typing furiously.

Morgan rarely came to Bardstown because she rarely left the farm. After reclaiming it as her home, she hadn't exactly felt much like venturing away. But Shonda's comment wedged itself like a sliver beneath Morgan's skin. She made a note to get out more and stepped toward Emmett's door, the first bedroom on the right of the old home.

"I know he's probably busy, but do you mind if I just—?"

Shonda cut her off, pursing her lips then clicking her tongue. "Oh, honey, I'm sorry. He just stepped out. Said he'd be back in an hour, tops."

"Oh." Morgan straightened, rolled her shoulders back, and moved her cross-body bag in front of her waist. "Do you know where he went?" She really didn't want to kill an hour in the office.

Shonda slashed the air with a long red fingernail. It pointed in the direction of the back of the office. "You might catch him, actually. He *just* left."

Morgan thanked Shonda and darted straight to the back door which led to a shallow porch and the grassy backyard beyond. Squinting into the bright morning light, she shielded her eyes and looked across the homey parking lot, but only two other cars were there. A red coupe—maybe Shonda's. A tan Tahoe. Not Emmett's truck. Probably his uncle's.

Morgan eased down the stoop and kept looking, out toward

where the backyard wrapped to the narrow driveway and back to Third Street.

There he was: the brake lights of his pickup truck glowing red and his right-hand turn signal flashing.

Morgan tried to jog his way, waving her arms in the air as she half-jogged, half-hobbled toward the street after Emmett, who eased onto Third and north into the square.

"Emmett!" She waved bigger and yelled, but he didn't see her.

Morgan couldn't run. She hadn't run since before the incident that had left her partially crippled. Instead, she took long strides with her left leg and pulled the right side of her body along toward her car, parked not too far away across the street. The traffic had ebbed and she started her car, stuttering out a cramped U-turn before trying in vain to spot Emmett. *He had to have gone around the old courthouse, but did he turn onto Stephen Foster? Or go around to the other side?* She drove slowly, peering through her windshield at any glimpse of blue metal that reflected the mid-morning sun.

Just as she was about to pass Court Square, where every famous picture in Bardstown had ever been taken—facing the courthouse and its towering red-brick glory, she spotted it. His blue truck rolled up the street and away from her.

Morgan had to complete another circle on the roundabout, and by the time she'd made it back to Court Square, there was no sign of him.

She finally punched his name on her list of recent calls and waited as it rang and she rolled down the street, glancing along for his truck.

Five rings in, and no answer.

Strange.

Morgan continued rolling down Stephen Foster, her eyes wide open as she glanced down side streets.

Ready to give up, she turned right onto the next street and

pulled to a stop beneath the shade of a blue ash tree and picked up her phone. Again, she tapped his name and pressed the screen to her ear.

Emmett picked up after the first ring. "MoJo! How ya been doin'?"

"Hey. Where are you?" Before she could explain she was just at his office then on his trail, Emmett replied with conflicting information.

"At the office?" He said this with a hitch in his tone. "Why do you ask?"

Morgan's heart sank in her chest. Emmett was lying to her.

But... why?

She had two options. Go along with his lie or confront it. Why should she go along with it, though? Why not just out him? And tell him that *no*, she was *just* at his office. She watched him drive down the street and away from the square. He was definitely *not* at his office.

But if she did that, then... well, what if he lied again?

And why was he lying to begin with? Morgan cranked her AC on high and stilled her breathing. "Your office?" She bought time.

"Yeah. Is everything okay?"

If she pointed out his lie, then the next thing would be for her to admit she was following him, and of course she was only following him in order to talk to him about wine recipe stuff, and there was no reason she'd look desperate, but then...

That's exactly how Morgan felt in this moment. Desperate. Strangely so.

"Everything's fine." Should she mention she was in Bard-stown? Why was she pausing? Why wasn't she asking him to explain himself?

"MoJo, I have to get off the line. I'm *right* in the middle of something."

"You are?" She frowned and craned her neck to see if she couldn't spot his truck. Nope. "What are you in the middle of?"

"What am I in the middle of?" His voice was weak. *Telling.*

"Yes. I mean, what is it you're working on?" She couldn't be suspicious or sound accusatory. Morgan knew this was the shortcut to relationship trouble. If she trusted Emmett, then she *trusted* him.

But what if he was lying?

How could she possibly trust a man who lied? Because if he lied about little things like this, then surely he'd lie about bigger things, too.

And Morgan knew exactly where that could get a person.

She thought she could trust Emmett. But maybe she was wrong. Maybe he was like most of the other men Morgan had known. Grant. Uncle Hank. Her own father... Maybe Emmett was nothing more than a leaver just like the others.

CHAPTER THIRTY-SIX

PRESENT DAY

Amber

Amber packed a few carefully considered props in her cross-body bag—a letter to mail, a book to return to the library, and a cat-shaped notepad and a pen—before leaving the farm and setting off for town.

In Brambleberry, much like in any other small town across America, if you wanted to learn something about something, then you'd best start in the heart of the place. The heart of Brambleberry was most assuredly Main Street.

The drive into town from the farm was short and sweet, across farmland that transformed into small-town USA.

She parked in a quiet little lot behind the market on Tenth Street and Main.

Before getting out the car, she sent a text message to her mother, who'd be at work by now. Barb cleaned homes and business offices, and she planned to meet Amber at the Dewdrop for a late lunch.

Just parking. Will make my rounds and check back when I get to the diner.

Her mother replied that she'd see Amber soon. Then she sent a second message: *Tiff is coming, too. Get a table for three!*

Amber reacted with a heart to the message, stowed her phone in her bag, and set off on foot heading south along the east side of Main Street.

She wore skinny jeans and a bright orange blouse with flowing short sleeves, strappy brown sandals, and a wrist full of bracelets. Amber felt *good* about herself. Not just because she'd trimmed down lately—losing five pounds was quite a boon to a short figure—but also because she'd toned down her beauty routine all around. Swapping heavy sweeps of rouge for a pat of pink cream blush and false glue-on lashes for a quick swipe of mascara was a freeing experience on the whole.

Plus, it was nice not to have to worry about wrapping her hair around a curling iron for an hour every day. Short and sweet, her fresh bob swayed as she walked with purpose to the first shop on her mission: the post office.

She withdrew the letter from her purse. It wasn't altogether a decoy, this letter. Before leaving home, she'd plucked a greeting card from her stationery set—all kitten-themed—scrawled a few lines to her old school friend, Shawna, then slipped the card into an envelope, added her friend's address, and smoothed a cat-whiskers sticker over the flap to secure the little note.

Now, Amber entered the town's lone post office with a need for knowledge.

Behind the Formica desk stood a black-haired woman who peered out over black-framed glasses with chains hanging down on either side. She pursed dark-red lips at Amber. "Mornin', Amber Lee."

"Mornin', Mrs. Tuelle." Amber trundled up to the desk and gave the woman a winning smile. "Slow day at the post office?"

Mrs. Tuelle didn't have time for small talk, even on slow days. "Mm."

"Well, I'm here to get stamps, mainly." Amber slid the note from her purse and pushed it across the desk toward Mrs. Tuelle. "How've you been lately? I feel like I don't come down much unless it's Christmastime, when I like to get those special holiday stamps the Humane Society puts out."

Mrs. Tuelle replied again with, "Mm." She plucked up the letter, glanced at the address, lifted her eyebrow at Amber. "Just one stamp, then? Or you want a book?"

"A book please." Amber removed her wallet from her purse, which was actually a small coin purse in which she kept a scant amount of cash, her driver's license, and a single debit card. She pulled out the card.

Amber cleared her throat as Mrs. Tuelle set about pulling out three different books, the various options of stamps the Brambleberry post office had to offer.

Glancing at each one with a discerning eye then making her selection, Amber dredged up the thing she'd planned to say. "So, how's Mr. Tuelle doing?"

"Oh, fine."

"I heard his daddy passed. Rather, I saw it in the paper."

Mrs. Tuelle looked up at Amber and narrowed her eyes over her glasses. "That's right."

"He was a friend of my grandad's, the deceased, I mean."

"Oh, that right? Your grandad on the Taylor side or the Coyle side?"

Amber felt her cheeks grow hot. It wasn't uncommon for locals who knew Amber's family to make subtle digs about the *problems* in Amber's family. Nelson-Coyle drama was the heartbeat of Main Street, Amber was beginning to realize.

"Grandad Bill. The Coyle side." Amber kept her voice light.

"In case you didn't hear, we're workin' up a new business plan. Morgan Jo and me."

"A new business, huh?" Mrs. Tuelle finished the transaction, tore a receipt from the feeder and slid it over the desk then propped her head in her hands and her elbows on the desk like she was settling in for a good story.

"That's right. Out on the Nelson farm."

"Tobacco?" Mrs. Tuelle snickered. "Hell, I remember when I was a girl you walk within a mile of that place and you came away smellin' like tobacco leaves."

"Not tobacco. Wine. It's in the early phases," Amber fibbed and moved the conversation along at a clip. "Anyhow, did you happen to know Grandad Bill made wine?"

"How would I know that?" Mrs. Tuelle pushed off the of desk, leaned back, and folded her arms.

"Oh, well, maybe Mr. Tuelle's daddy talked about it. They bein' friends and all."

"Honey, Bill Coyle wasn't friends with no one in this town." She checked her watch. "I'm about to go on lunch. See you at Christmas, Amber Lee."

CHAPTER THIRTY-SEVEN

1992

Bill

"Andddd... *action*."

"All right, well, since we started over, I got a new batch of grapes and cleared 'em off the vine and put 'em in this here crock." Bill tilted the crock for Hank to get a good shot of it. "You see, now next you're gon' want to pour water over 'em to soak 'em down." He remembered something else to make mention of. "We got this here whiskey barrel from town. We also use one for the crock, but you could use a plastic bucket, I'd guess."

Bill picked up an empty gallon jug. "This here ain't for tap water. You ain't gon' use tap water for your wine." He chuckled then made a pretend retching sound. "Aw, I'm messin'. It's just that you don't want no tap water, you want real good clean water. The best thing to do is if you've got a fresh spring. A fresh crick. Well anyway, we do, so we'll go and get water to cover the berries."

Hank followed behind Bill as they tracked their previously planned route out the barn, over the grass, through the fence gap at the back of the property, around the pond, and deep into the woods.

As they walked, Bill figured he might as well talk about the things on the farm, since this was supposed to be a teaching film. "Well, here in the woods we got all kinds of plants and trees, as all woods do. We got hickory and regular oak. Some evergreen types, though I don't know the name, but they never do lose their green. Poison oak and poison ivy, both, so watch out. When Essie's folks lived on here, they had the whiskey still down by the creek, but I reckon you knew that. Rest of the woods, well, they was just for hunting and playing. The usual."

They came to a clearing at the very end of the path that Bill had cleared with the Gator. If you didn't know what you was looking for, you might miss it, but right there was the crick, which sprung from what you might call a small shelf or even a cave in the side of a wall of rocks.

Bill held up a hand at the camera. "Be careful, now. There's moss down here, and the rocks are slick as oil." He took his time, picking taller rocks to tread across until he was right up against the stone shelf. "Now Essie's dad pulled water outta here for the still." He pointed to a dirt cove with big weeds growin' up around it. "Used to have the still right there. Copper pots and stuff." Bill adjusted his glasses then turned back to the shelf in the tower of rocks. He pulled a flashlight from his back pocket and shined it in. "Now, go on and look in here."

Bill moved his body back so Hank could get a great shot inside.

The water trickled down from somewhere else in the earth, moving through the stones and over moss and between crevasses until it made a small pool inside the little cave. Bill picked up a copper mug he'd kept there for show. He held it below where the fresh spring let down to the crick until it was half filled with cool, fresh water.

"Go on." He held the mug to Hank who fumbled with the video camera but took the cup and sipped.

As the camera operator, Hank wasn't supposed to make no sounds. But he did now, oh boy did he. "Wow, Bill. That tastes *so* good. I don't think I've ever had water taste so good."

Bill took the mug back. Hank had emptied it. He refilled it halfway and took his own drink. "Tastes like crystals or some-thin'," he remarked. Then, he reached for the plastic jug he'd left on the forest floor at the bank of the crick. He twisted off the cap and held it under the trickling waterfall.

"So, we'll use this here water to make our batch."

The stream of chilled water made an echoing sound in the jug at first, but by the time the jug was filled up, it was heavy. "Here, get out the way," he told Hank. "Hard to find good purchase on these here slick stones."

Hank moved back and Bill carefully passed from the crick to the bank, where he recapped the jug and gave a small shrug. "Well, now. We go on back and do the next part."

The red light on the camera blinked off, and Hank lowered the hulking machine. "Great job, Bill. Man, that is *awesome*. I've never seen a real fresh spring or creek."

"Sure you have, you just didn't knowed it, was all." Bill didn't believe that people had new experiences. He figured people had the same old experiences as ever and just didn't stop to pay attention. That was how he felt about aging, anyhow. Like you were just goin' along working, then one day you woke up and wondered why your back hurt or your knees ached, and you realized that it wasn't just one thing you woke up to. It was something you'd had in you all along and you just started noticing it. It was important in life to take notice of things.

"What happens after all the filming?" Bill asked Hank as they trudged back through the woods and to the barn.

"After filming?" Hank blew out a whistle. "Well, that's up to you. We've got options, Bill. You can slap a label on and shelve the tapes. We can put them in the bank. I mean, if we think we've got something really good, we send it to a production company. Or a film agent. I've got some contacts in Cali, but—"

Bill couldn't help himself. He broke out in laughter. "California? What, so I can be the next John-Boy Walton?" He waved his hand and smacked the idea right off. "I'm not a movie star or whatever you call 'em."

"Okay, well, then you go back to your purpose. Why are we making this series?"

"Series?" Bill scratched his head. They were standing in the green field just outside the barn. Shrieks and giggles poured out from the back of the house. Bill knew his reason. And two of them were right there, running wildly through the air toward Bill and Hank.

Morgan Jo tripped and sailed through the air, falling like a starfish on the grass at Bill's feet. He grabbed her arm and pulled her up. "You okay?"

The little girl laughed so hard she sounded all but drunk.

Bill grinned and looked over at Hank, who'd squatted down and opened his arms to Amber Lee, who was now a big sister.

Something was funny about it, though. Bill wasn't one to suspect things, but he was good at takin' notice of things, and something was most definitely off.

"What are you two crazies doing?" Hank asked Amber, who held his hand and smiled ear to ear. "We gon' go play!" she squealed.

"Where you off to?" Bill frowned and looked toward the house to be sure someone was comin' out to watch over the girls.

"The orchard." Morgan Jo pointed toward the trees beyond the fence.

"Who's comin' with ye?" Bill demanded as he looked from Morgan Jo to Amber Lee.

He saw it again. Amber's light hair—pin-straight and scraggly. Her plump face and bright eyes, light as the morning sky. So different from Hank, who stood lanky and tall with dark eyes and a face full of sharp angles. His shaggy hair, dark and heavy. Amber Lee was her mother incarnate. But there was something between her and Hank that didn't really remind Bill of his own relationship with his daughters.

Not in a *bad* way, in a gentle, soft way. A way that meant the pair of them were closer than any father and daughter Bill had ever seen. Maybe Amber's incident in the pond had something to do with that—with their closeness.

"Girls!" Barb's voice came from the back door. "Wait up for Aunt DanaSue!" Barb waved to them. "Dad, DanaSue's coming to go with the girls."

"I'll take them to play," Hank hollered back. "You girls go on in and gossip."

Bill frowned. They had more work to do on the video series. "The berries have to get set," Bill pointed out. He hated to fuss and especially in front of the kids, but this was a time thing.

"Oh. Can they come play in the barn for a bit?"

"In the barn?" Bill stifled seeping rage. "It's not a place for kids."

"How about I get them settled with something to do in there, and then we'll film quick?"

Bill didn't feel he had a choice. The desire to record this work for his family was fast becoming more than a desire. It was becoming a need. It was becoming the last thing Bill wanted to do in his life before he kicked the bucket. And Bill knew that even if today he was still as young and thick with energy as the hippie, Hank, that didn't mean he was promised another day on this earth.

Hell, neither was Hank.

CHAPTER THIRTY-EIGHT

PRESENT DAY

Morgan Jo

Morgan Jo drove home with fumes burnin' out her ears.

Once inside of the town limits, she picked up her phone and dialed Amber, who answered right away.

"Any luck?"

Amber replied, "Nope. I've just started though. Mrs. Tuelle at the post office says Grandad wasn't friends with anybody. When I returned your mom's book to the library, the librarian said she'd never met Grandad. That was when I realized I'd never seen the girl before in my life, so that was awkward. But she said I was welcome to look at the microfiche, whatever that is."

"Archives," Morgan answered. "That's not helpful. It wasn't like Grandad made the papers with his famous wine recipe."

"Well, anyway, I'm about to head into the *Observer* next. See what they've *observed* when it came to Grandad."

Morgan was getting another call coming through. She glanced at the screen: Julia. "Okay, well good luck. Remember, our goal is to get any scrap of information we can. The more we have to work from, the better we can build this business. If that means family history, great. If it means information on making wine locally, even better." Julia had stopped calling. "I gotta go."

Morgan dialed her best friend back. "Hey, are you at work?"

"On lunch. I saw your text. What's goin' on?"

"Amber and me, we tasted the wine Trav taught us to make."

"And?"

"And it was gross. Jules, I'm totally stuck."

"You're not stuck. What's our plan B, Mo?"

"There's no plan B." Morgan sighed into the phone and pulled down the drive at the farm. Her mouth was dry. Her head ached. "We're trying to scrape together more information. So much of how Grandad made the wine is missing from his notebook. It's like incomplete."

"What about the tapes Amber found?"

Morgan had kept her best friend well in the loop on all developments via text messages. "They don't work. We tried them on different machines. We cleaned them. Nothing. That's why we went with Travis's formula, which was also a bust."

"I could have told you that."

Morgan could practically hear Julia smirking on the line. "Desperate times."

"Yeah, I get it. Okay, so what can I do to help?"

"For starters, we need to understand the process better. The chemistry behind wine. We need to do the work we should have been doing since we decided to go this way. The *real* work, not just the orchard work."

"Meaning?"

"Meaning we need your science background."

Julia laughed. "What science background?"

"The science background that took you to working in the sciences. Right? The *medical* sciences?"

"Physical therapy is hardly science."

"Jules, we have to make this work, and that means we need to start experimenting with base formulas and stats."

"Why not buy wine from a distributor? At least for this year, to see if that works?"

"Because then we aren't a *winery*. Or a vineyard. We'd be a shell of the business we're purporting to be."

"Okay, that's fair, but—"

"But what?" Morgan was losing her patience with her best friend, which was an effect of her worries over her boyfriend more than anything else.

"But this can't be *that* hard. Hasn't Emmett been talking about basic wine recipes since we started the idea in the first place?"

Emmett.

Morgan killed the ignition on her car and squeezed her eyes shut. "Yes, and it's a starting point. But go ahead and look online. Every article has a different recipe. Every wine blogger boasts a different *bombshell* tip. It's a lot. I guess... I don't know where to start. And once we tested Travis's and saw just how bad wine can be..." Morgan slammed her hand against her forehead.

"Ouch. I could literally hear that."

Morgan laughed. "Yeah, well. I guess I just want that..." She groped for the right word.

Naturally, Julia read her mind. "Connection to your ancestors. I get it."

"You do?"

"Of course. My grandparents—all *four*—died so long ago. I don't have cousins or aunts and uncles like you. And the ones I *do* have? They're long gone from here. Sometimes, I feel like an outsider in my own communities. Even at the hospital, there are sister nursing duos. Uncles get their nieces gigs as receptionists. Everyone is related to someone else. Nobody knows a Miles."

"Well, they don't count because the Miles family is one of

the most important families this side of the Ohio." Morgan hated to hear her best friend feeling lonely.

"Thanks." Julia's voice was lifeless.

"I mean it, Jules."

"And I'm thankful," Julia answered, her tone lifting a bit. "Anyway, this isn't about me. It's about you."

"It's about *us*. The business. It's not even about my ancestors." Morgan felt an epiphany taking shape. "I don't even care about that—I mean, I *do*. But I have the connection. I'm here on the farm, living it. It's just that I want this winery thing to be real, to carry meaning. I don't want it to be a joke, and if we're churning out bad grapes then people will laugh. And they'll also laugh if we're just passing off other people's product, too. We can be more. We *have* to be more."

"That's a lot of pressure." Julia laughed nervously.

"I'm not trying to add pressure. Just... *clarity*. Purpose. Right?" Morgan's breathing and pulse had slowed. She'd nearly forgotten about Emmett and his lie.

CHAPTER THIRTY-NINE

PRESENT DAY

Amber

The staff at the *Observer* took an immediate interest in Amber. It wasn't often a potential story walked in off the street. However, by the time she'd explained what she was trying to accomplish—the recovery of old family recipes, or at least the clarification of said recipes—they'd shrugged.

She thanked them and turned to go, but just as Amber made her way to the door, one of the reporters who'd lingered around stopped her. "You said you found tapes? Like, VHS?"

"Yes, but they're broken or too old. I don't know which."

"Try that old video shop up off of Ninth. The guy there could help. He's a real AV whiz. Callum. Callum Dockerty."

"An AV whiz?"

"I know—I'm old." The reporter shrugged. "But he restored a bunch of 8-tracks for me." The guy made an okay symbol with his fingers and Amber left, intrigued but still feeling a little hopeless.

It wasn't that she thought she'd alight on something real helpful by casting a limp net across random Main Street folks, but she thought she'd at *least* get a lead. Maybe something like a friend of a friend's second cousin worked with Grandad on wine. Or so-and-so's grandma bought the recipe for her own personal kitchen, and Grandad walked her through it.

Amber was beginning to feel this was a dead-end mission. Of course, she couldn't say that to Morgan Jo. Not after making a big deal about *no backup plans*. Get 'er done. All that.

She checked her wristwatch for the time. Her mom would be close to finishing up at the bookstore—her client that morning. Amber called her.

"I'm in the diner. Where are you? Tiffany's starving. I swear she's gonna eat her own hand if you don't get here so we can order."

Amber shook her head. "Order me a sweet tea and a French dip. I'll be there in five."

She hung up and made her way farther south along Main, glancing into shop windows as she went. Nothing sparked an idea, so Amber crossed the street at the crosswalk and entered the diner to see her mom and her sister at the counter, lined up like old, retired men on a Monday morning. Newspapers spread out around them and everything.

"I thought you were getting a booth."

Her mom patted a red-vinyl-topped stool that sat between Tiff and herself. "No way. We're on an information-scouting mission."

Amber couldn't argue with that. The waitstaff at the Dewdrop probably hear more juicy news in half an hour than any other place on Main. "Fair enough." She pushed the lifestyle section of the paper over to Tiffany and the sports section to her mom. Then Amber did a double take. "Why are you two pouring over the paper?"

"Geddy's in here." Barb unfolded the section she'd had folded to her left and showed page four to Amber. "Take a look at this."

Amber read aloud from the small column on the bottom of the page. She began with the headline: *Hometown boy has big plans for Brambleberry.* Amber looked up at her mom. "What?"

"Go on," Barb answered, beaming. "Read it."

Garold "Geddy" Coyle Junior is promoted to Manager of The Market on Main Street. Since he was just a kid, Geddy Coyle has scrapped his way around Nelson County, finding odd jobs here and there as he wondered what his life would be.

From construction to property management, farming and more, Coyle never seemed to find his place in life, unlike his ancestors of local tobacco and moonshine fame.

Just last year, Coyle took a position as a grocer with The Market on Main Street, Brambleberry's hometown grocery and convenience store. He quickly found he liked being around people and says, "There's something nice about having a set schedule and knowing where I need to be when, and what I'm to do."

Coyle's supervisors took note of the young upstart's enthusiasm for the job and his work ethic. Just one year on and he's finding himself more secure in his stable position than ever, now as manager of the grocery store.

What's more, Coyle has big plans for Market on Main. He tells the Observer, *"We're already forming a partnership with farms in the greater Nelson County townships to offer a farmers' market experience to locals."*

When asked what new goods the market will stock, Coyle adds, "Everything from fresh butchered meat to free-range eggs, produce, and even alcoholic beverages."

It's hard not to hope that with Geddy's guidance at The Market, Brambleberry might be on the brink of greatness. And that's something we can all toast to.

Amber looked up. "The market already sells beer."

"It's not just that," Barb answered. "Tiff called him up."

Tiffany took over. "He says he's going to distribute wine from area vineyards. Like the one out in Elizabeth across the river. What's it called?"

"Great. Great Vineyards," Barb replied. "And that bigger one, too. Can't remember its name. Hocklebore or something or other?"

"So he'll distribute *our* wine, then." Amber was tickled pink by the idea. "How come Geddy didn't tell us he was gettin' promoted?"

"He told me," Tiff answered pompously.

"I knew it on account of talkin' to Jackie." Barb paused. "Plus—"

"What?"

"Well, Hank called me about it." Barb gripped her drink—a sweaty iced tea with a plastic straw poking out the top and a lemon wedge floating inside. She looked straight ahead at a line of plastic tumblers that sat along a stainless-steel shelf behind the bar.

"Hank? As in Daddy?" Amber asked.

Barb turned to Tiffany who smirked. Tiffany and Trav went along with Amber's scheme to force Hank to come home, but ultimately, they kind of hated him.

"He called her just this morning," Tiffany said sourly.

"How come you didn't tell me?" Amber accused her mother.

Barb's voice lifted, taking on an airy, breathless quality. "It just happened! We talked about Geddy and what's new and then he mentioned meeting. I decided I *would* tell you, then you ran late, so I had to tell Tiff. I had to get it out. Anyway, here I am. Telling you now."

"I wasn't that late..." Amber shook her head. "Why'd he call?"

Barb pointed to the article. "Well, he called because he read *this.* He wanted to send his congratulations to Geddy. You know your dad used to be close to the family. I think he probably felt bad for Garold way back when."

"But Dad's not in Brambleberry. How would he have read the *Observer*?"

"Online." Tiffany said the word slowly as if Amber had never heard of the internet before.

Amber rolled her eyes. "So—what, the article is on the *Observer* online? He read it? And why'd he care?" Amber was thirsty for the answer. She eyed her tea, which would satisfy her almost as much. She took a long swill of it, pinning the straw with her finger in order to drench her craving faster.

Barb replied, "He just said he wanted to congratulate the family. See how things were."

"That's all?" Amber was skeptical.

Tiffany snorted. Disgust filled her face. "Naw. He asked Mom to dinner again."

Amber froze, her drink still in her hand as the waiter arrived with a plate of food for each of them. Once Sam, the waiter, had left them to it, Amber recovered from her shock. "He just called you up this morning and asked you to dinner. He just... called?"

Amber had worked so hard and so awkwardly on making plans for Barb and Hank the first time around—The Dinner Train—only to hear that all it took was their cousin making the paper and suddenly Hank was moved to pick up the phone?

"Anyway," Tiffany went on. "She said yes. They're going this weekend." She pretended to stick a finger down her throat and made a gagging sound. Sometimes Tiffany acted half her age. Well, most of the time she acted half her age.

Amber ignored it. "Oh my gosh."

"Well. We'll see." Barb pursed her lips.

"Mom, this is awesome. Are you excited?" Amber was excited. She was gushing excitement. "Where are you going?

And when? Saturday? What time? What are you going to wear? Should I do your hair?"

"I think gray roots suit her fine." Tiffany was gobbling down her grilled cheese with fervor and spoke through a mouthful of food.

"Gross, Tiff. Swallow before you open your mouth." Amber returned her attention to her mother. "Well?"

"We don't have plans. It's just—loose. We're gon' get back in touch on Saturday and go from there."

"He'll call you back?"

Barb let her fork clatter to her plate—piled with salad—which was unusual for her. "Honey?" she blinked fast and smiled fake. "You know what? I think I'm gon' need both you all to stop talkin' about Hank now."

Amber frowned. Tiffany jutted out a thumbs up. "Fine by me."

"What?" Amber asked. "What do you mean stop talking about him?"

Barb pushed her plate away and laced her fingers together. "If something happens between us, you'll know. But for right now, I don't need the pressure. And neither does he, honestly."

Amber narrowed her eyes on her mother. After a beat, she said, "You've been talkin' to him."

Barb grunted. "What?"

"You and Dad. You've kept in touch. He didn't call you out of the clear blue. You talk regularly, don't you?"

Tiffany grabbed Amber's arm and squeezed. "Oh my Lord, I think you're right. They're hookin' up."

"Ew, what?" Barb made a face and shook her head and spat back, "*No*, we're not *hookin'* up. My word, child." She closed her eyes. "Listen, things with your dad and me—well, there aren't things between us. Just history. And if we decide to... to start talkin' again or spending time together, it'll be a slow thing."

Amber's face fell. There was nothing more she wanted than for her dad to come back into the fold. She wanted it worse than she wanted to open a tasting room and a winery or a vineyard or whatever. Ever since Amber was a little girl who played at running a restaurant with her cousins and sister and brother, there was one thing at the center of her world:

Her *people*.

Her *family*.

Since the day she woke up and her mother announced that "Daddy took a job out West," Amber had waited patiently for her family to be back together.

It wasn't until a few years later that Barb had confessed she'd fibbed. Daddy had taken a job out West, in California. But he wasn't coming back.

And yet, the previous autumn, he had.

As soon as Amber learned her dad was back, her focus shifted from everything—from Grant and the cats and her future—to her past.

Her mind swirled in the happy memories of her preschool days.

Precious memories but *clipped* memories.

When it came to Tiff and Trav, well, they didn't even know Dad. They were too young when he left.

By all accounts, Amber, Tiffany, and Travis—all three of them—shouldn't want a thing to do with the man who'd just up and left.

And yet... Amber knew in her heart there was more to the story. She didn't know what it was. But she knew there was more. Maybe it came down to a hunch, but it was there, growing like insatiable hope in her heart.

Barb cleared her throat. "Anyway, we aren't here to talk about Hank. We're here to talk about the wine business." Barb pointed her finger at Geddy's article. "He's your ticket, Amber Lee Taylor. Geddy can help you."

Amber pushed away thoughts of her father, for now. She took a bite of her sandwich and replied to her mom. "I don't know what Geddy can do unless he has a recipe pack complete with instructions on how to make Grandad's moonshine wine." She sighed. "It's useless."

"Who's to say you have to follow his recipe to the T, anyway? Why not make your own? Set aside a week and make a whole buncha batches, all different fruits—see what you get."

Amber agreed. "Morgan Jo thinks we need to know exactly what Grandad did and how he made the wine."

"She can't sit long enough to try and fail." Barb sipped her tea and looked thoughtfully ahead.

The waiter returned to refill their drinks, and Barb spoke to him. "Sam, you guys ever make homemade wine?"

"No, ma'am, but I got friends who do. It ain't hard."

Barb patted the tabletop and lifted her hand toward Sam, the friendly waiter who wasn't any older than Amber herself. "See? Tell Morgan Jo. Go on. Call her up and let her know that you all can do this on your own without Grandad."

Tiffany had finished her entire sandwich by now and was slurping her milkshake. "I thought you found Grandad's recipe book anyway? What happened to that? What was wrong with it?"

"It was vague. We tried to follow it, but the wine came out bad."

"You don't know how to make wine at all. None of you do. So you pick up a man's recipe book from, when? Thirty? Forty years ago? And you think, I'll just do exactly what's put down in here. And you do that, 'cept what you're followin' ain't a cookbook with specific times and measurements, it's nothing more than a diary."

Amber looked at her mother. "A diary? It's not a diary. How would you know, anyway? I don't even think I showed you."

"You didn't have to. I know what you what you found. It wasn't some secret buried treasure."

"Nothin' ever is," Tiffany cooed sagely. Amber wanted to slap her.

"Honey, Amber Lee, that notebook? I gave it to my dad for his birthday back before the twins were born. I told him he could write down how to do the wine."

"So you *know* it's a wine recipe book."

"I *know* my dad." Barb looked wistful. "He wasn't a writer or a *cook* with an eye for food or beverage chemistry."

"Well, what was he?"

Barb folded the paper napkin in her lap and laid it neatly over her partially eaten salad. "You know, accordin' to Hank, he was a movie star."

* * *

Amber asked her mother to explain. "A movie star? What?"

Barb smiled and chuckled. "Your dad, back when we was together, was *huge* into filming things. He filmed every last thing in our lives, I swear. I never knew where it went to. All that film, I mean. After a few years, I totally forgot about it, and then your Uncle Billy got a camcorder sometime in the nineties and started tapin' stuff, and it was enough. And I forgot. Well, I mentioned to Hank today that you and Morgan Jo was lookin' to make wine based on Grandad's recipes and he got all huffy and emotional."

"What do you mean huffy and emotional?"

"He said he'd filmed Grandad making wine."

"We knew someone did." Amber frowned. "I didn't know it was Daddy."

"Right, well. He said he left all the tapes with Bill before leaving and that he regretted it."

"Why?"

"I have no idea. That was just like Hank though. He got something in his head and got so sentimental about it that he never could do right by an idea. He was a lot like Grandad. A dreamer. Always thought something big was right around the corner for him."

"Is *that* why you divorced?"

Barb looked away. "It's why we didn't get married." She looked back at Amber and then to Tiff. "At *first*."

"What?" Amber was more confused than ever, but her mother shook her head and held her hand toward Sam.

"Sam, check please." Barb reached for her wallet. "I have another job after this. A home clean in lower Brambleberry. Here." She passed three ten-dollar bills to Amber. "Gotta run."

"Mom, wait. You're just getting started. You said you didn't marry Dad at first because he was a dreamer? So, what? Then you ended up marrying him anyway?"

"Well, yes, hon. You came along, and Hank was a family man at his heart. It just... it worked out." She patted the bills, then leaned in and kissed Amber on the check, stood, went to Tiffany and did the same. "Wish I could stay. Let's have supper soon."

"Mom," Amber blurted as Barb started away.

"Do you think Dad would tell me about how to make the wine? Do you think he remembers?"

Barb looked around the restaurant, which was filling up with the lunchtime rush now. She took two strides back to the bar and rested a hand on Amber's shoulder. "I don't think Hank wants to relive that time of his life. Of *our* lives." She squeezed Amber's shoulder. "Let it be. Find your way. Both you and Morgan Jo and whoever else you've got roped into that business. Find your *own* recipes. No sense in dragging up the past. Best to let sleeping dogs lie, if you know what I mean."

CHAPTER FORTY

1992

Bill

Inside the barn, there was plenty for little Morgan Jo and Amber Lee to get hurt with, from tools to heavy machinery to splintered wood. The seeping rage from earlier collected in the base of Bill's neck and turned to an ache.

"Girls, I've got a job for you, okay?" Hank grabbed a thermos he'd brought along, then pulled two copper pots from the workspace. Bill held back his protest. He didn't need the pots, but they were antiques.

"I need you two to whip up a potion, okay? Something magical."

Amber whined. "Not magic, Daddy."

"Yes! A potion!" Morgan Jo squealed. The pair of them couldn't be more different. Amber was a sensible little girl and Morgan Jo was a dreamer. Maybe one day they'd go in different directions, too far apart in their minds to get along. Bill had cousins like that. Some who were too math-smart and interested in keeping their hands clean to do any real work or have any *real* fun. In spite of himself, Bill liked to dream and have fun. He didn't always show it, but that's just exactly why he was doin' this video series with Hank.

Hank set the girls up in a corner of the barn with an ol' kettle, copper pots, and his thermos of water, which Bill thought was a funny thing for a man to carry around. And just like that, the girls were off in some fantasy world, mixing up a drink and serving it to one another while Bill and Hank got on with the winemaking.

Hank leveled the camera, and Bill hefted up the crick water. "We just pour this in the crock and cover up all the berries."

Hank leaned the camera closer to the workbench to get a good angle on the operation.

Bill took a long-handled wooden ladle and gave the berries and water a good stir. "They'll just float if you don't do something, so we gotta weigh the berries down that way they soak proper."

Bill had set out a variety of items that might be used for such a purpose to add a little flare to the film. A brick. A great big stone. The holy Bible. Essie had fussed at him calling him a heretic and a blasphemer, but it was just a joke. "I ain't really gon' use the Bible, but you get something heavy, like a stone or brick, to hold down the berries. Actually, we'll also need a board to keep the weight level across the batch. Bill picked up a board he'd cut just for this moment, a perfect cylinder of oak. "Depending on what type of wine you make you can even use the wood as a sort of, um, flavorin' or whatnot."

Easing the custom-cut board into the cork came next, and Bill did this awkwardly while Hank pointed the camera lens right over his shoulder. Bill was feelin' more and more like a real winemaker and even a bit like someone important. "Now that's in, you can add weight on top since the wood'll float, so here I'll put on this brick. Now it's important that what you put on ain't contaminated. So you can seal it up in a plastic bag or you can just add natural rocks from the crick which is what I'm gon' do here." Indeed, he added a smooth round stone from the crick bed to keep the board down and then pressed on all them grapes. "There's different ways of doin' it, but that's how I do it, anyhow." Bill knew the taste of the wine that came out after, and this made him feel confident in the whole thing.

He put the lid back on top of the barrel and folded his arms over himself. A hunk of cud was stuck inside of his lip, and it was about time to get a fresh one. "Well, that's it for now." He drew a finger across his neck. "Cut."

Hank laughed. Hank was always good for a laugh, which was one of the things that Bill really liked about the kid. The pair had grown on each other over time. He replied, "Cut," lowered the camera, then looked over his shoulder.

The girls was so damn quiet, Bill'd done near forgot all about 'em. "Girls? You want to come see this? What Grandaddy's makin'?"

"Aw, no. It ain't for kids, anyhow." Bill waved a hand and the girls carried on sippin' from their copper teacups like they was having a regular tea party. It was sorta cute, Bill figured.

He grabbed his spittoon from beneath the workbench and gave a big spit, then added a fresh wad of chew to his lip and lowered to the stool. "'Sgoin' good, I reckon."

"It's going great." Hank was always one to agree, too. Another likable thing about him, but also something to be wary about. When a person was keen to agree with you all the time, they might just be hidin' something. A'course, Bill didn't have no suspicions when it came to Hank, and it was best you just followed your gut about these things, anyhow.

Hank went on, "What's next in the process?"

"Next?" Bill pulled his glasses down and cleaned them with the handkerchief he kept in his breast pocket. "Well, we'll add the sugar. Some people add yeast at this part, too. I just add in the sugar. The more sugar you add, the more drunk this wine'll make ya. You know, it'll make the alcohol content way higher." Bill made a blast-off noise then whistled through his teeth. "Woo-ee boy, I got some stories about backyard wine."

Hank looked up fast. "Backyard wine? That's what you call it?"

Bill smirked. "Well, that's what we called it when we was kids makin' this stuff in the backyard." He laughed to himself.

"Backyard wine. It's great."

Hank could be a weirdo even when he was agreeable and quick for a laugh.

"Well, whatever."

"Should you add the sugar right now?"

"Right this minute?" Bill blinked. "Well, we could. If you want to get a shot of that, then we'll give it a spell and come right back to it." He was really getting the Hollywood lingo down. Shot this and angles that.

"I'll take the girls in. It's almost nap time for Amber Lee."

"Oh, right. And the twins'll be cranky. You goin' on home then? For their naps?" Bill lifted his eyebrows to Hank and buried his hands deep in the pockets of his jeans.

Hank gave him a thinking face in return. "They could probably nap here. Would that be okay with you?"

"Oh, I don't care. Plenty of room in the big house. Or anywhere on this farm." He chuckled. "Essie'll like to help, I'm sure."

"I'll have to ask Barb." Hank hooked a thumb toward the doors. "Mind if I just—"

"Go on. Go ahead." Bill waved him out. He understood when a man had to get permission from his wife. Any solid marriage worked this way, what with the woman havin' equal or greater say. And when it came to the children, well, the woman had all the say. Hank was a good-enough dad, but Bill sort of appreciated that he deferred to Barb when it came to Amber Lee and the twins.

"I'll come on in behind you." The sugar could wait an hour or even a day, and so Bill followed as Hank scooped up the girls, leaving their copper kettle and pots in the dirt floor; a little mess. Hank carried Morgan Jo in his right arm and Amber Lee in his left, and he looked nothing short of a good father.

Sometimes, Bill wondered why his oldest daughter couldn't have landed a better man. CarlaMay wasn't no idiot, and she was as pretty as any girl around. She had morals, and she was a Christian woman, brought up in a Christian home.

Where'd she gone wrong?

Then again, it wasn't like Bill to blame her. It wasn't Carla-May's fault that she fell for a man who knocked her up and left her like a whore in the street. That was on the *man*, whoever the scoundrel was. It was *his* fault for leaving a good girl in delicate condition. Bill felt for CarlaMay and he felt for Morgan Jo, which was why they could stay on for as long as they'd like.

Anyway, their situation gave a little more meaning to Barb and Hank's relationship.

After all, Hank mighta knocked Barb up, too, like a real dog.

But at least he stayed.

CHAPTER FORTY-ONE

PRESENT DAY

Morgan Jo

Amber called Morgan just as soon as she got off the phone with Julia. "Did you know my *dad* was the one to film Grandad makin' wine?"

"What?" Morgan's mouth could have hit the floor. "Oh my word, Amber Lee Taylor. Call him up now! Let's get him to meet us. He probably has a great memory. Wasn't he out in Hollywood all those years?" A million and one thoughts raced through Morgan's head. With someone smart like Hank Taylor on their side, they could whip up a great replica of the Coyle recipe, probably. This was the break they needed to settle into a process. Heck, Hank Taylor may even be able to *recite* the whole process.

"I can't." Amber sounded hollow.

"Where are you right now?"

"I'm out on Main Street about to walk north. I have a few more places to hit, but—"

"Just come home. We'll call your dad. Amber, this is *perfect!*" Morgan all but squealed.

"Morgan Jo, I can't."

"You can't, *what*? Call your dad? I thought you two were talkin'. Aren't you still trying to reunite him with your mom?" Morgan had never much appreciated Amber's recent drive to bring her parents together. Sure, Hank Taylor lived closer now, but he'd *left*. *Why did Amber care? Did she even still love him after what he'd done?* Morgan knew *she* didn't love *her* dad, wherever or *who*ever he was. But even if Morgan didn't give a rat's nest about ol' "Uncle" Hank, he was obviously the key to the family winemaking knowledge. Surely, the man could walk them through what he'd taped Grandad Bill doing. He'd have a sense of timeline. There wouldn't be a question about whether to wait four weeks or six or eight—they wouldn't ruin a whole batch by opening it too soon. They wouldn't ruin a batch with too much sugar or add too little and be forced to test for longer. They could take Grandad's specific recipes and run with it, and Morgan could declare to the world that the Moonshine Vine-yard—or whatever they called it—was *authentic*. It was all theirs. Totally family-based. No cheating. No copying. As pure as blood.

As pure as Brambleberry.

"Morgan Jo, I can't ask my dad. My mom told me to let it be. We'll go with Geddy's knowledge and Travis's and what we have at the orchard on the farm. We'll fill in the blanks with the internet. We don't need to keep harping on with something that's a pipe dream, Morgan Jo."

"A pipe dream?" Morgan Jo got back in her car, ready to drive straight to wherever the hell Amber was, pick her up, and choke her dad's phone number out of her. "This whole idea was based on the fact that we found Grandad's *recipes*, Amber Lee."

"They aren't recipes! They're... they're diary entries, Morgan Jo. There was nothing fancy about that book. My mom gave it to him as a journal to write stuff down in. To give

Grandad something to do. Then my dad filmed him, and it was just a... a *hobby*."

"Winemaking starts as a hobby. And it can become so much more."

"You're just like them, I guess. You're a dreamer, Morgan Jo. And that's nice and all, but if you aren't willing to be practical, I don't see how in the world we can open a business together. Emmett agrees. He's the one who's always lookin' stuff up online. He's out there in the fields testing the fruits. And Julia doesn't care at all. She's only in this 'cause she's your friend. She has a full-time job, Morgan Jo. And so does Emmett. Plus, he *loves* you. And what do I have? I have a part-time hair gig which I hate. I have a brother and sister who'd rather while away hours drinking and arguing and snooping on other family members than do anything productive with their lives. I have a dad who's back in the county and doesn't even want to *see* me. Do you know that, Morgan Jo? Did you know my daddy doesn't want to see me?"

"I thought it was you all who didn't want to see him," Morgan whispered. And she did, too. She distinctly remembered Trav spitting out into the wind at the very mention of the name Hank Taylor. And Tiffany had said she'd die before she gave five minutes to the father who'd left them for Hollywood.

It was just Amber who'd been so desperate to mend the past.

And it was Morgan who was so desperate to recreate it. Morgan was more convinced than ever that she and her cousin shared a common goal, it was just going to take some convincing.

"Amber, you want your parents to get back together. Let's... let's set something up. A barbecue, maybe? We can invite Hank to the farm, and your mom. They can meet on quasi-neutral ground here. No pressure. We can talk about wine and Grandad and—"

"Morgan Jo, I think I'm gonna be sick. I have to go."

CHAPTER FORTY-TWO

PRESENT DAY

Amber

Amber made it to a flower bed that trimmed Main Street before pukin' up her lunch right there, in the begonias.

It occurred to her, mid-puke, that she'd also puked the week before, first thing in the morning when she went to get her coffee.

And she'd felt sick enough to puke the month before, late April. That was food poisoning though.

Amber kept going back and back until she recalled the first time she'd puked in recent memory. The day she found out Grant was cheating. She'd gotten sick right there in the salon.

It was the stress. And the heat. And the fact that Amber was walkin' up and down Main Street. Talking to strangers on a mission she didn't *actually* believe in. And then there was Morgan Jo, laying on the pressure so thick that Amber felt like she couldn't breathe.

Taking deep, slow breaths, she gripped the trunk of the tree that sprouted up from the center of the well where the flowers grew.

"Are you okay?" The voice came from behind her. A friendly voice but unsure, even staccato, like the man asking the question was afraid Amber might turn around and projectile spew all over him.

Amber turned, one hand covering her mouth. "I'm okay." She blinked at the man—who didn't quite look like a man. More like what real adults might call a *young* man. Twenty-something, maybe thirty tops. "I think."

"Don't. Um. Please don't *Exorcist* me," he warned, passing over a paper napkin as he shielded himself with a paper to-go bag from the Dewdrop. Amber guessed he worked along Main Street and had come over to grab a bite on his lunch.

Humiliation mixed with amusement as Amber bashfully took the napkin and pressed it to her mouth. "I won't." She couldn't *not* laugh.

"What's so, so... funny?" The staccato effect of his speech remained. A pause came between each of his words. *Was it a stutter?* Amber wasn't sure, but she was... intrigued.

"I was thinking of that movie, too. After I barfed and right when I heard you ask me if I was okay." She closed her eyes and shook her head. "That's so awkward. Sorry." She wadded the napkin in her hand and raised it in her fist. "Thanks again. I really am okay. Just, um... the heat, I guess."

"I'm. Callum. Callum Dockerty." He stuck out a hand then pulled it back. His speech flowed more smoothly. "Maybe I won't shake your hand."

Again, Amber laughed. Then, his name clicked like a gear into place in her mind. "Callum Dockerty. You work at—"

"Olde Towne Video on Main and Ninth." He pointed up the sidewalk. "Just came down for my lunch." He held up his bag. "Saw you get sick." He pointed with his bag at the begonias.

"Olde Towne Video," Amber echoed. "Do you know how to fix VHS tapes?"

CHAPTER FORTY-THREE

1992

Bill

The day before, Barb had dragged Hank and the kids back to their apartment on Hickory in town.

Now it was Monday morning, and Hank had called the house at the crack of dawn. He had to go into work, and he couldn't come to film the sugar-adding until later in the day. "Was that all right by Bill?"

He'd asked all this of Essie, who'd relayed the phone call.

Bill was sore about it. He ought never to have taken that spittin' break. He ought to have stayed in the process, pulled the wood, added the sugar, stirred, added back the wood and stone, and sealed it up. Then they'd have time for things like naps and the video store.

Bill was so sore, in fact, that he wasn't sure he wanted to carry on with filming that day or any day. That's just how sore Bill was. Mainly, his soreness was aimed not at Hank, in fact, but at Barb. Sometimes, Bill's daughters acted too much like their mother, commandeering their men around like it was a woman's world. And it wasn't. It was a woman's home and hearth, but...

Well, even Bill couldn't argue that the world belonged to men. Look at him, for example. Bill Coyle had turned out to be good for nothing, that's what. The world certainly didn't belong to *him*. Even his own life didn't always feel like his own.

"Fine." Bill grumbled some other choice words, but he gave his blessing to Essie who gave the blessing to Hank, and it was settled. Hank would join Bill that afternoon to continue with the filming.

Come evening, Essie was fixin' supper and Hank still hadn't appeared. Bill had been pacing the front room, poking his nose out the front door, sweeping the porch, oiling the rocking chairs, and doing any other number of things to try and pass the time while keepin' an eye on the gravel drive.

"Billy, come on and eat. CarlaMay's goin' out for supper with a friend. It'll be just you and me tonight."

"What about Morgan Jo? She gon' come down and eat, too?"

"CarlaMay fed her earlier. She's down for a nap before CarlaMay leaves."

"I ain't hungry," Bill mumbled, but he ambled into the kitchen and started settin' the table anyhow. By the time plates and silverware were down, Essie had filled two glasses with sweet tea and the center of the table with a great big spread of food.

Bill helped himself to a chicken thigh and a heaping spoonful of collard greens. He added a lump of mashed potatoes and patted the center of it before filling it up with brown gravy. Essie was known the world over for her brown gravy.

Come to think of it, somethin' was goin' on. "What's all this about?" Bill accused her through a mouthful of food. He poked with his knife at the food on the table. "You don't ever cook a big meal just for you and me." It was true. Very rarely would Essie cook the pair of them a full supper. More likely, she threw together leftovers and food that had sat in the pantry so long it was growin' moss on it.

"Oh, what? This?" Essie kept her eyes on her own spoonful of potatoes. "Ain't nothin' but a nice supper."

"Where's CarlaMay?"

"I told you. Getting ready to go out. Probably getting the baby up and settled. Sooner we eat, sooner CarlaMay can leave and I can take Morgan Jo."

It made no sense at all. Bill parked an elbow on the table and gave it a quiet think. "And Hank said he'd be here this afternoon?"

Essie set her fork and knife down on her plate. They clanked against the porcelain. She wiped her mouth with the hem of her apron, which was an Essie habit that really got to gratin' on Bill, but he ignored it for now.

She rolled a mouthful of potatoes around and swallowed, then took a long pull of her drink. She still didn't look at him.

"Essie, what's goin' on?" He put his silverware down, too and crossed his arms. "You know somethin' and you ain't saying it."

"I did talk to Hank this morning. He had to go into work, Billy. Said he'd be here after. I don't know what time that is."

"You said the afternoon."

"Well, Barb has mentioned before he usually gets off around three or four, then the evening shift takes over. I don't know how video shops work, Bill." Her voice had a hollow, airy quality to it, and Bill could pin this down to a bald-faced lie. *Yes, sirree.*

The outside supper bell clanged loud. It served as a doorbell only to the sorts of dopes who didn't spend any time at the farm.

Hank wouldn't ring that thing, but who else could it be?

Bill whipped around.

Essie grabbed Bill's hand before he could launch out of his chair and give the kid a tongue lashin' for bein' late.

"Billy, just wait."

"Wait?" He twisted and leaned left to get a view. "Let me get the damn door, Essie. Prob'ly Hank, I'm sure."

Essie had a clear view of the door with its high-up window. She was starin' at it like she could tell straight away who was there. "It's not Hank, Bill." Essie's face was drawn and serious; her tone was flat and cold. "I didn't give you the full truth, but only on account of I didn't know how."

"Full truth of what?" Bill roared.

"Well, you'll just see. Go on now. Open that door. See who it is. Talk to the person."

He twisted and pushed up, heading to the front door to see if maybe it was Hank and Essie was just foolin'.

Before he got that far, footsteps on the stairs tore his attention up and away.

CarlaMay was coming down. She wore a checkered dress, red and white like a picnic blanket. At her waist she held her daughter's hand.

Morgan Jo had been crying. CarlaMay's face was awash in stress.

Bill might not know much, but he knew when Essie was lying.

Confused and angry, he pointed at CarlaMay. "You're sure dressed up for supper with a friend."

Essie joined Bill at the bottom of the steps. Bill didn't move toward the door now, but he could distinctly see the figure of a man beyond.

A man with short hair.

Essie was right.

It wasn't Hank.

Bill backed up. If it wasn't Hank there, he didn't give a damn who was callin'. He had no interest at all. Not one lick of it. And he showed this by crossing his arms and frownin' and saying, "What's goin' on?"

CHAPTER FORTY-FOUR

PRESENT DAY

Morgan Jo

Rattled after her conversation with Amber, Morgan went into the house. Her mother was away at work and Morgan needed someone to talk to. Julia had also gone back to work. Emmett was untrustworthy.

Maybe.

She studied her phone for a moment then took a chance.

The phone rang once.

"MoJo." Emmett's voice was chipper. More chipper than usual. Was this more evidence that he was lying? Was he covering his tracks with a bright mood?

Emmett was almost always in a good mood. But Morgan was certain that he sounded... excited.

"Where are you?" She tried to soften her tone, but it came out sharp.

"I'm at the office. I told you."

Never one to play games, and also on the threshold of convincing Amber to talk to Hank, Morgan didn't have time for this. "You weren't there earlier. I know."

"What?"

"When I called you before. You said you were at your office but you weren't. I went to your office. I needed to talk about business stuff." She hesitated. "Emmett, you lied."

He was silent a moment, and Morgan's grip tightened on the phone. She waited.

Another beat passed.

"Yeah. I did lie."

Morgan couldn't tell if the dropping of her stomach was a good reaction—one of relief—or a bad reaction—one of horror. "You lied to me?"

"I really don't want to talk about this over the phone." He sounded stretched. "But I have a client coming in. Can we meet?"

"Meet?" Lukewarm. That's what the suggestion was. Lukewarm.

"I'll come to the farm after work. Will you be there?"

"And what? Just wait for you? Just tell me now, Emmett."

"No," he shot back. "Listen, Morgan Jo. I love you. I lied— this is..." He made a noise somewhere between a growl and a laugh. *Was that even possible?* How could he find this funny at all? And why couldn't he just tell her where he *was*, for goodness' sake?

"Does this have to do with the vineyard? Just because I don't want to use internet recipes? Because I want Grandad's recipes? Do you even know why I want Grandad's recipes? No one gets it." She was working up to something; her chest clenched and her throat went dry. She felt like she might cry.

Morgan Jo continued, "It's about *family*, Emmett. No one gets that. Everyone wants to take the easy way. They don't want to hit the ground running and do it right. Do it like our ances- tors did. No one wants to restore houses anymore—they want to tear them down. Or better yet—they want to build a brand-new stucco box down the street. They want to tear down forests but they're afraid of a little foundational work." She stopped, took a breath.

Emmett said, "Wow." It came out on a whisper.

"Wow?" *Was this it?* Was this end of their relationship? After just a few months of rebuilding what they once had, falling in love all over again, and breaking ground on what could be a true future—what? He'd found someone else? Decided Morgan wasn't worth the work?

"Wow, you're right."

"I am?" She frowned. "Well." Her words sputtered in her head like an engine that wouldn't start. "You agree with me, then it's not the business. Then why'd you lie?"

"I, um." He cleared his throat. "I—can I just come to the farm? I'll be an hour. Two tops."

"Fine, I'll see you then."

CHAPTER FORTY-FIVE

PRESENT DAY

Amber

As Amber walked with Callum to the video shop up on Ninth, she tapped out a quick text to Morgan Jo: *Met the video store guy. Get the box of VHS from the basement and meet me on the corner of Ninth and Main. Hurry!*

She set aside their argument and the fact that it'd upset Amber so much that she'd barfed. Partly, Amber chalked up her anger to her father. The fact that he didn't want to see Amber. The fact that Amber'd never get back what she once had and that she didn't understand any of it—well, her obsession withdrew when Callum came up to her with that brown paper napkin.

He didn't get ahead of her, despite having long legs. This made it hard for Amber to sneak good looks, but she managed. It was strange she'd never seen him before, especially if he frequented the Dewdrop.

"How long you been in Brambleberry?" she asked by way of small talk.

He wore a forest-green bucket hat over longish brown hair,

and Amber wasn't altogether convinced bucket hats were actually in style, yet he looked good in it. Artsy but also preppy but also... indifferent. Like he didn't much care what people thought. He wore a *Goonies* T-shirt with a threadbare quality and well-fitting jeans. Amber could tell because they gave his butt a nice shape. Or maybe his butt just naturally had a nice shape too it, and that gave Amber a secret thrill.

She could hear her cousin Rachel's words in her ear, *"Don't ever follow a man into a place that isn't public."* Rachel would probably think that following a man with a nice butt was extra bad, but Amber reasoned that Olde Towne Video wasn't a private place. It was an objectively public place, in full view of any pedestrians or window shoppers. *Plus*, Morgan Jo was probably on her way right now.

"Just about a year. I came down from Louisville."

"Why Brambleberry?"

He tucked a strand of his dark hair behind his ear and gave her a big goofy grin. "Olde Towne Video."

Amber walked beside him, her eyebrows furrowed and her eyes moved left and right as she considered his answer for a beat. She noticed the nausea hadn't entirely left her but walking and talking was a good distraction. Maybe she had a stomach bug? Maybe she was exposing this kind—if nerdy—stranger to some sort of terrible virus. Amber once had the norovirus after eating canned turkey and it just about ruined Thanksgiving for her for life. But she'd gotten over it.

Her mind returned to Callum's reply. "You came to Brambleberry to work at Olde Town Video?"

They stopped at a crosswalk. Callum stepped forward slightly and leaned to look left and right, almost like a kindergartner might after just learning the famous tune: *Stop, look, and listen before you cross the street. First you use your eyes and ears, then you use your feet.*

Callum struck a sexy profile, Amber realized as he craned

his head to the right, around Amber, the stop sign, and a hickory tree. With a jaw that could cut glass and an Adam's apple like Ichabod Crane, he was all boy. Dark eyelashes, warm skin, and light-brown irises gave him the sort of quality that made girls pant.

And yet—he was no Lothario. That much was obvious.

Once the coast was clear, they crossed and Callum answered. "I read in the *Kentucky Standard* that it was going out of business. So I contacted the owner. Turns out he was this guy out in California who lived here forever ago. I guess he was ready to kiss the shop goodbye, but, like, it's got, like, a *cult* following around this area. Olde Towne Video is one of the last video rentals in Nelson County, for one. For two, it's always had this, like, impeccable reputation surrounding its acquisition of comics. It's like a secret thing in nerd circles." He was talking almost to himself as he unlocked the front door—a beautiful wooden thing that jangled beneath a bell as Callum pushed it open and gestured for Amber to walk through.

"Oh, right. I bet my ex was always in here."

"Your ex?"

"Grant Maycomb. He was a video-game type."

"Oh. No, we don't sell video games. It's more old school."

"Oh." Amber regretted mentioning she had an ex. It felt a shade too personal.

"So, you said you had some video tapes you wanted me to look at?" He rounded the counter and propped his hands in a neat pile of long fingers atop the counter, as if he thought she might pull the videos out of her small cross-body bag.

"I do. I just..." Amber glanced out the window to look for Morgan Jo, but there was no way that girl could get here so soon. Amber had to stall. "My cousin's bringin' 'em by. Maybe I'll just browse while I wait for her?"

Callum lifted his hand around the store. "Take your time. I'm here if you have any questions."

A little disappointed that their banter might be over, Amber departed from the counter. Her nausea returned in full force, and it got worse as she recalled her worry it could be a bug and now maybe she was spreading it around Main Street. But she didn't *feel* sick. Mostly, she felt... dizzy?

"Actually, is there a place I can just set down for a minute?"

Callum looked at her funny, like he didn't quite understand. He blinked. "Yes. I have a chair." It was like a switch flipped and when he was confronted with something he hadn't planned for or practiced, he stumbled. He shuffled down behind the counter, reaching for a chair that stood in the corner against a shelf of neatly organized books.

Then, with a quick lift, twirl, and plant, the chair was on the other side of the counter, facing Amber. Awkwardly.

"Thanks." She felt bad. "What time do you usually close shop?"

"My shift ends at six." He looked at his wristwatch. "That's in four and a half hours."

"Three," Amber repeated. She felt compelled to carry forth the small talk or else sit there like a weirdo while Callum organized a display of action figures. "So, who takes over for you at three? Or does the shop close?"

"Oh, no. It stays open until midnight. We pride ourselves on keeping *industry* hours."

"Industry? Which industry would that be?" Amber forced herself to breathe and talk, and as long as she did this, the nausea remained at bay. In fact, the feeling in her head and stomach—that swirling awful feeling—seemed to be slipping away entirely now. She relaxed her shoulders and set her purse on the floor, folding her hands in her lap neatly and pushing her knees together so as to avoid lookin' like a slouch.

She felt Callum's eyes flash on her briefly, like he noticed that she noticed that she might be noticeable. Or maybe this was all in her imagination.

Yes. It was. No chance could this cute, tall, dark, handsome shopkeeper take a real and true physical interest in Amber Lee Taylor.

Not a chance.

"The entertainment industry."

"Oh." Amber thought for a moment. "I always thought of this more as a radio shack meets electronic repair shop."

Callum leaned from the far side of the display he was cleaning. "Quite the opposite. We specialize in antiquated audiovisual media with an emphasis on curating and brokering equipment, entertainment media, and collectibles. I have a lot of experience in restoration, however. Anyway, the collectibles are a new focus. The owner gave me permission to pursue it in order to bring in more diverse clients."

Amber smiled. Callum was adorable.

A jangle sound came above the heavy wooden door as a trio of teenagers entered. Pimple-faced, bespectacled, and metal-mouthed, they could have stepped right out of the nineties. They beelined to the small comic shelving unit at the far corner.

"No touching," Callum told them.

"No touching?" Amber raised her eyebrows to him.

He shrugged. "It's summer now, and as I warned the owner, we'll get an influx of bored school children who want to see Wonder Woman's cleavage."

Amber laughed so hard she snorted, and Callum grinned at her.

"Well, then, I suppose it's a good rule. Teachin' those boys a little control."

"Yeah. I just enforce it, though. Actually, the idea was Hank's."

Amber froze. "Whose?"

Callum folded the cloth he'd been using to wipe the display and replied nonchalantly, without even looking at her. "The owner's idea. Hank. Hank Taylor."

CHAPTER FORTY-SIX

1992

Bill

Essie let forth a long low sigh. She looked up at CarlaMay on the stairs. "Well, cat's out of the bag. Thought you was drivin' to town to meet him." The bell, a Nelson Farm myth, that big ol' iron thing. Not a true doorbell but irresistible to strangers. Especially stupid ones. "Might as well make introductions."

Morgan Jo sniffled. CarlaMay said, "It's fine. I'll just go." She didn't meet Bill's eye.

"Anybody gon' tell me what in the hell is going on and who's at the door? And what kind of a friend we're talkin' about here? A man?"

The heavy boom of Bill's voice bounced around the house, but he had a right to raise his voice. He had a right to protect his family.

Morgan Jo sprouted tears all over again.

"Dad," CarlaMay shot back, her tone sharp and her eyes glaring. "It's nothing. A friend. Can't I have friends?"

At that, Bill laughed. "A friend. Here you are with a baby

who doesn't have a father. And what? You're goin' out to meet yet another man? And she's here to watch you leave?"

"Bill," Essie hissed as she moved to the staircase and pulled Morgan Jo into her arms, lifting the little thing up and bouncing her, shushing her. "You just worry about Hank. We'll handle this." She folded her arms but jutted a sharp chin toward the door and the shadowy figure that stood beyond it. Bill was surprised the guy hadn't left yet. Were it Bill, he'd have left by now.

"Hank." Bill scoffed. "You say that like I'm a girly man or something!" He was roaring now. All these wild accusations and lies buzzed about his head like flies. He couldn't slap them away fast enough. "I got a right to know what's goin' on in my house, just as surely as any one of you do!"

"Oh, is that so? Well, if you've got a right, Bill Coyle, then tell us why Hank comes by here? What you two are working on in that barn out there with the camera? What are you up to back there?"

Bill grunted. It wasn't like it was a secret, but if it was a secret then it was more along the lines of a surprise. What they were doing was going to be a gift to his children and grandchildren and all the ones that came after. What he was doin' with Hank was building a damn legacy. That's what. But he couldn't seem to say as much. The words floated away from him like cigarette smoke on the wind.

Instead, he bellowed, "Up to? We're up to exactly what men get up to. Drinkin' and smokin' and carryin' on!" It was crazy that he had to explain himself to Essie and CarlaMay. Just plain crazy.

And yet, he'd lied.

Bill looked at his feet. "We're not drinkin' and smokin'. Well, we smoked cigars one time. That was it."

From the corner of his eye, he could tell Essie was frownin' low and crossin' her arms and shakin' her head and clickin' her tongue. "Bill Coyle, I'm surprised at you. Lyin'. And after all this quietin' around in the barn with Hank."

"Hank is Barb's husband. So what if he helps me with some work?"

Essie's eyes narrowed like daggers on him. "Helps you, huh? If he's helpin' you, then why have the pears dropped to the grass, rottin' and drawin' critters? And the bunkhouses—the toilet in the first bunkhouse backs up every week. And the roof in the second house—it's been leakin' for a year. And that's not to mention the *mess* you got in the back of the barn, like a pack rat or somethin'! We're running a business here, and you'd rather spend your spare time with Hank. A guy you call the *loser*." Essie sneered.

A strange protectiveness twisted like a screw deep down in Bill. "Hank's not a loser," he spat acerbically. "But whoever that is out there—waiting on the porch like a John in the slums of Louie-vull—*that's* the real loser." Then he looked at CarlaMay. "And if you think it right to set this sorta example for your daughter, then I reckon you just might be a *loser*, too."

Bill might take back the words if he could, but it was too late. They were out of his mouth and ringing like bells in the ears of his wife, daughter, and granddaughter. Then again, maybe he wouldn't take them back. In fact, another thought came to his mind and made its way out his lips. "Whoever that person is out there—*pfft*." Then he added sourly, "At least Hank is *family*."

CarlaMay swung around the bannister and planted a kiss on Morgan Jo, who sucked her thumb and stared at the mess of them. CarlaMay whispered something to the little girl, then said, loud enough for Bill to hear, "Mom, take her out back to play or something." Lastly, she said, "Love you, Morgan Jo. Be back real soon." Then, CarlaMay cut across the floor, opened the front door, and slipped out into the night.

"She's not a loser." Essie stared at the door. "And if you'd just opened the door and greeted him, you'd find out that *he* ain't a stranger."

CHAPTER FORTY-SEVEN

PRESENT DAY

Morgan Jo

Morgan Jo received Amber's text message while she was on the phone with Emmett.

Bring the video tapes to the shop on Ninth? Did Amber really think they'd extract good info?

It was worth a shot.

She sent a message to Emmett letting him know that she had an errand to run. If she wasn't at the farm when he got there, please wait.

Then she went to the basement.

Amber had taken to leaving the door inside of the big house unlocked, which made egress simple enough.

Morgan eased down the staircase. The cats were asleep on the sofa, each tucked at opposite corners on little blankets. Amber's neatness was remarkable, really. On the coffee table, a small pale oak square, sat the box of tapes. Morgan had already looked through, but she wanted another moment to admire the haul of family history.

There weren't that many tapes with labels about wine,

which was interesting. If Grandad or whoever'd made the tapes —Hank, apparently—had labeled them so methodically, then why were others random dates? December 1992. April 1993. Nineteen ninety-four with a little American flag. Morgan suspected they were holidays, but then they could be related to wine. She figured that in December, bottling might begin. April was planting season. If he meant July 4 by the American flag, then it could be an early harvest.

It was maddening to own these pieces of history but to not be able to *open* them. Like a locked secret, the tapes belonged to Grandad and history.

Morgan went to lift the box, but it was heavier than she expected. She'd been lifting plenty lately, from buckets to boxes of wine glasses to power tools. This box, however, proved awkward to hold against her body.

For one, the box itself wasn't sturdy. Time and the introduction of moisture had broken its cardboard, so that you had to hold the bottom and one of the sides at the same time.

Morgan had to go get a hand truck. It'd be the most efficient and safest way for her to move the box to the car.

Getting it into the car would be hard, but not impossible.

As she left the basement to go out to the barn and grab the hand truck, she thought again about Emmett's stupid lie and stupider excuse. He *had* to lie. Who *has* to lie?

And if they *have* to lie, then *why*?

As she passed through the kitchen on her way to the mudroom and out back, the telephone rang.

The house phone rang at odd intervals, mostly on account of scammers and spammers, which drove everybody up the wall. Still, it was the family's habit to pick up the receiver anyhow. Morgan grabbed it, snapping a terse "Hello" into the line.

"Is this Morgan Jo?"

She frowned. The last time she'd answered for a telemarketer, they'd asked for Esther Coyle. The time before that was for William Coyle. Once or twice, it had been CarlaMay, but it hadn't ever been Morgan Jo. She was too recently a resident and owner of the property.

"Yes?" she answered by way of question.

"Morgan Jo. Hi! This is Father David."

She held back an eye-roll. Morgan Jo had been bad about going to church ever since she'd become an adult. Returning to Brambleberry, she'd occasionally go along with her mother, but her mother didn't attend St. Mary's any longer.

Even so, Father David seemed an ever-present figure in their lives, on account of Essie's seemingly close relationship with him in her final years. Yet CarlaMay had pushed him away every chance she got. She wasn't Catholic. Didn't ever want to be Catholic. And that was that. Father David was irrelevant to their lives, especially now that his favorite two parishioners were dead and gone.

"Sorry, Father David. Now isn't it a good time. I'm about to head out and—"

"Oh." He sounded disappointed. Like *she* was the reason he called. But then he said, "I read the article in the paper about Geddy. Just wanted to share my congratulations. If you'd pass it along to him? I didn't have his direct line."

Morgan frowned. *Geddy's article?* But if she asked, she'd get sucked into the details of her cousin's world. Right now, she was on mission.

"I'll tell him," she assured the priest, then hung up the phone, and returned to her task, wondering all the while why Father David called and what in the world Geddy had done to be featured in the newspaper.

CHAPTER FORTY-EIGHT

PRESENT DAY

Amber

Amber was in a panic now. An excited panic. Her nausea flared back up as she frantically phoned her mom to see if Barb knew this. When her mother didn't answer, Amber tried Tiff and Trav. Neither answered either. She sent a group text: *Daddy owns Olde Towne Video. Did anybody KNOW this???*

When Amber revealed to Callum that his boss was her dad, he stiffened up. His kindness retreated and he turned more professional.

She tried to reassure him, "We're... estranged. Don't worry."

"Estranged?" He looked at her with suspicion.

"It sounds dramatic. I know. I promise I've never been on *Maury Povich's* show or anything. I mean, we're really a nice, normal family," Amber said, referencing the words on a much-loved sign that graced the kitchen wall in the big house. It was the family's inside joke. But it was true. Their family was normal and everyone was generally quite nice. It was a good life that Amber led and that was in great deal thanks to who she called her own. Her mom, siblings, aunts, cousins, and so on.

"You said the owner takes over for you in the evenings?"

"That's right. He closes. But only a couple of days of the week. He lives in—"

"Bardstown. I know." And in Bardstown she figured he'd stayed. "So, a year ago, you called him?" Amber shook her head. She didn't even know that her dad had ever owned the video shop. Had her mother? Had *anyone*? It seemed impossible. Small towns were such that you couldn't just own a piece of Main Street without everybody having something to say about it. Asking you for donations or discounts or that kind of thing.

"He was hard to find. I guess at the time he was a silent investor or something. But he held the majority of the company, and he was ready to sell off his piece. That would have meant the store would close, though, because the other investors were only interested so long as it was making money." Callum's voice went even flatter, if that was possible. "It wasn't."

"You convinced my dad to keep it open? How?"

Callum raised a finger. "I'm sorry if this personal, but you really didn't know your father owned this place? It seems—"

"Hard to believe."

"Unfathomable." Callum used judgy words but on the whole, Amber didn't feel judged. She felt, interesting, even.

"Right. Well. Believe it. It's true."

"I know that families can be complicated. Anyway, I told him I'd take over on any aspect. I told him my ideas. I said all I needed was his backing, and I'd bring this place to life."

"Why did you care so much?"

Callum looked stumped. "It's... what I do?"

"It's what you do? Like, your *thing*?" Amber nodded slowly. "Your passion."

"Yes."

As Callum started tidying another display, Amber thought about her own world. Hairdressing. Grant. The basement apartment. Their cats. She thought about Morgan Jo and her passion

—the vineyard and winery. Finally, Amber thought about her place in all of that. It wasn't with the vineyard. Or the winery.

It definitely wasn't with Cutting Edge, sad to say.

"My thing is..." What *was* it? She knew what her childhood dream was, but childhood dreams never squared with adulthood. She knew what she wanted to do with the winery and Amber was over the moon to be part of a family business—and one in the service industry, too!—but that whole business was lookin' grimmer by the day. Especially if Barb said they weren't allowed to bother Hank with it.

Then again... here she was. In her daddy's shop which just so happened to deal in *antiquated* media. It hadn't been Amber's intention to get in touch with Hank, and even if he did show up, she was here for one person and one person, period.

Callum Dockerty. AV whiz.

CHAPTER FORTY-NINE

1992

Bill

Hank arrived an hour after CarlaMay had left. An hour after Essie told Bill who the guy was, what he was doin' here, and what his intentions with CarlaMay just might be.

It was enough to push Bill to make a plan. He wasn't usually one for plans. Essie was the plannin' one of the pair. Even so, a scheme cooked its way up into Bill's head like a boiling pot.

"Let's go," he grunted to Hank when the kid had arrived with his camera case in hand.

Hank hadn't rang the bell. He'd just come on in, like normal people did.

They went to the barn, and it wasn't until Bill set about adding the sugar and talkin' through the process that he realized Hank hadn't made a peep.

"What's wrong?" Bill asked after they'd filmed the scene and Hank had turned his camera back off.

"I gotta get going." Hank didn't seem himself. "It's late. I'm tired. Long day."

Bill frowned deep. "Well, it's a long day for me, too. I gotta take care of some business tonight, you know."

This was the sort of nugget that might get Hank talkin' and riled up. He was like a woman that way. A gossip.

It didn't though. "Okay. We can pick this back up in four or five weeks? Is that how long until the fermentation is over?"

Now Bill was real worried. "I just told you on the film that it's more like six weeks. You recorded it. What? You wasn't listening?"

"Sorry, Bill. Like I said—"

But Bill had started to the barn door, opening it wide for the two of them to spill out. "Just go on, then."

Hank moved onto the grass and turned to say something to Bill, but his father-in-law's rage had simmered for enough time now that he didn't care about Hank acting funny anymore. He slid the barn door shut and locked the padlock. "See you in six weeks."

Hank left the farm, and Bill set aside all thoughts of him acting so odd. Quiet and unexcited. That's how he'd been when they went into the barn to film the final scene for this step of winemaking.

It didn't matter too much to Bill that Hank was acting funny, though, because he had more important things to worry about. Mainly CarlaMay and the man who came to pick her up for supper.

He returned to the big house and trudged around looking for Essie. When she wasn't nowhere inside to be found, he went out through the mudroom door at the back of the house. It was late fall, and he knew better'n anyone that night fell faster this time of year. Winter would be swirling into Brambleberry, bringing cold snaps and maybe snow—if the farmers were lucky.

Even so, there was Essie in the grass with their little grand-daughter and a jar. Bill knew what a jar in the dusk-kissed grass meant. It meant lightning bug catchin'.

He had a mind to tell her off of it. She'd never find any of those glowing bugs and the little girl would get let down.

Something stopped him, however. He stood just outside of the screen door on the short porch that gave way to gentle rolling hills, and Bill thought quietly about his lot in life. He had a wife, a naggin' one but a good one. One who worked hard and loved fierce. He had kids—most of 'em good, too. He had a farm, complete with a money-making tobacco crop, outbuild-ings, and event income rentals if they ever decided to do some-thing with the bunkhouses. He had his faith in God, even if it was a private thing. Bill had his health, too. Really, he had everything.

When he compared what he had to others, Bill was a rich man. Bill knew that rich men had more obligations than poor men. They had responsibilities.

Bill also knew he sometimes failed at those responsibilities.

His youngest son, Garold, was proof of that. Bill had done somethin' wrong with Garold, though he didn't know what. Maybe too heavy a hand. Maybe too strict. But you had to be strict with children, that was just plain fact. Even so, Garold had gotten into drugs and drink at an early age. Sneaking out of the house and winding up in juvenile detention before he could even drive a car.

The rest of the family saw Garold in a different way than Bill saw him. They saw *Gary*, the good-time kid. They saw the soft side of masculinity. Barb especially loved Gary. They were two peas in a pod, those two. In fact, it was Gary who'd set Barb up with Hank. Gary had done a stint at Old Towne Video, and before the big boss fired him, he'd introduced Hank to Barb.

That had been the last of Gary, though. After he got canned for being drunk on the job, he took off on a bender up in Louie-vull. Bill decided he didn't want nothin' more to do with Gary, not until he got clean and pulled himself together.

Soon after all that went down, they'd had another visitor to the farm. Sort of like this one tonight, the strange man there to pick CarlaMay up for supper—except this visitor was a girl.

It was almost like the opposite experience to what had happened tonight, now that Bill thought about it. A girl had shown up with a toddler in her arms. Both were soaked wet from a good rain.

Essie ushered them in and told Bill to ring up the police, but the girl had said no, don't do that. He didn't. They were a little nervous, Essie and Bill, until the girl put the toddler down and spilled the beans.

She'd been with Garold—Gary, as she called him. They'd had a baby together—a wild, freckle-faced boy with moppish, strawberry-red hair and lungs so strong he could holler all the way up to Bardstown if he didn't get his way.

Essie didn't believe the girl. In fact, Essie had turned her out, shooing the baby with the girl and then takin' up the phone herself and calling the police.

Long story turned short, the police came around and took a lukewarm report. Months went on and Garold returned to the fold. The baby was his: Garold Junior. They called him Geddy.

Bill nor Essie ain't seen Geddy since.

Bill took it to heart that Essie had done that—turned out their own blood, and a baby nonetheless, and Bill had a soft spot for kids. Mark it up to his own childhood, which was less a childhood and more a what you might call a free-for-all. His mother didn't hold him to no standards, and his daddy was too busy with picking up odd jobs the county over. Bill spent his free time doin' nothing much, and it bothered him deep down.

It bothered him when Essie turned out their blood like that. And it bothered him that he'd done something so wrong with Garold that he couldn't be a father to his son.

All this explained the burning in Bill's chest that he'd better do something about the man who'd come for CarlaMay. If not for CarlaMay, then at least for Morgan Jo, who deserved better than her mother goin' out on the town like that.

Bill couldn't well sit with the burning. He gave Essie and Morgan Jo one last hard look. Then he turned to go in and do what he had to do.

CHAPTER FIFTY

PRESENT DAY

Morgan Jo

Morgan parked in the small lot just behind the video shop. It backed up to a residential home off of Main, and a wooden fence separated the house from the shop's square of parking. Hedges trimmed three sides, and Morgan found herself impressed with the modest yet neat display of landscaping for even such a small, hidden space.

As she pulled the box roughly from her back seat onto the hand truck, Morgan worried she'd possibly damaged the tapes even worse now.

Julia, Emmett, and even Amber's admonishments rang out in her head. *What's the rush?* But they didn't understand. There was a difference between a *rush* and *resolve*. Between *haste* and *determination*. In the eyes of the indifferent, the person on a mission was in a hurry. But in her own eyes, Morgan was fulfilling a commitment—one to herself, to her grandmother, her grandfather, and even the greater Nelson-Coyle brood. She was doing the thing she decided to do, and she was doing it *now*. Or, at least, that coming fall.

Morgan wheeled the hefty banker's box through the squat lot and up onto the sidewalk, taking her time moving from the pavement to the concrete path, then she continued toward Main Street, where the door to the shop stood.

On the short jaunt there, a million thoughts flashed through her brain. Emmett and his big reveal to be made in less than an hour, possibly. The efficacy of still pushing to use Grandad's recipe, even though she hadn't gotten it pinned down. The chance the tapes would work or that Amber would be able to verify any information with her dad...

And then there was Geddy and Father David's strange phone call. Whatever was going on there felt like a pricker in Morgan's side. A distraction carved out of the ether to bug her.

Forcing everything out of her mind, she pushed through the heavy wooden door, beneath a loud clanging bell, into a little shop she hadn't been in since she was a teenager.

Olde Towne Video.

It looked the same and different all at once. Two rows of shallow metal shelves bisected the shop and at the front end of each was a tower display shelf. In the far back-left corner, a trio of teenaged boys fell in a line along comic books. Morgan didn't remember the video shop having comics.

Along the counter nearest and adjacent to the front door sat a cash register and behind that a stool. Farther down the counter stood a tall young man. Maybe not so young, but certainly younger than Morgan. *Thirty at best?* Dark hair curled from beneath a floppy hat. He wore a movie shirt. Morgan recognized the actors but couldn't name the film. It was one of those 1980s classics that most people had seen hundreds of times, but Morgan had never seen once. The hazards of being partially raised by her grandparents, probably.

"Welcome to Olde Towne Video. How can..." He frowned and his eyes fell to her hand truck and the weighty box that sat on its metal platform. "Is. That..." His voice stuttered to a halt and he raised his eyebrows up at her in question. "Are. You...?" He cocked his head.

Morgan, confused, replied with a question of her own. "Is there a woman named Amber here? Or was there a woman named Amber here?"

He seemed more confident now. "Oh. Yes. She's in the restroom. She's ill."

"It passed." Amber emerged from a back room, her hand on her stomach. "I drank some water and I feel better now."

"Oh. Were you—did you—?" Morgan asked, referring to when Amber had quickly jumped off the phone earlier.

"I threw up."

"I watched." This came from the store clerk who said it without much emotion.

Amber smiled at him, and Morgan immediately pegged the fact that the pair had formed some bizarre bond over this.

"Oh." Morgan blinked. "Right." She left the hand truck by the door and walked toward Amber, lowering her voice and dipping her head to avoid the attention of the guy watching them. "Are you okay?"

"Morgan Jo," Amber said proudly, "meet Callum Dockerty."

Callum jutted a hand from his post at the counter. "Manager on duty of Olde Towne Video and Video Specialist. Nice to meet you, ma'am."

Morgan offered her hand to him and gave it a shake. "Nice to meet you, Callum. Did Amber tell you about our videos?"

"Yes, ma'am. I know all about them."

"He thinks he can help," Amber added.

"That's great." Morgan strode back to the box, ready to start unpacking the black cassettes, excitement coursing through her veins.

"But there might be a problem," Amber said more meekly now.

"What?" Morgan straightened, two video tapes crooked awkwardly in each hand. "What's the problem?"

Amber glanced at Callum, who answered for them both. "I have to get approval from my boss, the owner of the shop."

"Oh." Morgan stacked the four cassettes on the counter and bent to get more. "Well, that's no problem. Whoever it is, the owner, I'll talk to him. I'm sure he'll understand. I mean—we'll pay. If you don't already provide the repair service, we'll pay."

"We don't provide the service traditionally," he replied. "I get approval to use his equipment in the back room after hours."

Something shifted in the air.

Morgan said, "Okay. If you have to put in the work order with him first or whatever—that's okay." She looked at Amber. "Right, Amber?" She repeated to Callum, "We'll pay."

"Well, Callum says it's usually no problem. And he always puts in the orders, and gets the approvals, but, um—"

"What is it, Amber?" Morgan urged, confused and concerned.

"His boss? The owner of the shop?"

"Yeah...?"

"Is Hank."

Callum confirmed, "Hank Taylor."

Morgan's disbelief was palpable. *No. No, no, no.* This was the worst luck. What? "Hank Taylor. As in... my uncle?"

Amber murmured, miserably, "My dad."

CHAPTER FIFTY-ONE

PRESENT DAY

Amber

They left the tapes with Callum, but not before Amber gave him her phone number. As she did, she felt a flicker of something in her chest. Maybe Callum felt it, too. He asked if her last name was Taylor like Hank's.

Amber confirmed that yes, it was. She half expected him to put "Boss's Daughter" along with her name in his contacts but when he flashed her his screen to confirm the details, she saw he'd only written Amber Taylor.

Amber had never felt more disappointed in her life than when she and Morgan walked out onto the sidewalk on Main Street.

Morgan had left the hand truck with the box, in case she had to come back and get them alone at some point.

"What now?" Amber mused aloud.

"We go back to the farm, for starters. Invite the group together. Julia, I mean. Emmett'll be on his way soon if he isn't already there."

"But why? I mean, we have to wait to see what my dad tells Callum."

"Do you really think he'd turn away paying work?"

"Don't you mean, *do I really think he'd turn away his daughter?*" Amber shook her head dolefully. "And yes, I do." She looked at Morgan Jo. "Where did you park?"

Morgan Jo pointed to the lot behind the shop. Amber cocked her elbow for Morgan Jo to hold on to it, which she did, and together they made their way to Morgan Jo's car out back.

"Everything is going to be fine. It has to be. We'll figure out the wine thing. And—"

"Hank Taylor?" Morgan Jo lowered into her seat and looked up at Amber. "If he's really your dad, Amber, he'll want to help you. And if he doesn't want to help you, then he was never *really* your dad to begin with."

Amber understood what her cousin meant, and coming from Morgan Jo, who'd lived her life as a half-orphan, with no daddy to speak of, it meant a lot. Plus, Amber happened to agree. If Hank deserved to be in Amber's life at all, then he'd step up. He wouldn't do as Barb had said. He wouldn't want to give up hope for the future just because of the hardness of the past. Amber *knew* this.

But she didn't believe it.

CHAPTER FIFTY-TWO

1992

Bill

Bill sat in wait in a rocking chair on the front porch. He'd tucked his pistol into the back of his jeans waistband, but he didn't intend on usin' it.

Darkness had long since fallen across the farm, and he reckoned Essie had put Morgan Jo to bed a while back.

Nearly falling asleep himself, Bill was stirred by headlights washing over the drive. Where he rocked slowly in the corner, the lights missed him, as he expected they would. He moved forward and back, forward and back, in easy time on the easternmost side of the wide porch.

The car that had picked CarlaMay up—a little sedan that seemed vaguely familiar to Bill—turned right onto the long gravel drive, and its headlights swept the western stretch of porch, coursin' over the front window and the door and then around the corner and across the parlor.

It was there, tucked in the nook of the porch along the exterior wall of the parlor where Bill woke up all the way, felt for his gun, then planted his feet real firm on the wooden planks beneath his boots.

The car came to a slow stop at the end of the drive. The driver killed the ignition and with the engine, out went the lights. All Bill had to do to get a look at it was lean forward into the darkness of the night.

He could see movement behind the windshield, but nothin' was clear from his vantage.

Leaning back, he took up rockin' all over again. Wouldn't hurt to announce his presence ahead of time, rather than to spook 'em outright.

Bill didn't account for the fact that a man rockin' in the shadows was a spooky thing all on its own.

He listened on as one car door opened and shut. A few moments later another. Feet on gravel. There was no significant delay in the time between both doors had closed and the couple —if you could call 'em that—emerged along the pathway to the front door.

Bill kept on rockin', but he didn't say nothin'. Not quite yet. The ideal thing would be to catch this stranger on his own, without CarlaMay fudgin' things all up.

The couple passed, she ahead of him. Bill didn't detect no funny business, which was a strange thing in and of itself. Not until the man moved on up the steps behind CarlaMay, who turned to him at the door. They still didn't see Bill, which made him feel real funny now. He moved to get up just as the man went in to put a kiss on CarlaMay's cheek.

That's when Bill saw who he was.

Bill fumbled to get out of the chair. CarlaMay was all the way in the house and the man was goin' back down the steps once Bill finally launched out of that damn ol' chair and raised a finger to the man. He hadn't really practiced what he was gon' say, and now seein' who this guy was changed things.

They changed things quite a lot. And Essie even *knew*! She

knew and she never told him? So much confusion and pain flashed through Bill's mind that he hardly had the chance to holler at the guy.

But he did.

"You's a phony!" he shouted through spittle at the top of the steps.

The man turned, and even though it was darker than a cast-iron skillet, Bill could see plain that the guy was scared shitless. He sorta froze-like.

"Bill, please. Let me explain. It's not—it's—there's more to this than..."

Bill wasn't about to let this fraudster get a word out edge-wise, but the lights came on in the house, and Bill knew he'd really screwed up then. He'd alerted the women. Soon they'd be out there.

Bill didn't have much time to say his piece, so he stayed at the top of the steps and belched out a slew of curses and threats, ending again with, "You's nothin' but a big fat phony. I don't ever want to see your phony face 'round here or *anywhere* ev'r again. Not in town. Not *nowhere*. You hear me, *boy*? You blasted *phony*." Bill'd have spat if he was the type, but he saved spittin' for chew. Not for *losers. Pretenders.*

The guy backed up into a rosebush, and Bill hoped he poked himself with a thorn right up the butt. He scrambled away and into his car just as Essie fell out of the house, fumin' like a wood stove. "Bill *Coyle*, you idiot! Do you even know who that was?!" she screamed.

"Of course I do! I only see him every week at—"

"No." Essie's voice fell down low and flat and hard as a stone. "That was Morgan Jo's *daddy. That's* who."

CHAPTER FIFTY-THREE

PRESENT DAY

Morgan Jo

As Morgan pulled up to the farm, she glanced in her rearview mirror to see Amber's car in the near distance.

Returning her gaze to the drive, Morgan discerned not only Emmett's truck, but Julia's car, too.

Once she put her car in park, she tore out of it as fast as her body would let her, half-jogging and half-hobbling up the path and to the front door of the big house. She ripped open the screen then twisted the knob and burst into the house. "Jules?" Her heart raced with confusion that her best friend had left work early and shown up here, in some sort of overreaction, surely.

"Jules?" she called into the house.

No answer came. Morgan moved through the house and to the back, glancing through the kitchen window and seeing both Julia and Emmett in the backyard.

Embracing one another.

CHAPTER FIFTY-FOUR

PRESENT DAY

Amber

Amber watched from the driver's seat as Morgan Jo tore out of her car and raced inside fast as she could.

Her panic made little sense, but then again—so did Emmett's appearance at the farm ahead of Morgan.

Clearly, Amber was missing a piece of information. All she could do was show up and listen, probably. But before she could so much as park the car, she got a call.

Her mother.

"Amber Lee," Barb said, breathless. "Were you at the video shop on Main Street?"

"Yes. Did you get my text? Mom? Did you *know*?"

"Honey. Listen." She was panting, like she'd been running. "Hank's business was never... well, it's not like he was *here*. I just want you to know that. Trav thought he was here all along, but he wasn't. He was in California. Managing it from afar. Oh, hell, hon, he wasn't even managing it, he was just a partner. On this rinky-dink board. It was all so silly."

"When did he buy the shop? It couldn't have been when we

were little—when he left. You said he was just a manager at a store in town."

"Honey, he *was*. He used to be the manager at the video shop."

Amber shook her head and squeezed her eyes closed. "Okay, so what? He eventually bought the store? With other people? It's confusing."

"Not exactly. The store belonged to Hank's cousin or something. They left it to him in the will, and when they died, Hank didn't want to just let it go."

"When did this happen?"

"Oh, about twenty years ago, hon."

"Twenty years? And how did you know?"

Barb blew out a heavy sigh. "Small-town drama. Word got around."

"How come *I* didn't know? Or Tiff or Trav? They'd have said something?"

"Does it matter? Anyway, he brought on other people to manage it and started selling it off piece by piece until it looked like it wasn't gon' make it. Video shops are dying everywhere, I guess. Not like he held on to a piece of something his kids would be proud of." There was a hitch in her mother's voice, but Amber was too confused to give it any attention.

"Okay, so let me ask you *this*, Mom. Hank Taylor didn't move back to Bardstown on *business*."

"No, hon." Barb's voice was low and flat. "He moved back here for... well, I don't know why he moved back. I guess he got a call from some young kid who wanted to bring the video shop back to life. And we was all here, of course."

"But he didn't want to see us?"

"He did, honey, but it was *complicated*. Oh, Amber, when will you let this go? Hank Taylor wasn't a good dad to you. Why are you trying to drag him back into your life? Or my life?"

Amber shut off the engine and studied the other three vehicles here at the farm. She had a lot of people to lean on, but it was beginning to feel like her mother, her father, her brother, and her sister weren't among them.

"You're right." Amber said this with a new resolve. A new idea. She told her mom she had to go, ended the call, then placed one more.

To someone who was on the front of everyone's mind in Brambleberry.

At least, everyone who read the *Observer*.

CHAPTER FIFTY-FIVE

1992

Bill

After the mess with CarlaMay's date—well, *friend*—Bill realized he'd better turn his attention back to the things that didn't give him pains.

A month later, it was just about time to bring Hank to the farm, and Thanksgiving was creepin' up on Essie and Bill like the ghost of Christmas past.

This holiday was shapin' up to be a hectic one, what with four grandkids to tend to and possibly one more.

Essie had called Jackie. That was the woman who'd had Garold's baby. Jackie was a spitfire of a woman, and if Bill thought Hank was a hippie, he didn't know a hippie. Jackie was a hippy *mama*, as Essie took to callin' her. The aggravatin' thing about Jackie was how Essie had turned on a dime regarding her feelings towards her.

It was the Sunday of Thanksgivin' week, which Bill only knew was Thanksgivin' week on account of the fact that Billy Junior came around with a turkey he'd shot the spring before and had kept frozen up to that day.

Essie assigned Bill to coordinate the delivery and the thawing process of the turkey, which was a rough go, but Bill figured he didn't get a choice in the matter, so he went along.

Once Billy Junior had come and gone, Essie picked up the horn to start in on her plannin'. Bill knew better'n to hang around and listen to her on the phone, so he slipped out the back.

The first thing he figured could use doin' was testin' the wine. What with four weeks in, it ought to be close to if not done. If it was done, he could still seal it back up for when Hank arrived later in the week for the feast.

He tugged open the barn door and the familiar smell of earth and tools, oil and metal hit him. Bill's heart rate slowed and his shoulders relaxed as he made his way to the workbench where the crock sat, stewing up the wine.

He set about opening the lid, slowly so as not to crack it anywhere. Once it was pried up, he peeked inside.

The smell hit him instantly. He'd added enough sugar that just one sip would knock him on his butt, probably. But he didn't dare take a true sip quite yet. It wouldn't hurt the mixture to set for a few more days until Hank came around, so Bill closed the crock back up and smiled to himself. What he ought to do was he ought to call Hank right up and tell them they were good to go, but naw. Last he'd seen of Hank, they was both sore over something or other, though Bill hadn't a clue as to what Hank was sore over. Prob'ly nothin'. Bill decided it better just to wait until Thursday rolled around and he could steal Hank away from the gatherin' to come out to the barn and surprise him with the good news.

So, instead of makin' a call—not that he could anyway, what with Essie hoggin' the line—Bill tinkered about in the barn, oiling his machines and wipin' down surfaces. He kept the place neat as could be, considering just how much stuff he managed to store in there. He'd had ever'thang from the tractors on down to collectible antique-type things, such as his ol' campin' stool and a whole line up of spittoons. He had more along the back walls, like old license plates he'd found washed up on lake shores.

As he worked toward the back, checkin' old drawers from a metal filin' cabinet, he came across the recipe book he'd started so long before. Ever since Hank had gotten Bill set up with filmin', the book didn't seem necessary no more.

He flipped through the few pages he'd got started and found the blunt pencil wedged along the spine of the book.

Bill wasn't much for writin', he'd learned, but he also figured there might be more to put down on the page than he'd already got.

He carried the book and pencil back to his workbench and squared it up to him. First, a rereading reminded Bill where he'd left off. To Bill's great surprise, the words floated off the page pretty good.

The first thing you do is get a crock. These days they don't but sell 'em except as antiques. You'll find 'em all over the county but they'll want a hundred dollars. People don't use 'em for anything but to set in the house.

Anyway, you'll need a crock but you could get a plastic drum.

Next you'll need is grapes. It don't matter the kind, red or green or a mix unless yer particular. Now if you ain't got vines on yer property then you can go to the A and P. They hold the grapes they don't sell. Used to be they'd feed 'em to the hogs if they didn't sell but they don't do that no more. Or they'd feed 'em to a cow. Anyhow that's what you need to get yourself is the crock and the grapes and also a flour sack. And that'll be the first thing anyway.

Bill let out a long, low sigh. He'd hardly gotten anywhere. He still had to write down how to make the damn wine, and truth be told, he didn't much feel like writin' no more.

He flipped back to the first page of the book which he'd treated as a sort of list of recipes.

There was a whole slew of other things to explain.

PLUM WINE
WINE MADE OF PEECHS
PERRY WINE—PERR WINE (A.K.A.)
GOOSE BARY WINE
BOYS 'N' BARY WINE
STRAW BARY WINE
WINE MADE OFF THE BRAMBEL VINES –
BLACK OR RAZZ BARYS

Bill wondered if he had to finish the book. After all, he'd have the tapes from Hank in no time, now. Maybe writin' was overrated and filmin' was enough. Movies was a big business, anyway. Bill couldn't see it dying off like, for example, the continental railroad seemed to. People had a thirst to laugh and cry at other folks' foibles. Bill knew this sure as he knew a fence that needed mendin'.

Thinking for another long beat, Bill flipped all the way to the back of the book.

The answer to his question wasn't there, though. Just blank pages. Ample space to write a man's thoughts and feelings.

CHAPTER FIFTY-SIX

PRESENT DAY

Morgan Jo

Instinct told Morgan to back away from the window, storm out through the house, get in her car and drive far, far away.

And never look back.

Courage had something else to say.

She was sick of running, anyhow, so Morgan swallowed down instinct, opened the screen door and found Julia beaming, her hands clasped. She saw Morgan at the door and didn't look any less excited at all.

In fact, Julia looked even *more* excited to *see* Morgan Jo.

She narrowed her eyes on her best friend and boyfriend. "What's going on?"

Emmett turned to see Morgan, and he, too, didn't act embarrassed or *caught*. Mostly, he acted... normal.

"Oh, *nothing!*" Julia trilled, giving Morgan an obvious wink.

"You two were... *hugging?*" Morgan Jo walked out the question delicately. It was becoming clear there was nothing untoward happening, but why *were* they hugging? And why *was* Julia grinning from ear to ear and *winking* at Morgan?

There was only one plausible explanation.

"Tell me one of you did it," she said, accepting Julia's hands in hers.

"Did *what*, exactly?" Julia asked, her twang swimming in Morgan's ears.

Morgan looked past Julia to Emmett, who had his hands tucked down in his pockets and smirked, knowingly. "Who?" Morgan asked.

"Who, *what*?" Emmett replied, striding toward the friends.

"This is getting confusin', you all. First, Morgan accused us of doing something, I don't know what. And now she's asking *who*?"

But there really was only one thing Emmett and Julia could be celebrating together and then *sharing*, even a little teasingly, with Morgan. "You found someone who knows the recipes."

"What?" Emmett and Julia asked at once. Julia fell back a step. Emmett frowned deep.

Morgan felt herself turn hot. Was she wrong? And if she was, then... what was all this?

"You were hugging. And you..." Morgan pointed a shaky finger at Emmett. "You *lied* to me. You said you had to *lie* to me. Like it was... it was a *surprise*."

"Morgan Jo, what are you talking about? Found someone who knows the recipes?" This came from Emmett. The pain on his face communicated nothing. Morgan had no idea where they'd all gone wrong in communicating.

Morgan took a deep breath. She steadied herself with a hand against Julia's shoulder. "You two were out here. You were hugging. Why?"

Emmett and Julia exchanged a look. Each one looked crest-fallen. Morgan *felt* crestfallen. "What?" she repeated. "You were hugging. It's *not* because you found someone who knows Grandad's wine formula. But then..." she looked at Emmett, "why did you lie on the phone? About not being in your office?

Why did you come here?" She looked at Julia. "And you? Why are you here?"

Julia chewed on her lower lip. Her smile wasn't all gone, but there'd been a shift. Julia reached down and took up Morgan's hand. She tugged her in for a hug. "Let it go, okay?"

"Let what go?" Morgan whispered back.

Before Julia could answer, a booming holler tore Morgan's attention away. "You all!" It was Amber, waving wildly from around the side of the big house where it spread out to the gravel drive.

She wasn't alone. Behind her, striding half bow-legged like a rodeo cowboy in his Wranglers, flannel shirt, and dusty-brown boots, was Geddy.

CHAPTER FIFTY-SEVEN

PRESENT DAY

Amber

"You all!" Amber hollered again through cupped hands. She waved Geddy along through the grass. He wasn't all the way up to speed on Amber's idea, but there was no question he'd be able to help them.

Amber was counting on it.

"I have an idea!" she hollered again.

Ambling over the grass and up to the three of them— Morgan Jo, Emmett, and Julia—Amber felt her face flush with the heat of anticipation.

Geddy lagged behind her, and Amber didn't understand this—he had the longest legs of anyone in the family, probably— until she turned to see him tucking in his shirt and pushing his hand through his hair.

"Geddy, come on. Hurry."

"Amber, wait," he hissed. "You got a mint? Or a piece of gum?"

"A mint? No. Come on." Amber ignored his weirdness and

pulled him by the elbow like a reluctant teenager until they were at the back porch of the house.

"You all are gon' want to sit down," Amber declared proudly.

At her side, Geddy waved a hand. "Emmett, Morgan Jo. Hi." Then, he tipped his head toward Julia. "Miss Julia, how do you do?"

How do you do? Amber gave him a look of disgust.

Geddy winced like Amber might slap him then started to cross as if he was going to sit down, too. "Not you," Amber held him back and squared Geddy off so that he was on display. Then, Amber trained her gaze on her cousin and started in on what she hoped was going to fix *everything*.

CHAPTER FIFTY-EIGHT

1992

Bill

Still unsure whether he was gon' finish the recipe book or not, Bill carried it into the house.

Maybe now was the time to tell Essie what he was up to. She'd made a fuss over it anyway. And it was the holidays, and wasn't the holidays the time to come clean about things like home movies?

Bill wasn't sure, but he'd rather be an honest man than a secret-keeper. Coyles weren't secret-keepers, and he wasn't one to make a bad example.

Essie was still on the horn, still makin' holiday plans with the kids, when he came into the kitchen whistlin' like Yankee Doodle.

She looked him up and down and told whoever was on the line she had to go, then hung up the phone. "What're you gettin' up to, Bill Coyle?" she asked with a frisky look on her face. Essie knew how to tease, that was true. But she wasn't no tease, and her teasin' wasn't a joke but a promise.

Bill grinned. Maybe he ought to come clean right here and now. He flapped the book against his hand. "Oh, nothin'."

Essie's frisky face twisted and she looked harder. "Is that mine?"

"Yours?" Bill's voice sprang with surprise. "What'dya mean *yours*? It's *mine*."

"*Yours?*" Now Essie was gettin' wigged out. "Barb gave me a book exactly like that for my last birthday."

"She gave this to me for my birthday. I coulda swore you were there when I opened it."

"I don't ever remember seeing you open the exact same thing I got." Essie spun back to the phone and lifted the receiver to dial up Barb, prob'ly, but she hesitated. "I'd better not bother her."

"Why would you? She gave us the same present doesn't make it a bad present, I reckon." He had to salvage her *promise*. The frisky look. He moved toward Essie. "Anyway, ain't no big deal to put your thoughts to a page."

"I know. It's not that." Essie's face stayed scrunched and stressed. "I just shouldn't call her. It's a hard time on them right now."

Bill didn't know what she was talkin' about, but he pushed it aside and tickled her waist. Essie's face cleared of the stress.

"Why don't you show me what you write in your book, and I'll tell you what I write in mine?"

"*Billy*," Essie hissed, "you hush. Morgan Jo is upstairs nappin'."

"Then the timin' is perfect." He swayed his hips and moved hers in his hands. "Come on, I'm just dyin' to know what you write in your book, Essie Coyle." He applied a sing-song melody to his voice and it did the trick, *wowee*.

Essie melted into him in a fit of girlish giggles. "You can come back to the room with me," she answered through a great big smile. "But I ain't never tellin' you what I write in my diary."

CHAPTER FIFTY-NINE

PRESENT DAY

Morgan Jo

Morgan sat in a wooden, white-painted rocker matching the one into which Emmett had also lowered himself. Julia perched along a low white bench that spread between them. If it hadn't been for their situation—the awkward post-hug confrontation in the shadow of Emmett's lie and Julia's glee—the group would not have sat for Amber's so-called announcement.

That's what happened when the right place at the wrong time struck a person like Amber, though.

She got lucky.

The question was: *why was Geddy there?* Too aggravated and worried to ask, Morgan remained still as stone and quiet, too, waiting as Amber pursed her lips and glanced at Geddy and cleared her throat for a second time.

"Amber, spit it out, already," Julia urged.

Amber held up her hands as if to brace them. "Okay. This morning, I read in the paper that Geddy here is taking over at The Market as a manager." She glanced at Geddy who looked pleasantly, goofishly, and charmingly delighted to be in the spotlight. He even gave them a little bow.

Julia responded with girlish applause, but Morgan slashed her with a severe look. Now wasn't the time for *flirting*.

"In the article," Amber went on to explain, stealing glances at Geddy as she did, "Geddy mentioned *partnerships* with local or countywide distributors particularly relating to *alcohol*, including bourbon, whiskey, and wine."

"Not whiskey. At least, not *yet*. We're in talks, but nothing is concrete. The goal is all local, all the time. Sustainable. Community-oriented. And..." He rubbed his hands together like an evil villain waiting for a drum roll. Naturally, Julia obliged, rolling her tongue with a finesse Morgan didn't know her best friend possessed. She lifted an accusatory eyebrow at Julia, who shrugged impish shoulders but kept her eyes glued to Geddy.

"*Sorry. Can't help it you have a hot cousin,*" she whispered.

Morgan felt a headache growing. At least, if nothing else, this was further proof that Julia and Emmett's hug was innocent. She *hoped* it was true.

"Just come out with it," Morgan spurred Geddy on.

He bowed his head then looked up and declared, "Organic."

"Organic." Morgan clicked her tongue and dropped her face to her hands.

"Hate to break it to you, Ged, but that word's been circulating the grocery industry for some time now," Emmett said.

Morgan looked at Amber. "What is this? What's the great idea, Amber Lee? We're killing time when we could be checking back with Callum at the shop or even maybe with your mom and Hank." She didn't mean to ignore Amber's plea about keeping Hank Taylor out of the wine thing, but Morgan couldn't just drop it altogether. If something was worth doing, then it was worth fighting for. And with *no* plan B to speak of, she had to keep the pressure on.

"Okay. Geddy says he's working with local distilleries to offer their products, right? And he's going to stock wine from vineyards in the area." Amber moved to the white railing of the porch and leaned over it, fixing Morgan with a stare so intense it bordered on uncomfortable. "Morgan Jo, he can bring in the wine. It'll be local and organic. That's as close as we can get. Plus, we know it'll be *good*."

"Bring in the wine for what?" Geddy scratched his head behind Amber.

She turned and shushed him.

Morgan looked from Amber to Geddy and then across to Emmett. Finally, her gaze landed on Julia who still hadn't torn her eyes off of Geddy.

Morgan rolled around the words in her head then recited Amber's idea in a new way. "A wine distributor. Geddy brings in the product with his connections. Maybe a discount? Then... what? We just have the tasting room?"

"Well," Geddy interrupted, "depends on what you want to do." He frowned. "I mean, I know what you all are really up to, but the one product distributor I have in mind farms fruit trees and grapes. Unless you just want to sell fresh fruit and have people taste that, then—"

"Wait," Morgan held up her hand and leaned forward, elbows on knees. "You're saying you've got a contact with a local farm with *good* fruit? Is that it? And then we'd process the fruit? So, we'd operate the winery portion of our business and the tasting room. Just not the vineyard. At least, not at first."

"Well, yes. I mean, this guy sells his fruit to other wineries, I do believe, but he's looking for a new partnership." Geddy's face twisted into mischief and Morgan realized he was either fibbing, or there was a catch.

Morgan blinked. Emmett ran his hands down his thighs. Of all of them, he knew Geddy maybe even the best. After all, they'd been glued at the hip all growing up and when Geddy was away on a bender or on the lam, Emmett could always coax him back home.

"I can't believe I didn't think of this." Emmett stood up, and held his hand up to Geddy who gave it a hard slap. "Geddy. You're a genius. But—"

"What do you mean 'he's a genius'?" Morgan glanced quickly from Geddy to Emmett and back. "What do you all know that I don't?"

Julia and Amber were equally in the dark, if their gaping mouths were any indication, but Amber played it off. "Yes. Well, it was *my* idea, but once I read that article about you, Geddy—well it was obvious what we ought to do. I just can't believe you didn't think to tell us about your big news first."

"I'm not surprised he didn't tell us, but I still don't know about it." Morgan shook her head and thought. *Yes, it was as good an idea as any, for a backup plan. But Amber herself said no backup plans.*

She rose to her feet and folded her arms over her chest. "I don't know." A thought flitted back into her head, intrusive and unyielding. "Amber? Can you at least give me your dad's phone number? I'll call him myself. You can stay clear out of it."

Julia shot up from her seat. "MoJo, just drop it."

"Drop it?" Morgan threw her hands up in the air. "Drop what, you all? Drop Grandad's wine recipes? Drop what could make us great—set us apart?"

Emmett stepped behind Morgan and slipped an arm around her waist before dropping his chin to her shoulder and murmuring, "Morgan, it's time to drop your fear."

"Fear? You think I'm afraid? What would I be afraid of?" her voice climbed to a near shriek.

But Emmett's answer tumbled out soft and sweet even though it wasn't what she expected to hear—it wasn't what Morgan *wanted* to hear.

It was exactly what she needed to hear.

"Afraid of failing."

CHAPTER SIXTY

PRESENT DAY

Amber

Amber hadn't considered that Morgan Jo could be afraid of anything in the world. Heck, the universe. To Amber, Morgan Jo was the bravest woman alive. Next to Tiffany. Then again, Amber knew deep down that Tiffany wasn't fearless, she was just dumb. At least, she acted that way. There was a difference between being brave and being stupid, Amber realized.

Or was there?

She herself only found her courage when she turned her brain off and *let* go. A great example of that was Grant. The logical thing to do was to keep a hold of him and see through their relationship. But to really move forward in life, she had to silence that logic, that practicality that drove the idea that if she'd broken up with Grant, she'd have wasted all that *time*.

A quiet brain could be a bold one.

Amber turned her brain off right now, she silenced the over-thinking, the bad thinking, the useless thinking.

And she launched into her greatest sales pitch ever.

"Morgan, listen. Geddy can connect us with his contact—whoever that may be. We get the fruit. We ferment now, if we can. Heck, they might have frozen juice or ripe, fresh fruit—whatever. We start now with that product—just as soon as Geddy gets his hands on it. And we hit the ground running. We test the juice along with Grandad's flavors."

Geddy chuckled.

Amber shot him a look. "What's so funny?"

"You can be afraid to fail, Morgan Jo," Geddy answered, the humor falling away from his face now. "You can be afraid all you want. But that won't change whether or not you do fail."

Amber felt herself relax. Almost like *she* needed to hear that. Although there wasn't anything Amber was going to fail at.

Was there?

Again thoughts of her mom meeting up with her dad but telling Amber to keep a lid on things... it bothered Amber to no end. And that botherin' had frozen Amber up. That fear, that threat, it had worked. She obeyed her mother and respected that what Barb had relayed reflected Hank's wishes.

She wondered what Trav and Tiff thought about it—about their dad wanting to bury the past.

Something else bubbled up. If Hank Taylor wanted to bury the past so damn badly, then why'd he hung on to Olde Towne Video for so long? Why'd he agreed to come back and work there? So close to home—to his kids?

Still, nothing made sense.

She wanted desperately now to ask her dad for his help with the wine. It could reunite them. And maybe it'd be the only way to bring Morgan Jo around and help them get a good start on this. She was so stubborn, Morgan Jo. Even Geddy's nagging wasn't going to work.

"Okay," Morgan Jo said, plain and clear and calm.

Everyone whipped their head to her.

Amber eked out, "Okay?"

"I'm listening," Morgan Jo went on. "Geddy, do you have any distributors who aren't already committed with you? Who might be willing to shift their contracts to us? And if so, who are they? Can we rely on them? Are their crops mature? Good?"

"Why don't you see for yourself," Geddy replied, smirking.

CHAPTER SIXTY-ONE

1992

Bill

As the week wore on and Essie's excitement about Thanksgiving rolled like thunder across the farm, Bill got more and more aggravated.

The whole matter of a diary ate away at Bill so bad that he was just about ready to say somethin'. It wasn't that Bill figured a woman didn't have a right to private thoughts. It was that here she was throwing around in his face some *private life* she wrote about.

Meanwhile all he was doing was jottin' down *wine* recipes for the love of God.

The only good thing about Essie's tellin' him about her own diary was that it pushed Bill to take to his book, too.

Come Thursday morning, he'd not only finished writing every last recipe in that book, but he'd even thought about addin' some of his own private thoughts.

Before he'd go to that extreme, though, Bill figured he'd tell Essie she was actin' wrong.

"Essie," Bill grunted at her. She stood at the sink, apron

strings wrapped in crisscross around her waist and her hair tied back with a red kerchief. She was peelin' 'taters at the sink and looked flat-out pretty. For a quick second, he thought maybe he shouldn't say anything to her, but then again it really aggravated Bill, what Essie had said and what she was doin'. It wasn't right to keep secrets that weren't supposed to be surprises or presents or somethin'.

"Hi, Billy," she cooed as sweet as honey. But before he had a chance to come forth with his piece she turned and pointed to a bowlful of green beans. "You go on and snap the ends off those, Billy. Rolls is gonna go in the oven next, but it'd be good to have the beans ready to roast. Oh my Lord, do we have our work cut out. You know that CarlaMay is up in Louisville tryin' to find canned pumpkin for the pie. I guess we missed it on our trip to the market, and nothin' around here is open—"

"Essie," he grunted again, frownin' and tryin' to keep himself focused on the thing he came in for.

She went on yabbering without turning around. "Did you get the fold-out table from the barn? Clean it? It'll need scrubbin', Billy. I got wire brushes in the mudroom if you can't find SOS pads."

"I need to talk to you." He was gettin' itchy with annoyance now and scratched at his neck.

Essie turned and looked over the top of her glasses at him, her eyebrows raised and lips flat over her mouth. "I ain't got time for that, honey. We're settin' up for supper. Lotta guests comin'. Did I tell you I invited Jackie after all? Oh, sure I did. Well, she's bringin' the baby and maybe even her *sister*. I don't know, but I think maybe we could get Gary back here if we try hard enough. I don't like Jackie and I won't like her sister, I tell you, but it don't hurt to make a go of things."

"What do you write in your notebook?"

"What notebook?" she returned to peelin' while a crush of wailing came from the staircase. "Oh, heavens, no. No, no, *no*."

She shook her head and moved around Bill and hollered up at Morgan Jo. "You go back to bed *now*, Morgan Jo. And hush *up!*"

Bill winced at her screamin' and boiled about gettin' ignored like this.

"Billy, go on and get the beans done. I ain't got time."

"I just want to know—what do you put in that notebook?"

"What notebook?" Essie ran the back of her hand over her forehead and Bill could see beads of sweat sprouting beneath her ink-black hair.

He took up the beans and started on snappin', but only on account of it needin' to be done, and he might as well help if he was gonna get any answers outta that woman. "All right, fine." He set about workin', and after a minute tried once again. "The notebook. The one Barb gave you and gave me. What's so private in there, anyway?"

At his question, Essie erupted into a peel of laughter, and Bill got real aggravated at that. She was laughing at him. At his question and at his feelings. Bill gritted his teeth and snapped the beans harder.

"I write a bit of everything in there. Local gossip, you know. Family news."

"You write about me?"

Essie turned and looked at him straight on. "I'm not tellin' you no more about it. I'm done talkin' about it, Bill. A woman's sole personal thing in life is her diary. It's the only thing she has to herself. The only thing that's her own."

"You've got plenty of your own," he snorted, losing his grip on his control of the conversation.

"I'll tell you something right now, Bill Coyle. When a woman gets married, she has to share her life. When she has babies, it's her body she shares. By the time a woman has a moment to herself, she's got to find a way to capture it. That's where a diary comes in, anyway. And that's the end of it." She turned back around.

"Well, where in the hell do you keep it, anyway! I ain't never seen it!" His heart was aching like it got scratched, and Bill couldn't put down a reason for that. He tried to slow his breathing and not get so damn worked up, but it was hard. While Essie figured her diary was the only thing that belonged to her and her alone, Bill was wondering what in the world belonged to him and him alone.

"Somewhere *private*. That no one goes."

Bill grumbled, "If you'd just be honest with me you wouldn't gotta hide anythin' from me."

At that, Essie turned and smiled. "Billy, all girls hide their diaries. It's just a thing of life. Women ought to keep a book to write their thoughts, and they know to hide it away from the world so that their thoughts is safe." She blinked. "Maybe that's why Barb got you a notebook, too."

"Huh?"

"She probably figured you could do with writin' down your thoughts. Could be a good help to ya, Billy."

"Help? I don't need help, least of all from my own daughter." Bill boiled. He snapped another pea and tossed it into the second bowl.

Another set of wails came from the stairs. Morgan Jo was trippin' down them and cryin' her head off.

Essie ran her hands down her apron and threw them up. "Lord Jesus!" She crossed the kitchen and grabbed Morgan Jo's little hand and dragged the girl to the kitchen table. Essie took a chair and shoved it up against the corner of the room, facing a black space where two walls converged, then she lifted the little girl and sat her down hard on the chair. "Now you sit there and hush up."

Bill hated listening to children cryin', too, but he didn't figure treatin' a kid like that would do well to change anything. Could only make the hollerin' worse.

Edginess cut over his skin like cat scratches. He was

annoyed about his wife keepin' secrets in a book, he was annoyed at Morgan Jo cryin' and Essie slammin' her around. Mostly, he was annoyed with himself.

Why couldn't Bill just say what he felt?

He went on snapping peas and realized maybe there was somethin' to be said about this whole notebook business. Something *more* than wine recipes.

CHAPTER SIXTY-TWO

PRESENT DAY

Morgan Jo

They went together on Geddy's wild goose hunt in Emmett's truck.

"Don't worry," Geddy assured them. "This guy doesn't live too far."

Amber, Julia, and Geddy climbed into the back seat. And Morgan Jo took the front passenger. Not necessarily because she wanted to sit close to Emmett, but more because it was easier for her if she didn't have to squeeze back into the stunted rear seat. Emmett didn't drive a King Cab or a four-door. His truck was borderline classic and, as such, the back row of seats was more for storage than people.

Geddy gave them directions from the back seat, and they went a way Morgan had rarely ever been: east of Brambleberry.

"Take a left up on Twelfth," Geddy commanded from the back seat.

Emmett put the truck in gear, and they bumped along Twelfth, crossing over the old railroad tracks that divided Brambleberry from the woods.

Technically, the area to the east was a small rural town all its own. At a population of just over 200 people, Widow's Hollow—pronounced Widda Holler to anyone within a one-hundred-mile radius—was less a town and more of a backwater place.

Fed by the same creek that sprung on the Nelson farm and trickled southeast, there were just four major landmarks in Widow's Hollow.

The first was a cemetery that took overflow from the private family cemeteries so common in Brambleberry. Used to be that people just buried their own out on the backfields of their land. Once that became a known issue, people needed more space to plot an official burial ground, and the land out east was soft and bare, and it made sense to clear a few acres for the souls of those whose families didn't want their bodies leeching into the soil and well water.

After the cemetery, Widow's Hollow boasted two plantations. One which belonged to relatives of Daniel Boone, or so the legend went. The other which had long since grown over in weeds. Nobody knew who'd once manned that space, and no one cared. The dark history of Kentucky and, indeed, Nelson County didn't escape locals. Some were fine about it. Some were uncomfortable over it. And some just wanted to do right by it.

The three prevailing attitudes left age-old plantations to rot into the earth, mainly.

So, with the cemetery and the two great swaths of private farmland, most of the small-town limits were accounted for.

The last thing, though, in Widow's Hollow, was a private Catholic boarding school which once had been an orphanage.

Morgan was certain they'd only pass by all four landmarks in Widow's Hollow.

Instead, Geddy told Emmett, "Turn right here," as they

approached the main north-south artery of the town: Widow's Way.

This artery fed all four locales, from the cemetery to the school to the two plantations down south.

Smaller dirt roads spread off the main artery like minor veins. You could prick one but it'd only bleed a house or two, a gas station, maybe a little café, and that was all. The residents of Widow's Hollow amounted to poverty-stricken descendants who couldn't get out and weirdos who'd decided they wanted to get stuck in.

They headed south now. "Where are we going, Geddy? Nobody lives down here."

"That's what you think." Geddy grabbed Morgan's headrest and pulled himself up roughly. "Turn!" he hollered, piercing Morgan's ear.

Emmett tore the wheel to the right onto a dusty dirt road that every one of them knew.

It was the long drive to one of the old, run-down, should-be abandoned plantations.

"Geddy, I know you know this," Emmett said, "But I'm not about to trespass on a backwoods plantation from the 1700s."

"And you think *I* am!" Geddy cackled. He had a point. Geddy's mom was the descendent of slaves, and sure as the day was long, he wasn't about to step foot on a plantation if he didn't have to.

Which begged another question.

"One of your distributing partners lives *here?*" Morgan asked, leaning forward to get a good look at the tree-lined drive. Reminders of days gone by sprouted along the way. Overgrown, weedy bluegrass pawed at the truck at it rumbled down the single narrow lane and up toward a Federalist-style white mansion.

As they got closer, the house—if you could call it that— looked less like a house and more like a tumbledown, haunted asylum from a scary movie. The columns along the front were grown over in ivy and brambles. The white facade was more gray. Its chipping appeared to have taken on a life of its own.

All along the bottom of the building weeds threatened to break into the foundation. Cracks and crumbles appeared in corners everywhere.

"Well, we aren't partners yet, but I've known the guy my whole life," Geddy answered.

Morgan didn't buy it. Geddy was too flaky to have known anyone, save for family, his whole entire life.

"Are you sure about this?" Emmett asked. He wasn't asking Geddy, though. It was Morgan he looked at as he slowed the truck to a stop and put it in park.

In fact, this was Morgan's decision. Whether they potentially trespassed on a remaining set of ruins from the darkest time in American history. Whether they trusted Geddy, who could hardly be counted on to remember to lock his front door, much less take on a managerial position at The Market in town.

Morgan knew what she wanted. She wanted to open that winery. She wanted to take her grandmother's advice and make something of that old hangar. She wanted to succeed, and if that success meant she'd have to deviate from Grandad's recipes, then so be it.

She grabbed Emmett's hand and squeezed it, and her fear left her body. "Yes," Morgan replied, looking at Emmett then twisting to the others. "Geddy, introduce us."

CHAPTER SIXTY-THREE

PRESENT DAY

Amber

Geddy helped Julia out of the back of the truck first and then Amber, yanking her through the narrow slit between the inclined front passenger seat and the doorframe.

She came out on the dirt lane with a thud, and little clouds of dust pillowed at her sandaled feet. "This place is old," she marveled.

"He's workin' on it, though. I've been helping."

Geddy took the lead of the group of five and they made their way toward the door.

Amber could see in the distance, behind the tall gray-white building, green rows, neat and maintained. Even just a peek at them contradicted the building.

"Your friend *lives* here?" Julia asked, giving voice to a question on everyone's mind, no doubt.

"He isn't my friend, but yeah." Geddy stepped aside to let the girls climb the steps.

Amber whipped around to see Geddy and Emmett. She

couldn't read Geddy's expression but Emmett was just as confused as Amber, that much was clear.

On the drive down, Amber had checked her phone compulsively, as if Callum, back at the shop, might have gotten permission to fix the tapes, fixed them and watched them, all in just the short amount of time since Amber had been there.

Callum hadn't called or texted, though.

It felt like it had been days since Amber had dropped the tapes with him and told Morgan the bad news about Barb condemning their entire plan.

Now here they were, though. At a veritable *backup* plan. Amber knew better than to trust backup plans, and she definitely knew better than to trust her ne'er-do-well cousin, Geddy, but that's what happened when you had a great big venture and no way to get there.

You took desperate measures.

"What's his name again?" Morgan asked, smoothing her white T-shirt like it was a button-down blouse on a business suit.

But Geddy was too busy looking at his phone and tapping away. He murmured in a vague reply, "No doorbell."

Julia stepped up beside Geddy, though. "Well, here's a knocker."

She lifted the heavy iron knocker and Geddy grabbed for her wrist. "No!" he hollered, but it was too late, Julia had pulled the iron up to give it a knock, but as she did, the entire thing came away in her hand, pulling the whole right side of her body with it, straight down to the half-rotted wooden planks of the creaking porch below their feet.

At the same time that the rusted-out iron knocker hit the planks, breaking through the wood and sending a shriek out of Julia, a loud howling came.

Geddy, Emmett, and Morgan Jo tended to Julia as Amber

moved down the narrow porch toward the source of the howl-ing. A scruffy gray mutt trotted up out of nowhere.

"Hey there, pup." Amber squatted and offered the back of her hand. The old dog sniffed it then fell to the porch on his back, four legs up and tongue hanging out the side of his mouth, as Amber gave him a belly rub.

Geddy joined her, patting the hound's hind as he said, "This here is Jim Beam, but you can call him J.B.," Geddy said.

Amber felt an immediate connection with the dog. He had a name like her cats. Mint and Julep were called for Kentucky's most famous cocktail, Amber figured: the Derby special. And now here was their counterpart in an ugly ol' mutt with a good ol' boy's moniker to fit. "Hey J.B." It didn't occur to Amber just how much Geddy seemed to know about this would-be partner they were visiting.

She gave the dog one last rub and stood, following Morgan Jo's example and smoothing her shirt. After all, they were about to meet someone who might help them make their business take flight. She'd best look presentable, even if he was an odd stranger who lived out on an old abandoned plantation just a stone's throw from the farm.

All of it, Amber realized, was *very* odd.

"Hey there, Old Man!"

Amber and the others held back as Geddy threw up an arm and started around the porch toward an oncoming figure in baggy denim overalls and a straw hat. "I brought 'em by."

Morgan Jo looked at Amber and whispered, "He knew we were coming?"

"Maybe Geddy told him. I mean, obviously," Amber whis-pered back.

Morgan Jo stepped ahead, joining Geddy at the front of their group, but Amber wasn't too far back.

Geddy moved aside and out of the way, and Amber got a

good look at the man. But it wasn't until Morgan Jo spoke, her voice soaked with disbelief, that Amber finally recognized the man in front of them. "Uncle Gary?"

CHAPTER SIXTY-FOUR

1992

Bill

The family started tricklin' in just before four o'clock in the afternoon. First came DanaSue, her husband, Rick, and their daughter, Rachel.

Then Bill's cousin, Randall and Randall's wife, Mona. Next came along Karen Miles and her husband—they was friends of CarlaMay and had a kid just the same age as Morgan Jo. Then one of Essie's church lady friends and then Billy Junior and his best friend, Jimmy.

Last to show were Barb, Hank, and the kids. On account of the fact they didn't get there 'til after four and Essie was strict about startin' on time, Bill didn't get a chance to edge closer to Hank before Essie rounded the group to stand for grace.

After the supper prayer, Essie made everyone go 'round and say what they was thankful for, which Bill hated since he hated to say that sort of thing aloud.

Most of the family said they was thankful for family and their health, of course. Bill figured he could lighten things up with a joke and so when it was his turn, he said, "I'm thankful we're almost done saying what we're thankful for."

Half the group roared with laughter—mostly the guys, and this made Bill feel good.

But Essie dug her fingers into the palm of his hand, nearly stabbing straight through his callouses. "What the *hell?*" Bill hissed, but she laced her fingers into his and smiled up at him, sweet as a doe.

After Bill's turn, Billy Junior went, then Jimmy, then it came up to Hank, who was the last to go.

Bill looked over with interest at Hank who wasn't his usual grinnin'-like-a-fool self. He seemed an awful lot like he had last Bill had seen him. In a bad mood and irritated, like.

Bill was startin' to wonder what was *up*, as Hank might say.

Hank cleared his throat and pressed his mouth into a line. "I'm thankful for..." He looked down and back up then slid his gaze to Bill who didn't know what to do or say. It wasn't like Bill knew Hank's mind or what he was thankful for. Maybe the guy was tryin' to make a joke and needed help, but that wasn't on Bill to do.

Hank licked his lips and started over again. "I'm thankful for, um..."

Bill was waiting for the hippie to say something that would bring the group to tears it was so damn sweet. That was Hank's personality, to say the right thing or the kind thing.

Instead, though, Hank stammered, "I'm thankful for..." He looked up fast and sharp and a fiendish smile lit up his features, castin' him all but creepy. Hank found his words and recited them as clear and icy as the moonshine crick in winter. As he spoke, he looked not at Bill or his kids or at the group, but instead, right at Barb. "I'm thankful for such a loving and faithful wife."

CHAPTER SIXTY-FIVE

PRESENT DAY

Morgan Jo

It had been years—no—*decades* since anyone had seen Garold Coyle. Morgan had even assumed Geddy didn't know where his own father was. At least, that had been the company line.

After a scramble of smiles and shock and a fresh set of introductions between Garold and Julia and Emmett—who'd met him long before but hadn't exactly lingered in the recluse's mind—the five of them followed Uncle Gary around the side of the big house and out back, toward what could only be described as a hobo camp.

The set up proved that if Uncle Gary was living on this plantation, he surely wasn't living inside of the house. A little enclosure was built out of crude logs and rusted wire. Inside of it, a cot. Over the top, corrugated metal leaned into an old oak tree that sprouted up the middle.

Outside of the enclosure, a small fire flickered in the dying light of day. Morgan checked her watch. It was later than she realized. Getting well on to supper time now. Her stomach growled as if it, too, could read time.

Wooden chairs, probably taken from inside the house, stood around the fire.

Then, there was the beyond.

Beyond the camp at the back of the property spread neat green rows and rows and rows of trees. Orchards. Vineyards. Acres of well-cared for fruit of so many varieties, Morgan's heart leapt at the possibilities.

"Uncle Gary," she said, breathless, "how long have you been here?" A more burning inquiry rang like a school bell in her head.

Amber snatched the words from her mouth. "And how is it your crops look like they're—"

"Alive?" Morgan supplied the missing term.

"I been here for years," Uncle Gary replied. Then he chuckled. "Them crops, well, we got the forest here as a buffer, for one. For another thing, I threw down mulch, which I have a lot of on account of it being a plantation here. Plus, I use row covers." Uncle Gary spit out behind himself, which should have grossed Morgan out, but ever since she'd moved back to Kentucky, she'd gotten used to men who spat, again. Thanks to Travis. "Also, just plain luck."

"The farm—I mean the family farm—isn't but five miles west of here. How did we get hit and you didn't?"

Emmett interjected. "Our crops aren't as hardy, most likely. They'd sat for some years without help. That'll make them more susceptible."

"Plus, that hail event turned out to be a microburst. It only hit within about two square miles of the farm," Julia added softly. "It was in the paper the next day, Morgan. I didn't want you to feel bad, so I didn't tell you."

Morgan realized she'd better start reading the paper. Still, she felt stupid for not having done *any* of the frost prep. Some of that was within her control, but she was so preoccupied with —with what? Well, with everything else, apparently.

Geddy was quick to add, "Farming is my dad's only gig, right now. This here farm, I mean. He's got resources, time, and know-how. Thanks to Grandad, of course."

Morgan caught him glance Julia's way, and she felt something soft in her heart for her cousin. It wasn't often she got to see Geddy and even less often she saw this part of him. This tenderness and eagerness. This hope for the future and maybe, just maybe, a commitment to something in life. To hard work and legacy.

Hard to say, but Morgan was glad enough that Julia smiled sweetly and seemed altogether unfazed by the situation. If anything, she looked... charmed.

Encouraged, Morgan thought, Geddy dragged over three more camping chairs, and the group lowered together around the fire.

Over the next hour, Uncle Gary told them everything about his past that Morgan and Amber didn't know. It started with his childhood, and how he'd never quite felt loved by his parents. He told them about his teenage years and how he looked outside the home for attention. He paused for effect and gave Geddy's shoulder a squeeze when he explained he'd fallen for a girl, had a son, and been so scared out of his mind that he'd run for a while and gotten lost.

Some ten years back, Geddy and Gary found each other thanks to a letter written by Memaw. She wanted to talk to the boys about a property she knew of. Uncle Gary implied that she'd helped them acquire the plantation, but he wasn't specific.

By this point in the story, darkness had fallen over the camp, and everyone's stomach was growling.

"I'll cook up pork and beans," Uncle Garry offered, "and Geddy—you take 'em on out into the crops."

The group let Geddy lead them away from the camp and into the thickets of green rows, a headlamp affixed to his forehead and one wrapped onto Emmett's to light the way.

"When did you two reconnect?" Morgan asked Geddy, still in awe of all of this. It was as though a faction of her very own family had hidden away a secret in plain sight. So near and yet in a different world, here in Widow's Hollow.

"Oh, we never lost contact. Not since I was grown," Geddy assured them, picking his way through the overgrown grass and stepping onto the smooth soil of a row of pear trees. "He came on by a site where I was working and told me about this place and said he had big ideas. That was probably ten years back. I visited from time to time, and soon enough—poof. He'd come here almost every day, though he lived up north. And now look." Geddy held out his hands and though the crops were only lit by two headlights and a smattering of stars overhead, what Geddy and Uncle Gary had here was nothing to spit at.

"And you've been helping him?" Julia poked into the conversation.

"Yeah."

"Well, how come you didn't tell us?" Amber swatted at something, although it was too early in the season for bugs to appear at night. They had at least a month before they had to worry about bugs eating the crops. At least, that's what Morgan had been counting on. Bugs were just one of the little stitches in her neck. In fact, ever since she'd decided she was going to start a family business—a vineyard and a winery and a tasting room, too—it was as though she'd had her spine taken in. It was like a seamstress had come and hemmed up every other vertebra.

But *now*.

Now?

Well, now, seeing her family's work, even in the dimness of dusk, was like that old seamstress had returned. She'd come back and slipped her hand beneath Morgan's white cotton shirt, and she snipped away those little stitches with her seam ripper, one at a time.

As Morgan followed Emmett, her hand in his as he led her

way down the row of pear trees, her shoulders rolled back and a full breath filled her lungs with the smell of sweet fruit and acrid leaves. It was the feeling she ought to have back home, on the farm, in the beautiful age-old orchards there.

Why hadn't she? Why couldn't she walk through her own vineyard without the looseness of relief coursing through her body?

Geddy turned his head down a different row. "Come on over here. This is where he grows the grapes," he said. Julia and Amber started after him, but Emmett pulled Morgan's hand gently in the opposite direction.

"I think I saw strawberry bushes this way."

He didn't turn to look at her. Emmett was smarter than to blast Morgan with the glare of his light. Instead, he removed the lamp and held it down to shine their way opposite the three others.

Without question, Morgan followed him. It occurred to her, as they padded their way over the earth, that Morgan would always follow Emmett. Always trust him. She trusted that though he'd not given her the truth back in Bardstown, he had his reason. She trusted that though she came upon him embracing her best friend in Morgan's own backyard, he had his reason.

She trusted that right now, he was pulling her away from the group under the cover of night in an unfamiliar and enchantingly fragrant grove of berry brambles and bushes because he had his reason.

They passed through the bushes and came upon a clearing before a group of apple trees. Near the trees, a wooden ladder leaned. Emmett stopped here.

In this moment, the final stitch at the very top of Morgan's neck came loose, and she let her head roll back as Emmett laced his fingers through hers and he tipped his mouth to hers; his body pressed against hers, and they kissed.

In this moment, Morgan realized that not only did she trust Emmett, but she trusted Amber. And Julia. Geddy, too. All of them.

Mostly, Morgan realized that she trusted *herself*. She trusted herself not to fail, but she also trusted that maybe she would fail. She might fail to get Grandad's recipe. And then again, she might find a way to recover his recipe from Uncle Gary and use Gary's produce and then still manage to fail... but she'd get through. All she needed was to find that *trust*.

"I'm sorry I've been difficult," Morgan whispered to Emmett after their kiss.

"You're worth it." Though there was a smile in his eyes, his mouth remained parted, his face somber in the night.

Emmett rubbed her lower lip with his thumb, sending warmth through Morgan's whole body, deepening her relief until she felt like melting into him and falling asleep right there, beneath an apple tree in a plantation orchard just miles away from her home.

Home.

Morgan closed hers and let herself feel Emmet's thumb linger there, tugging down her lower lip as he dipped his face to hers and kissed her again. Funny, how the very idea of home could be such a movable, changeable thing.

Once upon a time, the farm was the only home Morgan had ever known. After all, it wasn't only *her* home, it was also home to her family, and even to her friends. She silently suspected that Emmett himself considered Moonshine Creek to be like a home.

Even so, Morgan had grown up and tried to strike out and find a place to call home anywhere but the farm. New cities, different apartments, new states, renovated condos...

Nothing stuck.

Yet when she returned to Moonshine Creek, Morgan found that the whole idea about home was wanting. As if it had once been in her heart but was no longer there. Then Emmett came back, and the feeling ebbed. Or rather, the hollowness in her heart filled. Memaw's death didn't help matters, but the hollow feeling didn't return. Then, once Morgan made the decision to move forward with a family business, once she started to read Grandad's thin recipe book and explore the property, all with Emmett by her side, she found herself sated.

It was as though Morgan was looking for something she'd never really lost. And now, leaning into Emmett and resting her head against his chest, it occurred to Morgan that she'd found it. She'd known this. She'd known this since she first met him. But sometimes it took inner struggle to come to terms with the truth.

Morgan frowned. She'd been so caught up in *her* feelings and with her own need to overcome the problem of Grandad's recipes, among other things, that she hadn't really stopped to check in on the man she loved.

She pushed her hands gently against his chest and peered up. "Serious question," she said.

He groaned. "The lie. MoJo, I—"

"No. I don't care about that. I know you had your reason. Whatever it may be." She looked him in the eye. "How are you?"

Emmett blinked at her. A smile broke out along his lips. "I'm doing well. Thanks. How are you?"

"No." Morgan shook her head and clenched his shirt—the blue Oxford he'd worn into the office, unbuttoned at the neck with its sleeves rolled back to his elbows. He never looked quite comfortable in business attire, but he sure as hell looked sexy in it. "I mean, how are you? How was your day? How's your mom? You haven't mentioned her in at least a week. What about that client you had that was bothering you—you know, the one with the will he wants to dissolve and start over on?"

"Oh." Emmett took in a breath and let it out as he stared out over Morgan's head. "Okay, we're talking like, how are things in my world? Usually, that all depends on you, but since you're asking about my mom and my work, well, let's see. Client's fine. We got the new will rolling and seems like it might be a winner." He took in another breath and let it out like he was thinking. "Mom's good. She's going to a baby shower up in Louisville. It's my second cousin's baby, and they actually live in Bardstown, but all the venues where they wanted to have the shower were booked, you see. So, they had to move it up into the city."

Morgan stifled a laugh. "Sorry," she interjected, "Amber thinks we should host events at the farm. You know, like baby showers."

Emmett raised an eyebrow. "She could be onto something. I mean, I figure a baby shower can fit inside somebody's living room, but new moms these days? They aren't settling for anyone's living room."

"It's not the moms so much as their moms. And their friends. And all that you have to live up to, what with social media and gender reveal parties—"

"Wow." Emmett whistled low. "Sounds like a lot."

"I know. And that's *before* the baby comes."

"Well, it's worth it."

"You think so?" Morgan bit her lower lip. They hadn't really talked about kids yet. Not since they'd gotten back together, at least. Sure, when they were teenagers, Morgan daydreamed aloud to Emmett, gushing over baby names she'd loved. But that was forever ago.

Now Morgan wasn't even sure it was possible. *What if it wasn't?*

Her gut clenched as she braced for his reply. Maybe Emmett didn't even want kids.

"Of course they are." He looked at her. Crickets chirped in the backdrop and they heard movement come their way, but Emmett didn't seem concerned. Morgan followed his lead.

"So, you definitely want kids?"

"Don't you?" He frowned, but a nervous smile quickly filled the fleeting silence. "I guess I figured you did. You used to talk about it before."

"I know. And I do." Morgan's insides fluttered with butterflies. "It's just—"

"I know. It's a heavy thing. Can we talk about heavy things?"

Morgan's cheeks flushed with heat. "Heavy things? You mean—"

"Like, the future? We haven't really—"

They were talking over each other, excitedly. She finished his sentence. "We haven't discussed the future."

"Morgan Jo, I... I, um, well, I mean... Okay, so you want kids."

"And I love you," Morgan added.

"And I love you, too," he replied.

Her chest burned with the throbbing of anticipation and worry. She had to tell him. He had to know. Maybe he did. Maybe he was clever enough to piece together that Morgan wasn't whole. She wasn't a complete woman. She was maimed. There was just one way to get over this little hill, and so Morgan blurted, "What if I can't have kids?"

Emmett's Adam's apple bobbed and he fell back a step. "You mean, like, biologically?"

"Well, yeah. The incident." She brushed her right hand over her hip, and he looked down, squinting through the minimal light offered by the headlamp he'd set on the ground, flashing away from them. Emmett rested his hand on Morgan's hip with his left hand. With his right, he lifted her chin to him. "I *love* you. Do you understand that?"

"But if I can't give you kids—"

"Morgan. You don't know that. I don't know that."

"It's a big deal though. You don't want to marry a woman

who can't give you kids." The threat of tears stung the backs of her eyes. Was Morgan really bringing this up right now? Was she insane? She had enough on her plate. Why add more angst?

Maybe because she was still sort of searching for that little spot somewhere in the world to call home.

Maybe, while Morgan *knew* that Emmett was her home, maybe she wasn't *totally* convinced that she was *his*.

"There you are!" Geddy bounded over to them. "Come on. Fire's goin', and Dad's cookin' up weiners."

Emmett kissed the top of Morgan's head, and they left the conversation to rest.

For now.

CHAPTER SIXTY-SIX

PRESENT DAY

Amber

Amber and Julia sat by the flickering campfire, and Amber lost herself in the flames. Inside of her, a quiet calm simmered. With that calm, something else. She was pretty sure it was hope. Maybe even joy.

Morgan Jo and Emmett appeared from the opposite end of the fields, converging on the camp just ahead of Geddy, who'd gone off to hunt them down.

Amber studied Morgan Jo. Her face was awash in the glow of the fire but betrayed something other than the excitement and hope that Amber felt.

Trying to get her cousin's attention, Amber gave a small wave and patted the empty camping chair next to her.

"Actually it's late. Can we, um—can we raincheck this?" Morgan asked.

Amber's jaw dropped. "What? *No*. Morgan Jo Coyle, this is *it*. Uncle Gary is going to save our hind ends. Now sit yours down and crack open a beer with us."

Emmett gave Morgan a nod and let go of her hand. Geddy passed over two beers.

The thought of the beer turned Amber's stomach, though, which surprised even her. "I'll stick to water. Got any bottles?"

"Bottled water?" Geddy laughed. "Here, go get you a spittoon and you can fill it up at the crick."

Amber didn't find this funny, but Uncle Gary rustled around in his cooler for a minute before emerging with an orange soda.

"That'll work." Amber drank it down greedily, unaware of how thirsty she'd been.

Uncle Gary manned the fire with wire sticks of wieners and a small table with hot dog buns and condiments.

"Seems like you were ready for us," Julia commented, sitting by Amber with a hot dog in one hand and a can of Bud Light in the other.

"A house this big, and you're just about always ready for comp'ny," replied Gary. "Not that we get much out this way. Just Geddy, mostly. Some of my ol' buddies from up north when they're fixin' to ditch the old ball 'n' chain."

Geddy handed Amber a beer, but she pushed it back, picking up her can of orange soda and cracking the top. The sizzle of bubbles tickled her mouth as she took a sip. Amber wasn't much for drink, but she didn't mind it, and beers went well enough with hot dogs that she couldn't complain. Besides, she was fit to be starved and needed something to do with her hands. Otherwise, they'd be tugging down the message thread she had opened with Callum, trying desperately to refresh it.

Now that his audience—or part of it at least—had returned, Uncle Gary picked up where he'd left off with the story of how he came to be the sole proprietor of one of the two infamous plantations in Widow's Hollow.

"None of us knew this, y'see, but this here parcel belonged to Bill's dad."

Amber stopped chewing, swallowed a too-big chunk of food and nearly choked but recovered fast enough to hold up her hand and stop him. "Wait, *what?*"

"Oh yeah. This piece of land here, this house and the acres and acres, they belonged to *my* grandpa and grandma. Me-maw and Pe-paw Coyle, you can bet your bottom dollar."

Amber knew enough about her lineage to know this had to be a lie. She looked at Geddy, hoping he'd help her refute the truth.

He didn't, though. Instead, he stared into the flickering sparks, mesmerized, wholly unaware Amber was having something akin to an identity crisis right then and there, with half a hot dog in one hand and a nearly full beer in the other.

"You're jokin', Uncle Gary. We'd have known if Grandad had property out this way."

Uncle Gary looked at her across the campfire, mustard dribbling into his wiry beard, his eyes as serious as a heart attack. "It was a family secret."

"A family secret? But why?" Morgan Jo cut in.

"Well, basically it was granted down from the Widder Holler township's funereal commission as a gift to Curtis J. Coyle in exchange for his work on the cemetery."

"The one here?" Julia asked.

Despite his hifalutin language and crazy-as-a-bat demeanor, there was no doubt Uncle Gary believed all this. "Yes."

Geddy yawned. "It's true. It wasn't in Memaw's will for some reason, but when Grandad's kin died off, the gifted land went straight to him."

"Grandad *owned* this place? And we didn't know about it?" Amber felt weird but also... strangely... captivated? All her life, she'd known Uncle Gary as the black sheep. The one who ran away to join a circus and never looked back. Geddy had been called names on account of Uncle Gary, and Grandad had never once spoken kindly of Amber's estranged uncle. "Are you saying Grandad sold this place to you? When he was still alive?"

"Kind of." Geddy looked at Amber heavily. "He told me about it. He said he wanted my dad to have something when he was gone, and he was worried."

"Worried about the family."

"Taking advantage." Geddy shifted uncomfortably now. "No one would have, but Grandad came to me and said he had this piece of land out here, and did I think my dad would want it? I was just twenty, but I was in touch with Gary." Geddy had the strange habit of calling his dad by his name. "I saw the process through."

"He gave it to me, basically. The sale wasn't for more than a thousand bucks or so. Transfer the title. Taxes. But he gave it to me, and by using the sale, made sure I'd get it." Uncle Gary's head was dipped low. "Ain't nothin' I'm proud of, being a charity case. Anyway, as the time wore on, Grandad stowed away seeds from the farm from different crops. Geddy brought 'em to me."

"And you planted 'em." Amber looked out into the black night. Her throat closed up and shallow breaths chanted in her chest. "Wow," she said on a short breath. Grandad was a better man than most people realized. Amber always knew this but hearing that he'd made sure Gary and Geddy would be provided for, in spite of the hard feelings, it was almost too much to take.

Plus, Morgan Jo was probably dying inside right now. It would solve everything for her. Amber had to tell her cousin that there was such a thing as a viable backup plan, and *this* was it. It was a heritage project. It had Morgan Jo's name all over it.

Amber elbowed her, and Morgan flashed a quick smile. She said, "It's incredible. It's—" Morgan Jo's eyes slid to Uncle Gary and then Geddy. "You two, you'll help us then?"

"Help you? Hell!" Uncle Gary roared. "I'll supply everything. I owe it all to you all." His voice quieted. "I owe it to my dad."

Morgan's tension seemed to break. She popped out of her chair and crossed to Uncle Gary and Geddy and looped her arms over each of them. They hugged her back, and soon enough, a group hug was unfolding. Amber joined in, reaching around her cousin, and then Emmett came over, and Julia, too.

Beer cans were raised and toasts were made. Geddy and Emmett started going over plans. Morgan Jo again wondered aloud if they couldn't get back to the farm.

Amber wasn't quite ready, and just when she went to check her phone to see what time it was, it buzzed in her back pocket.

She frowned and dug it out.

There, sitting like a wrapped gift in Amber's text message inbox, a notification.

A message glowed from none other than Callum Dockerty: AV Whiz.

CHAPTER SIXTY-SEVEN

1992

Bill

The gatherin' carried on normal as could be, but Bill wasn't no dummy.

There was something weird in Hank's words and weirder yet in Barb's face after he said 'em.

Essie musta thought so, too, because she pushed on like something awkward had happened and had to be swept out like grass blades that sprinkled the deck after Bill had run the ride-on over the hills.

Essie was real good at handlin' awkward. Bill had known this, but to watch her at work turned his heart soft on his wife all over again. Maybe it was because of Bill's own love for Hank, but he appreciated that Essie followed Hank's weirdness with good ol' fashioned bossiness.

"Now I been workin' and Bill too—all day. All you all have, just look at this spread." Essie pointed to the metal table Bill had laid out with all the food and fixin's. "Help yourselves, fill up your plates, and now let's get to the main event, which is eatin'."

Eat they did. The food was just as delicious as always, and Bill was proud he'd been a big part of the set up and even the beans. He cracked jokes and filled his belly, and beneath the table, he and Essie held each other's hands.

They weren't resolved on the matter of the diary. It was something that would bug Bill until the day he died. But it *was* something he could live with, and sometimes, that was what you had to do as a man.

Live with it.

CHAPTER SIXTY-EIGHT

PRESENT DAY

Amber

Best-case scenario, Callum was texting to say that Hank had given him permission to work the tapes.

Worst-case scenario, Callum was texting to say that Hank forbade him from touching those tapes.

If the worst case happened, then Amber was dying to know: *why?* Why was her father so repulsed with the history of his life and that of his children's? Why was Amber's mother covering up for him? What was there to be so ashamed of?

Regardless of whatever it was Callum had to say, Amber felt distinctly that she was excited simply to hear from him, no matter what news he had.

She tapped the screen and read his message.

Hi Amber. This is Callum. She smiled at his introduction. They'd *exchanged* numbers. He knew she knew it was him. Still, she liked the southern gentlemanliness of his formality. But that was it. Just the introductory text.

Just then, three little dots pulsed across beneath the

message. He was writing another message right now, as she was reading his first.

Hope bloomed back up in her chest as she watched the dots cascade. Amber moved farther from the campfire and into the yellow light of the back porch. As her eyes trained on her phone, she willed good news to come through. Or, if not good news, then at least the chance to prolong their interaction.

The dots disappeared.

No message came.

Amber tapped out a quick reply. Maybe he was waiting for one before he sent over the verdict. *Hey Callum!*

Short and sweet. That was her style, anyway.

She waited a moment, and then a red exclamation mark screamed back at her.

Message failed to send. Try again?

It didn't go through.

Amber's eyes darted to the top corner of the screen. *No service.*

She looked up, as if there were a visible satellite floating overhead and she'd lost track of it. Stepping back to where she'd been at the campfire, Amber watched as her phone slowly regained one bar, tried for two, and got stuck at one.

"Um, Geddy?" she asked, shamefully. "Is there, like, Wi-Fi here?"

Geddy had been in deep conversation with Julia, but he looked up at Amber. "Wi-Fi? As in internet?" He shook his head. "Naw, but we aren't too far from the boarding school. If you go to the front of property you might pick up the service they get?"

Amber didn't really want to walk around the big white house alone, in the night.

"Maybe we could, um, *leave* now? I mean, Morgan Jo is

right. It's gettin' late. And you—Julia—you have to work tomorrow, probably."

"Nope." Julia shrugged politely, and Amber wanted to strangle her.

"Well, I really need service. It's about those tapes," she pleaded.

"Geddy, let's go," Morgan Jo commanded. Though she'd perked up considerably since her low mood earlier, she jumped at the chance to get off the plantation and back to the farm. Amber watched as Emmett strode up to Morgan Jo and reached for her hand.

"Mr. Coyle," he spoke to Garold, ever the cowboy—or *gentleman*, rather. "We really appreciate your time tonight." Then he looked at Geddy. "Geddy, you bring your dad on by the farm tomorrow, won't you?"

Uncle Gary grabbed his hat in his hand and held it over his ample stomach. "Only if it's okay with my sisters. I don't need no drama."

"I'll talk to my mom," Morgan Jo assured him. "Come tomorrow. It's Saturday, after all."

Amber smiled at that, and soon enough, they were back in Geddy's truck, bumping along down back roads all the way home.

CHAPTER SIXTY-NINE

PRESENT DAY

Amber

As soon as Emmett put the truck in park and popped his front seat to let her out, Amber hollered out a mass goodnight and sped off to her exterior entrance. She'd catch Morgan Jo up later. Anyway, the two lovebirds seemed to want some alone time.

Once inside her basement apartment, Amber withdrew her phone and looked at it.

The signal was back.

And a new notification burned in her inbox.

She tapped it open to see that not only had her message gone through, but a new message had come in from Callum.

Amber read it, her eyes flying across the words and making no sense of them.

She read it again.

This was it, Amber thought. The real deal. They could pair this with the plan involving Uncle Gary.

Amber read Callum's message for a third time: *Hank says I can work on the tapes.*

Amber raced to respond: *Callum! This is incredible! When do you think you can start?*

She hated to rush him, but if Amber could bring back Grandad's tapes to Morgan Jo, then it would be icing on top of the perfect banana split. Amber would fast become Morgan Jo's new favorite person and together they'd open the Nelson Family Vineyards, Winery, and Tasting Room. Amber could picture it now, her on an online advertisement reciting their company line: *Your one-stop shop for Moonshine Wine, the best wine on God's green earth.*

She watched as Callum's little dots undulated beneath her message:

Maybe you could help me?

CHAPTER SEVENTY

PRESENT DAY

Morgan

Morgan grabbed Emmett's hand and tore him away from his truck and through the gravel, past the other five or so cars parked in the drive, beyond the barn and all the way toward the hangar.

She wanted a private place to talk to her boyfriend. To *finish* what they'd started.

A thick want had built up in her, but not only that. Morgan had to know if what she wanted was what *he* wanted too. And if he could accept that their future could look different than bare-foot and pregnant.

"Come on." She pulled him, and after he waved to Geddy and Morgan hollered goodbye to Julia, Emmett gave in to her, releasing Morgan's hand to loop his arm around her waist, half-guiding her, half-colliding into her as they picked their way through the thick carpet of bluegrass up the hill that led them to the very back of the property.

They came to the hangar, and Morgan was tempted to go in, but they'd have no light inside.

Instead, they continued on, wordlessly. To the pond beyond the fence that once might have been meant to keep animals in and now served only to keep others out.

At least, that's how it all felt to Morgan, living on the farm. Like a princess pinned up inside of a false fortress.

She liked it. Feeling like a princess.

But even spoiled, contented princesses needed to get their kicks. They needed to escape. All the better if a handsome prince came around to rescue them from their imprisonment, and threw them down into a flower-filled meadow, unweaving their braids and loosening the buttons along their dress and...

Both of them tripped and stumbled through the gap in the fence, tipsy from the wine and their success.

"Where are we going?" Emmett asked, half-laughing. "What are we doing?"

Morgan stopped at the soft green bank of the pond, turned to him. He lifted her chin with his hand, and she looked right into Emmett's lake-blue eyes. "What lovers do."

She tugged him down to the bed of grass with her. Her hunger for this—whatever *this* was—consumed her. She reclined back, and Emmett slid his body on top of hers, bracing himself on his elbows—each tucked tight against her.

He brought his face close to Morgan's, his breath warm and sweet with strawberry wine. Hot kisses set every inch of her skin on fire. His lips glanced off her forehead, moving down her nose, lingering on her mouth then moving again. Her chin and jaw. Her neck.

She wanted them back on her mouth.

"I love you," Morgan murmured, pulling his face squarely in front of hers. She lifted her face and pressed her parted lips against Emmett's, then slipped her tongue into his mouth where it met with his. The taste of him thrilled her, stilled her.

"Wait." Emmett drew back.

Morgan grabbed his face again, his rough, stubbled jaw was

everything. "No," she argued. "I want you to know I love you. I love you, but—"

"But what?" He ran his thumb up her cheek and then took both hands and pulled her arms down to her sides.

"What if I can't give you what you want, Emmett?" Her eyes cast downward at their feet.

"What do you think I want?" he murmured back, lifting her chin with his hand.

She looked at him, sad and sincere and so damn turned on that she wanted to lie and just tell him what he wanted to hear. But she didn't. "Emmett, what if I can't have kids?"

He laughed.

Laughed.

"This isn't funny," Morgan insisted.

"Morgan Jo Coyle," he whispered, combing his fingers through her hair and smiling wide. "What if *I* can't have kids? What if we get another hard freeze tonight and it kills your uncle's crops? What if the world ends tomorrow?"

"What if I'm not good at this," she whispered back, far more seriously.

Emmett's lips twisted in a grimace. His eyebrows dropped into a frown and he was looking down to where her hands rested on her belly.

He leaned back onto his knees, then off of her entirely, kneeling beside her.

"What are you doing?" Panic painted Morgan's voice.

Instead of an answer, Emmett pulled her up with him and they both stood.

She looked around. *Had someone come along? Seen them? Was a fish leaping out of the pond? Had a family of deer wondered past, nonplussed by the human affection evolving in the grass nearby?* "What?" she repeated, turning around again, back to Emmett.

He wasn't standing anymore. He was on the grass again. One knee down. The other bent.

Morgan drew her hands to her mouth. "What's happening?" she whispered. A chill flashed across her skin from her fingertips to her scalp and deep into her body, settling at last in her chest and taking the shape of butterflies. "Emmett?"

His hand emerged from his pocket and in it, a burgundy velvet box.

"Oh my." Morgan couldn't tell if she was breathing. Or living. Or dying. Or...

"Morgan Jo Coyle," Emmett started, his eyes creeping slowly from the box up the length of her body to her face, fixing on her eyes with such intensity that Morgan dared not look away.

"Yes?" she nearly wept the word.

He opened the box, and the precious jewel inside sparkled like top-shelf champagne. It wasn't a hulking solitaire embedded centrally in a ribbon of smaller diamonds. It wasn't anything that one might see in a jewelry catalogue or shimmering from the window of a department store like a prize pig at the county fair.

It was so much better.

The ring was the same one Morgan had seen her entire childhood on the finger of a woman who meant everything to her. It was Memaw's ring.

Emmett's voice dropped low and he asked Morgan, "I don't care if you've got a bum hip or a bum crop. And I know you're going to be good at this, because you're so damn good at loving me. Morgan Jo, will you marry me?"

And then Morgan did weep. She cried. She cried for all the years she'd been away and all the things she'd done that she thought were the right and good things. All the secrets in her life, in her heart. The greatest one being that she had always loved Emmett.

When she was young. When they broke up. When she left Brambleberry and figured she'd never look back. She loved him then just
as she loved him right now. And all Morgan knew was that despite
it all—despite her greatest secret: her inner damage, she knew that
Emmett *loved* her. She looked back at him with all the intensity of
a million butterflies breaking free of her chest and soaring out into
the open air above the farm and the town and all Kentucky—all of
the world. Morgan pulled him up from the grass, the box with its
brilliantly gleaming diamond sparkling like the North Star.

Emmett rubbed the tears from her cheeks with his left hand,
the box propped open between their bodies.

"*Yes.*"

* * *

Meanwhile, back on the farm, Geddy and Julia stood close and
spoke in sweet whispers on the front porch.

Amber Lee grinned like a fool as she and Callum wrote
back and forth, in short form, on their phones, miles apart but in
the very same town of Brambleberry.

And inside the house of Moonshine Creek, CarlaMay sat at
the kitchen table.

With a man.

CHAPTER SEVENTY-ONE

1992

Bill

After supper, the usual routine was that little groups took up. Essie and her daughters left for the back grass to let the kids roll around. Extra guests, like the friends, often tore off and left for their own supper at home or somewhere else.

Come sundown, it was just family that remained at the farm, and Bill spotted Hank alone, a beer in his hand, standing and staring at the kids as they played in the grass.

Bill wondered where the video camera was, and so he went right up to Hank and asked him. "We gon' film tonight?"

Hank looked back at Bill with something akin to shock, maybe, like he'd forgotten all about the wine. Bill closed his lips tight and pushed down the aggravation buildin' up in his chest. "It's ready." He hated to just spit it out like that, but what was wrong with Hank, anyhow?

"Oh, is it?" he asked, returning his stare to the kids.

Bill frowned. "Well, yeah. Do you have the camera with ya?"

Hank's jaw muscles worked left and right and up and

down. Hank tipped his bottle to his mouth, lifting it up, up, up, until it was empty as a holler log.

"As a matter of fact," Hank replied, "I do."

They agreed to meet up in the barn, and Bill ought to be excited now that they were onto the final steps of the process. But he had the feelin' that Hank's attitude hadn't shaken out since his strange comment at supper. How he was thankful. It wasn't what he'd said. It was in how he'd said it. How he'd looked at Bill's daughter. How he'd later drank his beer and stared at his kids. It wasn't like Hank to watch the kids. He was the sort to get in there and wrestle 'em.

As soon as Hank came in, he revealed two more boxes to go along with the camera case. One was more like a bag than a box, long, like it held a small tent or something. The other was just a cardboard banker's box type thing with a lid on top.

Bill was ready to get goin', but Hank didn't haul the recorder up onto his shoulder, instead, he fixed the device on top of what looked like a pair of legs he'd pulled out of the tent bag. No—not a pair of legs but rather three of them. "What in the hell is that?"

"It's a tripod. The camera goes on this to free up my hands. I just bought it, actually."

"Well then what's the point of a cameraman?" Bill chuckled, but Hank hit a button on the camera then shoved his hands back into his pockets, leaning back on his heels and watching without a smile on his face.

Hank spoke flat. "Action."

"Oh, hell." Bill got the jitters on account of Hank's attitude, but he was giddy enough to get the wine out that he set Hank's behavior aside and went on with the show.

"All right, now that the wine's set for some weeks—almost six now—we gon' go ahead and run the juice through a flour sack." Bill held up the sack he'd gotten from town. "You could use a cloth feed sack or anythin' like it. Anyway. We got a second crock here, and I'll just go on and squeeze the juice into the sack." Come to think of it, Bill could use an extra set of hands in order to avoid spillin'.

"Hank, uh, do you mind comin' here and doin' this?"

Hank raised his eyebrows and seemed to *wake* up as if he'd been asleep. He pointed his finger at his own chest. "What, me?"

"Well, if you ain't holdin' that thing up on your shoulder, I could use you to hold the flour bag over the crock here while I pour."

Hank joined Bill at the workbench and took the bag, opening its mouth wide as the bottom of it dangled in the second crock.

Bill poured slow and grapes and juice flowed into the second crock within the camera's view.

"Alright now, if you got a second person to help, that person just squeezes the sack until you got all the juice. If you don't got a second person you can just fix the sack to the top of the crock and do it on your own. Since I got Hank here, I'll go on and squeeze while he holds." Bill looked up to Hank for permission. He gave Bill a small nod.

Bill set to squeezing and talked while he did. "You'll have all the leftovers in the sack when you're done. Grape skin, seeds, all that. You don't gotta keep none of it."

"You throw it away?" Hank asked.

Bill chuckled. "Used to be we fed it to the hogs, and they'd fight and fall over drunk. Funniest thing you seen."

Hank cracked a smile. "I bet."

"Anyway, we ain't got hogs right now. We could feed it to the chickens. They'll eat anything. You don't want to feed it to cows or horses, not that they'd eat it, but you don't want a big animal like that fallin' over. Too high up. They'd break a leg and you'd have to put 'em down."

Bill finished squeezing then took the bag from Hank and put it in the first crock to deal with later. "Next you go ahead and add more sugar if you want, which I'll do here." Bill tossed in a scoop of sugar and stirred the new juice. "We'll go on and ferment it again with the sugar, then drain it again. It'll be potent by then. It already is, in fact."

"Wait a minute," Hank interrupted. "You already added sugar before and let it ferment. You mean you do the whole thing a second time?"

This was the first Hank had ever asked any specific questions on the process, and Bill got flustered, like.

"Well, depends on how sweet and how alcoholic you want it. This right here? We could drink now."

"Oh." Hank folded his arms over his chest. He was bein' obstinate, is what Bill would call it. Bill had an idea. "Here we go." He took the ladle and scooped juice from the crock and poured it into one of the copper mugs he kept on the workbench. "Try it."

Hank took the mug, peered inside, then he looked at the camera, winked, and slugged the entire thing back. He finished with a slurp and ran the back of his hand over his mouth. "Awesome."

Bill's jaw about hit the floor. "Wow*ee*."

They were pretty much done with the film, but before shutting off the camera and turning Hank out of the barn and closing up, Bill figured he'd go on and take a slug of the drink, too.

"Can I get another?" Hank asked once Bill poured himself half a mug.

Bill chuckled. It was good to have the old Hank back. And who cared if they both got drunk as hogs? That's what family get-togethers was for, Bill reckoned. "Go on," Bill said.

Hank filled his gleaming, dimpled copper mug then held it up in a toast. "To moonshine wine."

Bill's heart slowed and a smile broke out on his mouth. He held his mug up, too. "To family."

But Hank didn't smile back.

And soon enough, both men had forgot all about the camera.

They passed out in the barn, Hank and Bill did.

It wasn't the sort of sleep you plan, like when you go to bed and you're expectin' to drift right off any minute. It was the kind of sleep that happened on accident.

Sometime later, the squealing of the rusty hinges of the barn door slidin' open stirred Bill awake.

Essie stood in the darkness of the gapin' barn door, her hands on her hips. Bill squinted back at her through a splinterin' headache.

"What the hell time is it?" Bill asked, his throat dry and his breath thick with the bitter taste of the wine.

"It's past nine o'clock," Essie answered, not botherin' to keep her voice low. "Is Hank in here?"

By the time Bill cleared his head and looked around in the dim light of the lantern Essie had flickered to life, Hank was scramblin' nearby.

Bill watched him pack his bag and the camera case. He said, "I'm sorry, Essie." Then he looked at Bill. "Sorry, Bill."

"Hank, wait, honey," Essie replied, reaching for him. But he slipped out of the barn and into the night.

And that was the last time Bill ever saw Hank.

In person, at least.

Of course, that damn hippie had left behind a box full of video cassette tapes.

EPILOGUE

PRESENT DAY

Amber

Amber woke up early on Tuesday to a raging headache and the swirling, horrible feeling that she might be sick. Upon the realization that she might have the flu, she called her mom.

Barb answered on the first ring. "Amber Lee," she hissed. "What's wrong?"

Miserable but functional, Amber whined, "*Nothing, why?*"

"You're calling me at the whip crack of dawn, that's *why*. You sound awful. What is it?"

"I'm sick, Mom," Amber groaned as the swell of nausea rose in her throat. She curled herself into a ball.

Amber could all but hear Barb fly into action on the other end of the line. Before she knew it, her mother was coming down from the stairs inside the big house, with Trav and Morgan flanking her.

On the brink of tears, Amber allowed them to roll her from the bed and into Barb's awaiting car just outside.

"I called Dr. Maycomb," Barb said as Trav got Amber situated in the back seat and closed the door. Morgan waved the three of them off.

Amber protested immediately. "*No*, Mom!" She knew she sounded like a kid, but she didn't care. "I'm not going to see Dr. Maycomb."

Dr. Maycomb was the family's physician and had been ever since Amber was ten or so. He also just so happened to be Grant's uncle. Amber hadn't had the chance yet to switch doctors. Then again, it wasn't like she had many options in Brambleberry.

Her mother ignored her and drove. "Urgent care doesn't open until eight. Maycomb'll take you as early as seven."

Amber didn't have the strength to argue. Instead, she leaned into the window and took shallow breaths, trying to ward off the nausea with little pants.

As soon as they were whisked back into the exam room—a small white box with a collage of children's artwork—Amber was beginning to feel better.

Especially once the nurse, a kind but unfamiliar woman, put her mind at ease. "Date of your last cycle?" she asked.

Amber answered that one easily. "I don't have a cycle."

The nurse glanced up from her electronic chart. "What do you mean, sweetheart?"

Amber took a sip of the water she'd gotten in the waiting room. "I have polycystic ovary syndrome. So I don't have my period. I haven't had a period in about five years. Dr. Maycomb knows my history."

The nurse glanced back down the chart, and Amber watched her eyes flit down, down. "Oh. Yes. Right here." She appeared to read the notes. "Right. PCOS. And for treatment... ah. I see." She glanced up. "Oral contraceptives?"

"That's right. They keep the symptoms at bay."

Barb, who insisted on sitting in on the exam, chimed in, "Could this be linked to her PCOS?"

The woman gave a friendly smile. "Possibly. We'll know more once the doc comes in. I'll just get him."

Dr. Maycomb pretended he didn't know about Amber and Grant's breakup. Or maybe he didn't care. Amber was grateful, and they went about the check-up as if it were any other. But just seeing Grant's kin was enough to remind Amber how far she'd come. And how far left she had to go.

"What's going on today, Ms. Taylor?" he asked, running through vitals as she explained.

"She's been having waves of not feelin' well. I'n't that right, Amber Lee?" Barb prompted.

"Nothing consistent. Just—some days I don't feel right."

Dr. Maycomb told her to take three deep breaths as he listened to her lungs through her shirt. "Been out of the country?"

"Haven't even been out of the county," she shot back. "And now I'm here, I'm feeling a little better anyhow."

"Any big life changes?" he asked.

Barb clicked her tongue and shook her head.

Amber shot her a look. "Well, yes. A breakup." Amber kept her gaze ahead as Dr. Maycomb peered into her ears.

"Well, *that* woulda been a positive life change." He leaned back and lowered his ear-checkin' tool. He gave her a crooked grin. "Ain't my business, but I reckon you can do a lot better than my ne'er-do-well nephew."

Amber let out a breath she didn't know she was holding. The queasy feeling had almost entirely ebbed. All that remained now was a pounding headache. "Grant's not a bad guy," she added, stealing a glance at her mom who lifted a Coyle eyebrow. "We've both moved on."

"Anything other than that?" the doctor asked.

"What do you mean?" Amber finished her water with one final long sip.

"Sometimes, stress can manifest physically," Dr. Maycomb explained. "It can come on as headaches, stomach upset, and many other physical symptoms."

"Are you stressed?" Barb asked Amber.

She shook her head. "I don't *feel* stressed. Actually, I feel the opposite."

A smile broke over the doctor's face. "Any other big changes in your life, then?"

At that, Amber nodded slowly. "I mean, I'm taking fewer hairdressing appointments, so I can help more at the farm. And I don't have Grant around—which you'd think would *help* with the headaches."

Dr. Maycomb studied her then turned his head to Barb and then back to Amber again. He lowered his voice. "Is there something we ought to talk about *privately?*"

"Privately?" Amber was aghast. "No."

He was unfazed. "I'm not accusing, I'm just saying that sometimes people come in here with *secrets*, and then I can't do my job."

"Secrets?" Amber felt her gut twist. She didn't have any secrets. That she could think of at least.

Did she?

Barb cleared her throat. "We aren't a family who keeps secrets from each other. Anyhow, I'll just step out if that's best. Amber Lee."

Amber got hung up on her mother's first point, though. It was a lie. Of course the family kept secrets. It was perhaps the number-one thing the Coyle clan did: keep secrets. From each other. From the world.

Even so, that wasn't why Amber was here. She didn't have any secrets. Medical or otherwise. Unless you counted one's private, innermost thoughts. Amber had quite a few of those...

Amber was 99.99 percent positive there wasn't anything secretive she ought to cough up. But that 0.01 percent nagged at her. Even so, she looked up at the doctor. "I can't think of anything," she said weakly.

The doctor chuckled and then lowered his iPad and stood from the rolling stool. "Amber Lee Taylor, I hereby declare you healthy as a horse."

"Healthy as a horse?" Amber asked, wary. "But the nausea?"

"You're not throwing up now, are you?"

"The headache?"

"Stress," he shot back, then pushed his free hand into his trouser pocket before moving for the door. "Listen, if your issues persist, come back. We'll run labs. But as a rule, I don't like to treat psychosomatic symptoms. I like to treat *disease*. You seem fit as a fiddle to me, and the feeling has passed, right?"

Amber nodded.

"If it comes back, give us a call. For now, though?" Dr. Maycomb twisted the handle of the door. "Go out, get some sunshine, eat your greens, and don't keep any secrets."

Amber left with her mother, and though she felt physically better, her mind and heart were swirling with what-ifs and questions. What if she *was* sick? What if Dr. Maycomb was right and she *wasn't* sick? What if her occasional headaches and stomachaches were a result of all those open threads in her life? Like her father's absence, and worries about how they would get a winery up and running within a year's time?

But the biggest what-ifs were so faint in Amber's little world that they were more like wisps than what-ifs, at all.

Callum Dockerty, the cute "AV whiz" who made her heart pound.

The tapes, and what Amber might find on them.

And the future, and what it might hold.

As Barb and Amber left the offices and headed back down

to the farm, Amber resolved silently that her feelings toward her what-ifs were only hurting her. She needed to follow the doctor's orders as well as she could.

Sunshine.

Veggies.

But secrets? Well, secrets took more work.

A LETTER FROM ELIZABETH

Dear reader,

Thank you most sincerely for reading *Second Chances at Brambleberry Creek*. If you'd like to keep up to date with all my latest releases, just sign up at the following link.

Your email address will never be shared and you can unsubscribe at any time.

www.bookouture.com/elizabeth-bromke

I hope you enjoyed *Second Chances at Brambleberry Creek*. If you did, I would be so grateful if you could write a review. I'd love to hear what you think, and it makes such a difference helping new readers to discover one of my books for the first time.

I love hearing from my readers! You can always get in touch with me on my Facebook, Twitter, or Instagram pages, or through my website.

Sincerely,

Elizabeth Bromke

KEEP IN TOUCH WITH ELIZABETH

www.elizabethbromke.com

 facebook.com/elizabethbromke
twitter.com/elizabethbromke
instagram.com/authorelizabethbromke

ACKNOWLEDGMENTS

As always, I have so many fabulous people to thank.

Wilbert Best, of Best Vineyards, thank you so much for sharing your plethora of regional and subject-based knowledge with me. To the fine people at Wine Mountains in Pinetop, Arizona, especially Michael, thank you for going above and beyond and solving my plot problem all while teaching me the ropes of winemaking and tasting. I look forward to coming back soon!

Natasha Harding, thank you so sincerely for helping me shape this story and then fine tune it. And, thank you immensely for your continued encouragement and support. You are the best!

Likewise, thank you Lucy Cowie for your careful eye on this big story. Your skillful hand has elevated my manuscript into a novel. Thank you! And to my wonderful proofreader, Shirley Khan, thank you for polishing this story into a shine!

Mandy Kullar and Emily Boyce, thank you for handling all the important aspects of taking *Brambleberry* to print and sharing my work with the world. Saidah Graham, thank you for navigating audio for us. My fabulous cover designer, Debbie Clement, thank you for giving life to *Brambleberry* with your beautiful work. Indeed, all of the terrific people at Bookouture: thank you!

Of course, this book would not be what it is without the well of knowledge of my own grandfather, Grandbob Flanagan. Thank you Grandbob, and Grandma too, for picking up the phone and taking me down memory lane. If I've brought *Brambleberry* to life in an authentic way, it's all thanks to the two of you. I love you.

Bridget Durbin, Kris Durbin, Jackie Durbin—thank you for the regional information and for being terrific folks and family!

To my parents and brother, sisters, nieces and nephews, in-laws, aunts, uncles, cousins... you've provided unwitting support in acting as the inspiration in my storytelling. Thank you all.

Last but never least, Ed and Eddie: thank you for being the boots on the ground—for reminding me to lug my laptop everywhere we go, talking me through plot and characters, encouraging me, being proud of me, and thank you for being the reason I write. I love you both to the moon.